THE 19TH
HIJACKER

ALSO BY JAMES RESTON, JR.

To Defend, To Destroy, A novel 1971

The Amnesty of John David Herndon, 1973

The Knock at Midnight, A novel 1975

The Innocence of Joan Little: A Southern Mystery, 1977

Our Father Who Art in Hell: the Life and Death of Jim Jones, 1981

Sherman's March and Vietnam, 1984

The Lone Star: the Life of John Connally, 1987

Collision at Home Plate: the Lives of Pete Rose and Bart Giamatti, 1991

Galileo: A Life, 1994

The Last Apocalypse: Europe at the Year 1000 A.D., 1999

*Warriors of God: Richard the Lionheart and Saladin
    in the Third Crusade*, 2001

Dogs of God: Columbus, the Inquisition, and the Defeat of the Moors, 2005

*Fragile Innocence: A Father's Memoir of His
    Daughter's Courageous Journey*, 2006

*The Conviction of Richard Nixon: The Untold Story
    of the Frost/Nixon Interviews*, 2007

*Defenders of the Faith: Christianity and Islam
    Battle for the Soul of Europe*, 2009

*The Accidental Victim: JFK, Lee Harvey Oswald,
    and the Real Target in Dallas*, 2013

Luther's Fortress: Martin Luther and His Reformation Under Siege, 2015

*A Rift in the Earth: Art, Memory, and the Fight for
    a Vietnam War Memorial*, 2018

THE 19TH HIJACKER

A NOVEL OF 9/11

JAMES RESTON, JR.

REPUBLIC

BOOK PUBLISHERS

THE 19TH HIJACKER

2021 © James Reston Jr.
FIRST EDITION

ISBN 9781645720201 (Hardcover)
9781645720218 (ebook)

For inquiries about volume orders, please contact:
Republic Book Publishers
27 West 20th Street, Suite 1103
New York, NY 10011
editor@republicbookpublishers.com

Published in the United States by Republic Book Publishers
Distributed by Independent Publishers Group
www.ipgbook.com

Book designed by Mark Karis
Author photo by Christopher Casler

Printed in the United States of America

For Lee Hamilton

AUTHOR'S NOTE

THIS BOOK IS DEDICATED TO LEE HAMILTON, who in thirty-five years in Congress became a legendary figure for his folksy wisdom and expertise in foreign policy and national security matters. After his retirement from Congress in 1999, he became president of the Woodrow Wilson International Center for Scholars in Washington, where I have had a long association. He was also been the co-chairman (with ex-governor of New Jersey Tom Kean) of the blue-ribbon 9/11 Commission that had the thankless task of sorting out and explaining how the attack on America happened.

The inspiration for this book came at a luncheon some ten years ago when I sat with Lee, as he regaled us with his fascinating stories about political life in Washington, for he is a great storyteller. The conversation drifted to 9/11 and eventually to the nineteen perpetrators. The Commission, he said, did not have the time, or perhaps the inclination, to delve deeply into the psychology and motivations of the villains. But one of them interested him immensely: the pilot who brought down Flight 93 into the mud of Shanksville, Pennsylvania.

Several things intrigued Hamilton about the figure I came to think of as the nineteenth hijacker. He came from a fine, middle-class family in Beirut, Lebanon. He was handsome and smart. Many options were open to him in life. His death was a waste. More importantly, the Commission Report made clear that Number 19 nearly pulled out of the operation a month before September 11 because of a romantic relationship with a lovely Turkish-German woman. I was immediately interested. Hamilton encouraged me to write a book about him.

I thank him once again for steering me toward such a compelling and important story. Very little is known about the nineteen hijackers, and what little is known remains classified. While in my research for this book (which included trips to Beirut and Hamburg), I was able to track down several witnesses and participants to the events and gained access to a variety of significant documents, the hijacker's wife had disappeared, and the hijacker himself, of course could not be interviewed. His life and death had to be imagined.

I will call him Sami Haddad.

You cannot stop martyrs. You can only reduce their number.

—GRAHAM GREENE, *THE COMEDIANS*

When you stare long into an abyss, the abyss also stares into you.

—FREDERICK NIETZSCHE, *APHORISM 146*

SERGEANT BRAUN SHIFTED HIS WEIGHT uncomfortably in the car and looked again at his watch. Four o'clock. One more hour of this detail, and he would finally be off. The boys were going to a bar on the Elbchaussee and then on to a disco near the Reeperbahn. Braun was tired of the Reeperbahn. He used to enjoy the pantomime with those fleshy, half-naked whores behind glass, beckoning to him with their vulgar gestures, while he mugged back at them with a chimpanzee smile and thumbs-up. Now it made him feel dirty and stupid. Call Inge again? No, he was tired of Inge too. It was time to make some changes in his life. That's what Kommissar Recht kept telling him, when the old curmudgeon said anything at all personal to him. What did Recht know about women anyway?

At least, from the pictures and the videos in her file, Suspect 21 looked pretty. Olive skin, thick, shiny brown hair, perfect figure, a scent of the Orient. He imagined her on a couch in the harem. She had a certain grace about her when she walked, even as he had watched the footage of her leaving the hospital, with her face slightly bloated. Someone this lovely couldn't possibly be involved in something this big, no matter what the first kommissar thought. And anyway, she had never been seen at the Marienstrasse apartment by any surveillance.

A stubby postman came up the block, pushing his bag of mail ahead of him in a three-wheel cart. The detective watched the little man load the boxes one by one with care. A large, padded envelope came out of his mailbag. The postman looked at it briefly and then put it in its proper slot. He stepped back, glancing up at the windows of the apartment building. And then he waved to someone with evident pleasure—Braun could not see who—and pointed to the box. His job finished, the postman ambled down the street; 4:13 p.m.

The stakeout showed Braun where he stood in the office. The first kommissar had given the principal villains to others. Braun had asked to be put on the task force in search of Omar, but the assignment had been given to someone else. The newspapers were now talking about a "Hamburg cell," and in the chaos of gearing up the huge investigation in the past week, other colleagues got the plum jobs of tracking down those who had actually been seen going in and out of Marienstrasse 54 with Samir Haddad and the ringleader or Omar. Braun, with only five years' experience, had to work the second tier—with this peripheral figure—a girlfriend. What does a girlfriend ever know? And he had to work under the annoying vice kommissar.

The door of the apartment block opened, and Braun sat up. It was her, in the flesh. She was wearing slippers, an overcoat thrown over what looked like pink pajamas. Her hair was disheveled. Nice, Braun thought: sleeping at four o'clock in the afternoon. But then she was still recuperating. He thought about her throat.

She walked languidly to the bank of postal boxes, where she struggled to insert her key. Braun made a mental note. Vice Kommissar Recht liked this kind of detail. Maybe she was still on heavy sedatives, he planned to say, but then he remembered that Recht did not appreciate his speculations. Only the facts; that's all he ever wanted. As the girl pulled the bulky envelope from her slot, the detective reached for his squawker.

"She's just come out of her apartment, Vice Kommissar. Now she's pulled a package from her postal slot. Should I move in and detain her?"

The voice on the other end garbled an answer.

"But don't we want that package?"

Again he strained to hear the answer over the static.

"Okay, Herr Recht, your decision . . . Standing by."

Instinctively, Braun reached for his binoculars and then remembered they were in the trunk. *Verdammtnochmal.* When the suspect looked at the packet, he thought he saw a startled look cross her face, or was it only surprise?

And then she walked briskly back to the apartment house door. Her gait was different, Braun thought, hurried.

***

Karima had awoken that morning with a start and glanced at the clock. It was late, already past ten. She had missed her rounds. She was in for another scolding. She had had sufficient time to bounce back from her procedure, they would say, and didn't she remember that the office was shorthanded? It had already been three days since her release from the hospital—tonsillectomies are not brain surgery after all—and they would expect her at least to make an appearance. For five full days she had lain in a hospital bed in that fugue state of painkillers. She was glad she had been out of commission on September 11. It gave her an excuse not to think about the news. Through the haze of Demerol, she had seen the buildings collapse into clouds of dust on the snowy television above her bed. Through her delirium she could hear the nurses whispering about the attacks in America.

Sami still had not called, and he had not answered his phone in

Florida when she called him. She hated these tiffs. He always brooded and cut her off, and then, in a few days or weeks, he would call as if nothing had happened. He was probably still mad about July, she thought, but that was just not fair. It was not her fault she had gotten sick.

Sami could be so selfish sometimes. He had to know she was in pain. A simple call, that's all she asked, no matter how busy he was or what he was feeling about her just then. She barely remembered his last call, just before they wheeled her into the operating room, except for his strange proclamation of love. If only life could be lived backward, she thought. In the months before her visit to Sami in Florida in July, she had found her stride as a resident. There had always been a morning ritual, a final, satisfying check before she went to work. She prided herself in her professional look: confident, well-kept, proper, her demeanor as starched as her white lab coat, her name embroidered proudly over the left pocket, Dr. Karima Ilgun, in longhand script—her ceremonial rite of passage into the profession. In the year since she had become confident in preparing a crown, in suturing and pulling a tooth without asking for help.

She couldn't believe that Sami would do something deliberately to hurt her, and yet there had been times in Florida when he was aloof and distracted and at times, tense.

Now, she was eager to talk to him about the attacks. Where had he been when the towers came down, and what did he think about the whole thing? Was he still posturing? She felt like teasing him about his rhetoric. How did it sound to him now?

She looked around her simple flat. How many happy times they had spent here. He could always make her laugh. She loved that more than anything. Some thought they made an odd couple, Lebanese and Turkish, or Turkish-German, as she preferred to think of herself. Tabbouleh and kebabs complement each other, someone had said. They were meze and sweet, syrupy Turkish coffee. Even in the wake of their quarrels and separations, their reunions had always been glorious. Despite his insensitivity, that was what she was focusing on now.

Until the last few weeks, Sami had called her from Florida nearly every night. In July he had shown her his flight school and introduced her to his funny, quirky instructors. They'd flown to Miami, drank planter's punch at sunset, and watched a man swallow a fiery sword. They'd run together on the white sand of the beach. They had mused about their next time together when his sister was getting married in Beirut. And they'd talked a little about their future, even about children . . .

It was too late for the clinic. Her throat was throbbing. She went to the bathroom to rummage around for another pill and gazed at herself in the mirror. She looked terrible, eyes bloodshot, hair a mess. She blew into her hand and smelled the odor. What would Sami think? She needed to rest.

***

It was late afternoon when she awoke. Idly, for the first time in days, she switched on the television. The American president again, talking about evildoers and proclaiming a crusade against the whole Arab world and against Islam itself. She heard the name Mohamed Atta. Sami had not called. He was probably in the classroom or in the simulator. Usually he called about midnight her time anyway, so there was still a chance. The shrill ring of the telephone startled her, and she leapt for it.

"Sami!" There was a pause. "Sami?"

"Hello, sister. This is Omar, Sami's friend. Remember me?" The flat, accented voice was strange, faraway.

"Oh, I'm sorry. I thought you were someone else. Who is this again?"

"This is Omar. We talked a month ago, remember? After Sami asked me to call you, to see if you were all right, and if you needed anything."

She remembered vaguely. "Yes, I guess so."

"I know our beloved Sami now only by his warrior name, Abu Tariq," the voice continued. "Let us honor the heroism of Abu Tariq."

"Sami? A hero? I don't know what you're talking about."

There was a pause, then, "I hope you are well."

"I've just had an operation."

"Yes, we know."

"You know?"

"I hope you're feeling better."

"I don't understand. Why are you calling, Omar?"

The voice paused again. Then deeper, slower, as if to underscore the gravity of what he was saying next. "I may want to come to see you, Karima. Sami would want me to have any of his papers he might have left with you."

"Well, I don't know about that," she said with rising annoyance. "He can come and get them *himself* if he wants his things. I haven't heard from him."

"I'll be in touch." The phone clicked.

Weird, she thought. Sami and his secretive friends, with their posturing and grandiose ideas. She had never liked them. She never understood what he saw in them.

She could hear the postman fiddling with her mail slot outside. She shuffled to the window and peeked out to see the adorable Herr Schmitt, in his rumpled, postman's uniform, smiling and pointing to her mailbox. She waved back. She grabbed a coat and went out to the street to get her mail. In her box was a large, lumpy, padded envelope, its flap copiously taped. She turned it over to see an American label and froze. *From Sami.*

Inside, she closed the blinds and sat on the couch again, staring at the lumpy, padded envelope. She looked at the stamps, an image of the US Capitol, and the postmark, September 11, 2001. She turned the envelope over to see the return address: Super 8 Motel, Newark, New Jersey. New Jersey? Where was that? Her address was in Sami's unmistakable scrawl. Instinctively—she did not know why—she put the envelope to her nose to smell it.

The tape came off effortlessly, and she poured the contents onto her coffee table: a spiral notebook, a sheaf of papers, a pocket Koran, one gold coin, his engagement ring, a lollipop, two toothpicks, ten microcassettes, and a business envelope with her name on it. Carefully, her fingers trembling, she opened the letter, intent not to tear its flap.

"*My dear Karima,*" she read.

"*My love. My beloved lady. My heart. You are my life . . .*"

The telephone ring made her jump. For a moment she was disoriented. Her head was spinning. Hurriedly, instinctively, she stuffed the mess back into its padded envelope. At last. At last. She reached for the phone.

"Sami?"

"Hello." Male voice. Unfamiliar.

"Sami? Is that you?"

"Karima Ilgun?"

She stiffened. "This is Dr. Ilgun."

"This is Vice Kommissar Günther Recht of the *Bundeskriminalamt.*"

"From where?"

"From the BKA. German Federal Police."

"Oh."

"Yes, I'm calling about your boyfriend."

"My boyfriend? He's not here. I mean, he's in America."

"May I come to see you, Fräulein?"

"Come to see me? Here? You want to come here?"

"Yes. There. We will be there in an hour."

"In an hour? But I'm not dressed. I just had an operation. I took a pill."

"In an hour, Fräulein. Please be ready to receive us."

The vice kommissar rang off.

Karima looked down at Sami's package and carefully pulled out the letter again.

Most of all, I want you to believe truly that I love you with all my heart. You must not have any doubts about this. I love you, and I will always love you, until eternity. Do not be sad when I depart for somewhere else, in a place where you can neither see nor hear me. But I will see you, and I will know how you are. And I will wait for you until you come to me. I feel guilty about giving you hope about marriage, wedding, children, and family. And many other things.

Were they breaking up? Without even a final conversation? God willing, no!

I regret that you must wait until we come together again. I did not run from you. I did what I was supposed to. Everyone has his time. And this is my time. You should be proud of me. This is an honor. You will see the results, and everybody will be happy . . .

Her eyes floated to the ceiling as she clutched the letter to her chest. What was he talking about? *I will see you, and I will know how you are . . . This is an honor . . .* What on earth?

You must remain very strong as I always knew you. Remember always who you are and what you are. Whatever you do, always have a goal. Keep your head high. The victors never bow their heads. Hold on to what you have until we see each other again. And then we will live an eternal life together, where no problems and no sorrow exist, in castles of gold and silver.

I do not leave you alone. Allah is with you and with my parents. If you need anything, ask him for what you need. He is listening and knows what is inside of you.

If you marry, have no fear. Think about who, besides me, could deserve you. I kiss you on the hands. And I thank you. I say I am sorry for the difficult years you spent with me. Your patience has a price.

I am your prince.
God willing, I will see you again!!!
Your man always, Sami, brave as a lion.

***

High in a corner office at police headquarters in Bruno-Georges-Platz, Vice Kommissar Günther Recht and his deputy, Heinrich Braun, had been summoned for a brief meeting with the chief kommissar. Subject: Suspect 21. The chief had only a few minutes to spare for this sideshow. The kommissar was feeling overwhelmed. Annoyed as Recht was at his deputy over the binoculars, he allowed Sergeant Braun to report on his surveillance.

"You say she looked startled," the first kommissar said.

"Yes, sir. She stood there for a long minute just staring at it, and then, as I said, she walked briskly back to the door."

"We must have that package, Recht," the kommissar snapped. "I suggest you move right in and take her into custody."

Recht's gaze drifted to the window, and his hand lifted to his mouth reflectively. It was one of his signature gestures, when he was stalling for time and collecting his thoughts. The mannerism always exasperated the chief.

"Well? Come, come, Recht. I'm a busy man."

"I'm not sure that's the right course," Recht said slowly. "It might be illegal."

"*Scheisse*, Recht. What about the second wave? You *have* heard about the second wave, haven't you?"

Recht ignored the insult. "At this point we have no cause to arrest her, or to seize her property. We have no evidence whatsoever that she's involved."

The first kommissar spat out his contempt. "We must assume she is part of the cell. She was certainly involved with Samir Haddad!"

"Yes," Recht continued in his slow deliberate manner, "but he was in America, and she was here. She was never seen at Marienstrasse, and her voice has never turned up on any tape. I think we must proceed carefully, Herr Kommissar, even under these circumstances."

"A second wave, Recht! This woman is a perfect candidate for a meaningful suicide . . . Catch my drift? How would you feel if you were in her situation? Think about it: a high-rise in Frankfurt . . . or the Reichstag! No one will complain later if we bend the rules a little."

"Judge Schneider might," Braun piped up.

The moment was awkward. "The judge appreciates the gravity," the chief said finally. "The clock may be ticking."

Recht glowered at Braun and then turned back to the first kommissar.

"If a second wave is in the works . . . if she really is somehow involved, well—"

"Well what?"

"Well, we would lose her immediately if we arrested her now. And on what charge? We'd look pretty silly if that packet contained fancy leather gloves from Alsterhaus."

The kommissar sputtered his frustration. "Do you have any idea the pressure I'm under, Recht?" he said gruffly.

Again, Recht ignored him. "I propose we work her for a while. See where she leads us. If she is part of the cell, let her lead us to the others. Find a way to get the package legally, in a way that Judge Schneider won't complain about. Track her movements, listen to her calls—"

"All right, Recht. It's your case . . . For the time being it's your case, I should say. I'm prepared to give you a second chance after your last screwup. No screwups this time, please."

As the detectives rose to leave, Recht asked, "How goes the hunt for Muktar, Herr Kommissar?"

"If there are any developments there, you'll be the first to know."

"And Omar?"

"Nothing yet. *Good day.*"

***

When Karima opened the door, before her stood a tall, beefy man with a pasty face and a prominent mole. His overcoat was wrinkled and had a stain near his right pocket. He was accompanied by a younger officer in uniform.

"*Guten Abend, Fraulein Ilgun,*" said Recht with a slight bow, "I am Vice Kommissar Günther Recht. And this is Sergeant Braun. May we come in?"

She tried to speak, but no words came out. She had a stock image of policemen: gruff, hostile, cynical, dangerous. She had heard many stories in the community. Kommissar Recht's manner was proper enough. She didn't like the way the uniformed policeman was leering at her.

They sat around her coffee table.

"You have a very nice apartment," the vice kommissar said, as his eyes wandered around the room. "You are a dentist, I believe."

"Yes."

"We all have a certain awe . . . and fear of dentists, you know."

"I have heard so."

"I have just had a tooth taken out actually. Fortunately, it was in my lower jaw, so you can't see the hole when I smile."

Karima felt his discomfort at small talk and said nothing.

"Well," he said, slapping his knees. "I must come to the point. Do you know this man?" He nodded to Braun, who placed a picture on the table in front of her, as if playing a trump card. It was Sami's passport photo . . . his second passport photo after he had claimed to lose his first.

"Yes, that's my boyfriend."

"*Ja . . . und?*"

"His name is Samir Haddad. You called about him. But he's not here. He's in Florida, the United States. Has something happened to him?"

He looked at her curiously, as if she had told some sort of sick joke. "Tell me about him," he said.

"Tell you about him? Kommissar, is Sami okay?"

"Please, Dr. Ilgun, try to be responsive. This is a formal interview."

"Formal?"

"Yes, formal. Tell me about your boyfriend."

"I don't know what you mean," she protested. "Five foot, eleven inches, brown hair, green eyes, that sort of thing?"

"No."

"He's from Lebanon. Perhaps you know that. From a very fine family . . . What is this about, Kommissar Recht?"

"I will get to that," he snapped. "What about his friends?"

"His friends? Oh no, I don't know any of his friends."

"You don't know any of his friends?"

"I mean, I've met a few, but I don't know them. He didn't want me to know his friends, you see."

"Continue."

"Continue what? That's all I know . . . about his friends, I mean."

"He had a friend named Omar. Do you know about him?"

"No."

"You never heard of him?"

"No, I haven't."

"What about his family, then?"

"His family has roots in the Bekaa Valley going back to ancient times."

"And in present times? Where was he raised?"

"He grew up in a Mazraa apartment in Beirut."

"Mazraa, what is that?"

"Mazraa is the name of the neighborhood in the southern part of the city. I remember the name because Sami told me never to confuse it with the town of Mazra'a."

"Mazra'a?"

"Yes, that's an Arab town in occupied Palestine."

"I see. In Israel."

"In Palestine."

"What do you know about the rest of his family?"

"Well . . . he has an uncle who is a well-to-do banker and a member of Lebanon's parliament, I believe."

"Do you know about another uncle named Assem?" he asked.

"I know about him, but I haven't met him."

"Haddad never mentioned him?"

"Oh yes, he's mentioned him. Often, actually," Karima replied. "He idolizes him."

"Did you know that this Dr. Assem was a secret agent for the East Germans in the 1980s?"

Karima tried to control herself. "No, I was not aware of that. Has Uncle Assem done something wrong?"

"Later this uncle worked for Libyan secret service in an operation code-named 'the Dealer.' Its purpose was to collect information on the notorious Abu Nidal. You know who that is, don't you?"

"I've heard the name. Really, Kommissar—"

"He was the founder of Fatah, the 'father of the struggle,' the one the West called a psychopath, the most dangerous and ruthless of the Palestinian 'terrorists'—at least, until Saddam Hussein had him murdered."

"Kommissar Recht, you're talking about things I know nothing about. I'm a dentist. I'm busy learning how to extract an impacted tooth."

"But you said Haddad spoke of him."

"He talked about his uncle's powerful personality. That's all I know. I never heard about that other stuff. I can ask him more about his uncle when he calls, if you like. I'm expecting to hear from him soon."

Recht and Braun exchanged glances. "All right. Where did you meet Samir Haddad?"

Karima exhaled in exasperation. "In Greifswald. At the university. In a class."

"And you say you have been together for four years."

"I didn't say that, but yes, on and off, for four years."

"Then you know him very, very well."

She stood up. She had had enough. "Really, Kommissar Recht, I've just had an operation, and I'm not feeling well. I am on medication. Please come to the point. I'm quite tired, as you can see. What is this about?"

"Don't you know, Dr. Ilgun?"

"No."

"Then I'm afraid I have some very bad news for you."

***

Kommissar Recht stared at the floor as Karima wept, her hands over her face, and then squirmed into a ball on her couch. The policeman had been the bearer of bad news many times before, but nothing like this. As unlikely as it was, if this were truly the first she had heard the news, he could understand how shattering it was. He was prepared to wait as long as he had to. As Karima howled, Braun gazed blankly at Haddad's picture on the glass table.

When her sobs subsided, Recht reached in his pocket and offered a crumpled handkerchief. She shook her head and rushed to the bathroom. The officers glanced at one another, and Recht nodded his head toward the desk. Braun slipped over to it and noticed the package facedown among other papers. He reached under the desk and placed his bug expertly. The toilet flushed, and they heard tissues being pulled from their box. Karima emerged, clutching a small towel in her hand, her face contorted and her eyes glazed.

"I'm sorry," she whimpered.

"Dr. Ilgun, I want you to listen closely," Recht said softly. "We believe that you may be in danger."

"In danger? In danger for what? From what?"

"I cannot be sure. For your protection we will be assigning a security detail to watch over you."

"Security detail? You're telling me you're spying on me?"

"*Nein, nein, nein.* We're assigning you bodyguards for the time being. I must inform you that a massive investigation is underway, and I'm afraid there's a bit of chaos at the moment. We want to be sure that no one else gets hurt."

"Will I be able to come and go?"

"Certainly. But you must be very careful. A guard will be posted overnight on the street outside." He paused. "And by the way, do you have any written documents of Samir Haddad?"

Karima thought for a moment. The officers followed her glance toward the desk.

"I'm not very organized, I'm afraid," she answered.

"Yes, I see that," the Kommissar replied, nodding at the desk.

"I have a few postcards, I think," she continued. "Oh, and there is a letter from his college health insurance office, detailing dental charges. I may still have some travel receipts. It would take a little time to find everything."

"Fine," the Kommissar answered politely. "If you could gather them together and put them in an envelope for us, that would be appreciated. An officer will come by for them in the morning."

When the officers were out on the street, Braun turned to Recht. "She's a pretty good actor, huh, chief?"

Recht nodded. "And she's lying," he said.

***

Inside, Karima collapsed again in sobs on the couch. The spasms came in waves, one after another. Why had the kommissar been so interested in Uncle Assem? Once, Sami had quoted Assem's philosophy of life: "To live life fully, risk must play a part." Was he somehow involved too? But Sami had other mentors, with other credos. Sami, a terrorist? a murderer? Dead in a field in Pennsylvania, swallowed up by the mud of the earth? It was unbelievable.

She went to the bathroom again to wash her face. Suddenly, she saw in the mirror the image of a convict, someone on the run. She heard the bang of the gavel and the clang of her prison door.

And then her telephone did start to ring. First, her mother in Stuttgart, befuddled and frightened; she thought she had seen a picture on television of a man who looked a little like Sami. After that call she let her answering machine take over. There was a call from Gretchen, her old roommate from Greifswald, offering to come to stay with her for comfort. And a call from Sami's fellow student at his flight school in Florida, wondering whether she was okay. Another call from Omar terrified her most.

It was true. She was going to need protection.

She fell to her knees. "*Whoever forgives and makes reconciliation, his reward is with Allah,*" she mumbled, and then she rose and seated herself again at the desk. She reached for the package and opened it again, gingerly, and retrieved its contents, then began examining them more carefully, one by one. Sami's fingerprints would be all over the stuff, and now hers would be too. She glanced out at the street. "Please, God, nothing important," she whispered. Trembling, she put the first cassette in her machine, half-hoping it would be blank. But Sami's voice was calm, soft.

***

September 10, 2001, 10:00 p.m.

"Karima, sweetheart,

"I was never really sure about this. You must have sensed my conflict in July. You must believe this. Even to this last day. Yahabibti— *May God forever protect and nourish you—I lied to you. I lied to you so many times. I am so sorry. But you did not realize that with each lie, you fueled my doubts all the more.*

"In a few hours, I will do what I am supposed to do. They want me to think of this as an act of courage and nobility. But it feels more like an act of cowardice. I want to walk away, but I am not brave enough, even at this last moment.

"For three months, even when I saw you in July, I was unsure if I would go forward. I was so torn between you and the mission. I got tired of my deception, both to you and to my comrades. You, and only you, must know the whole story. How I came down this path. I cannot bear the thought that I will disappear from your life forever without a word of explanation. And so, I put these recollections in the mail to you now. I have been recording them for you in the past few months, just so you will know, as I tried to figure things out and decide what to do.

"Tonight, I think only about you, yahayati. *I miss you terribly. My thoughts dwell on how we first met. Your lovely round face, your luscious brown hair, your sparkling green eyes. I can see them even now sparkle all the way across the room. You were wearing your favorite earrings, the ones with little emerald balls at the end, and that lace blouse with a collar covering your long neck. How I miss you! And your laugh. It was your laugh that first caught my attention . . .*

ON THE FIRST DAY of Karima's new existence, a uniformed policeman arrived at her door and drove her to police headquarters at Bruno-Georges-Platz. At the daunting, five-pronged modernist building, she was escorted to its central core, taken to a top floor and down a long corridor, jammed with talkative detectives. As Karima passed through this scrum, their chatter subsided. Curiosity and recognition showed on their faces. At last, she came to a door where the small sign announced "Vice Kommissar Günther Recht, Chief of Counterintelligence." A woman emerged to say that the kommissar would be with her as soon as he could.

The day became a blur of interviews in confined, smoke-filled spaces with Kommissar Recht and a procession of German and American authorities. Time and again, Karima described Sami Haddad: tall, glasses, athletic build, an intelligent face, a really handsome guy when he was clean-shaven, a charming smile, a raucous laugh. It was as she remembered him in the wonderful days. She described their stormy relationship, the good times and the breakups and the tearful reunions. She talked about his hot temper and sullen moods, about the change in his demeanor over the three years they had been together before he went off to America. She could sense their skepticism. How could she blame them? She was aware that she had lied to them. She felt herself losing her bearings, unsure anymore of what was true and what was not, what had really happened and what she was making up.

Late in the session, Kommissar Recht leafed through pages and pages of her telephone records in 2001. Eighty-three international calls from Sami! He let out a whistle. "He must have had some bill!" An average of every other day, sometimes twice in a day, the last one on September 11. What did they talk about? She tried to think of all the mundane things. He let her tick them off without interruption, but she could tell he was not really listening. And then he asked about Sami's six trips back to Germany over the past two years, when he stayed with her for weeks at a time, and then about her last trip to see him in Florida.

"Isn't it true, Dr. Ilgun, that you were closer to Haddad than anyone else?"

She paused. "I thought I was."

"And you still say that you knew nothing whatever about his real purpose?"

"Yes."

"When did you first meet him?"

"In Greifswald."

She remembered the moment vividly. She was in the cafeteria, flirting with a clutch of Arab boys. They had stood around her, attentive and adoring, shyly giggling, vying for her attention, as she smoked and made fun of their awkward ways. And then she'd felt Sami's steady stare from across the room.

"And you started dating one another immediately."

"Yes."

The memories flooded her brain. Her periodontics class in the fall term of 1997, and how things had developed from there. The crazy day trips to Rostock and to the nearby bay of Dänische Wieck. The bike rides along the river Ryck. The local döner joint and a pathetic little dive bar in Greifswald called Fly-Boy. "Greifswald is no Beirut," Sami would say with a shrug. Sami the sophisticate.

"Did you meet his friends?"

"Yes."

Karima despised his Moroccan friends, especially the religious ones. They were dirty and rude. It amused her to goad them. She flaunted her disdain for prayer and made fun of other Muslim girls who wore the headscarf. Deliberately, she violated all the taboos: smoking, drinking, eating pork. "How can you be German and not eat pork?" she had baited his friends.

"Did you go to the mosque with him?"

"No," she lied.

Her rebellion had annoyed Sami. Occasionally, he'd asked her to tone it down, but his complaints had only made her more irreverent. Because they had so much fun together, he had chosen to ignore her quirks, at least early on. Karima's mother had disapproved of the budding romance, and this had upset Karima. Sami had consigned her mother's attitude to the superiority complex that Turks feel toward Arabs. Karima had asked him to be more generous. Her mother was old-fashioned, proud of the fact that the Ottomans had ruled the Arabs for four hundred years. Sami wasn't having it, and Karima resented the way he had disparaged her parents in July. They fit a mold, he'd told her scornfully: immigrants in the great wave of the seventies, settling in Stuttgart, her late father with a good job in a chemical plant, trying to fit in, trying to be European.

Questions. More questions. She answered Recht flatly, giving only the bare minimum.

Eventually, mercifully, there was a break. Recht handed her a newspaper and left the room. Whatever she said could be so easily twisted. She rose from her seat and looked at herself in the mirror on the side wall. She had to be strong. Wasn't that what Sami's letter had said? *Be strong as I always knew you. Remember always who you are and what you are.* She had to be strong—and smart—and consistent. She returned to her seat, paper in hand.

As she thumbed through the newspaper, her eye fell on a story about German intelligence agents overhearing terrorists talk about a new operation involving thirty people. "As authorities around the world try to piece together the conspiracy, the inquiry is focusing more than ever on Germany, and more American FBI agents are being sent here," the story read. Just then, Recht returned.

When he took his seat again, he was almost a silhouette behind the desk beneath a window. She sat in a single chair in front of him, bathed in the sunlight from the window. She had to squint to see him clearly, occasionally holding up her hand to shade her eyes from the shaft of sunlight.

"Let me be frank, Dr. Ilgun," he began. "There are still some very dangerous people at large."

"Who? Here in Germany?"

"We will get to that. Many more lives could be in danger. We must know about others who might have been associated with Sami Haddad. Their motives are important, and in the past days a lot of thought has gone into this, both here and in America. You have acknowledged that you were closer to Samir Haddad than anybody else. We must know what motivated him. We need your help."

Karima nodded, sitting erect, as she squinted against the glare of strong sunlight that streamed through the window.

"I'm not learning that much from you. We keep talking, but we don't seem to be getting anywhere," he said.

"But I've told you: he said nothing to me about any of this."

"So you have said. If I am to believe you, I need you to try harder.

There must have been clues, some side remark, some items inadvertently left behind, perhaps. Your Sami . . ."

"My Sami?"

He cleared his throat. "Haddad is a central figure in this calamity. He's directly responsible for the deaths of forty people and by implication for another three thousand. He probably slit the throat of the American pilot with his own hand, the hand that you knew so well."

She winced at the cruelty of his remark.

"If he had lived, he would have been tried in some dark and distant place for all those deaths," Recht continued. "And then hanged in disgrace and buried in an unmarked grave."

"He is already buried in an unmarked grave."

Recht noted the snide remark. "I need you to try harder, Fräulein Ilgun."

She sensed that he had restrained himself from adding the word *otherwise*. She struggled to control herself. A breakdown would not help her.

"Are you sure you have provided us with everything from Haddad?"

"Yes."

"Every document?"

"Yes."

She pulled a tissue from her purse. "I want to be helpful," she said unconvincingly.

He leveled a skeptical stare at her and paused for a long moment. Finally, he said sharply. "This is no simple criminal investigation, Fräulein Ilgun. The Americans are frantic for answers. The FBI is pounding on my door. Another attack could happen at any moment. Your boyfriend was a ringleader. A ringleader! Do you understand the gravity of that?"

"Yes."

"For the other eighteen hijackers, all of them, we have no one who was as close to them as you were to Haddad."

"I've come to wonder how close I really was to him, to the whole man," she replied.

"The whole man?"

"Yes, I've thought a lot about that in the last day."

"In the years ahead," he continued, as if he were speaking to the gallery, "thousands of Americans will go to that little town in Pennsylvania called Shanksville, where Flight 93 crashed, to pay tribute and to pay their respects. Little boys will look up at their fathers and say, 'Why did they do it?'"

"It's not for me to answer these little boys," Karima muttered.

Recht stared at her coldly, holding her in an uncomfortable gaze, silent, disapproving.

Finally, she said, "If I was closest to him, I was more deceived than anyone."

Again, there was an uncomfortable pause. "I will tell you bluntly, Dr. Ilgun," he said at last, "we are not satisfied with your testimony. We don't think you are telling us everything you know. I must warn you: you could be in very serious trouble."

"I have told you everything I know," she whimpered.

**

Karima returned to her apartment that evening to find her answering machine blinking ominously.

"Hello again, sister," the eerie, distant voice intoned. "I hope you and your mother are well, God willing. Remember what Allah says: *Do not backbite one another. Would one of you like to eat the flesh of your dead brother?* Remember your dead brother, Karima. Let us honor his martyrdom and carry on his work. We know what you have." The tape whirred and stopped. His time had run out. But there was no second call.

She felt the chill in the back of her neck and grabbed a robe, pulling it tightly around her, replaying his last words: *We know what you have.* The mention of her mother frightened her. Quickly, she picked up the telephone and called Stuttgart, but the call was unsatisfactory. Her mother was groggy from her sleep aid. Before Omar's call, Karima had supposed that she would soon turn over the tapes to Recht. Now she realized she couldn't.

Her thoughts returned—for the thousandth time, it seemed—to when all this had started for Sami. *Greifswald*, she thought. When he'd told her he'd realized he didn't want to be a dentist.

"Spending my whole life looking down people's throats?" he'd said. "No disrespect, Karima. It's not for me. I'm twenty-four, old enough to begin thinking about what I really wanted to do in life." Why not go for what he really loved? He heard about a program in aeronautical engineering at Hamburg's Faculty of Applied Sciences.

They had talked about his move from Greifswald to Hamburg and decided that they could manage the separation. Hamburg was not so far away. They could spend their weekends together. When Karima had offered to transfer to someplace closer by, perhaps to the University of Bochum, Sami was pleased. On one of his infrequent trips back to Beirut, he had discussed his ambition about a career in aviation with his father. As always, the old man had been supportive. For his only son, the future leader of his clan, to get his professional training abroad was a great and laudable thing. Sami could always depend on getting his monthly stipend right on time, Karima remembered.

Then, in September 1997, he had moved to Hamburg and met his new friends. With a gasp she remembered. Atta. She peeked out the window, then reached for Sami's journal, flipping through to find the name. Mohamed Atta. One of the nineteen. The ringleader.

Her mind drifted back to her last session with Recht. Had she really been Sami's accomplice? She remembered questioning him about his life in Hamburg, but it was true: she had accepted his evasions. And she had acceded to his constant demand to become "more Islamic." She had put up with his flashes of anger and his sullen moods. Was that enabling? In all those telephone conversations that interested Kommissar Recht so much, she had been honest—technically—in saying that Sami had never conveyed the slightest hint of his plot. What would have happened if she had just insisted he shave and stop spending so much time at the mosque? With all that she had learned about him since his death, she could not see him as a religious fanatic. Something other than religion was driving him. Sami Haddad. Brave as a lion? She guffawed.

She gazed at his material on her coffee table and at the telephone and at the clock. She wondered if she shouldn't tell Kommissar Recht about Omar's call for her own protection. It was midnight. The kommissar would be asleep. There was no point in disturbing him now. If she told him about it, he would want to hear the message. He wouldn't be available until office hours in the morning, if then. Kommissar Recht was an important man. She went to the answering machine and deleted Omar's message.

She set the journal aside and began to leaf through the loose sheets of paper that had come in the package. For the most part, they contained passages from the Koran, with headings such as "Verse of Repentance" or "From the Family of Imran, Verses 123–125." The notations were in Sami's hand but written in his labored scrawl. Here he had formed his letters slowly, as if he had been struggling to be precise. Several passages were written in someone else's hand—*Was it Omar's?* she wondered—and this handwriting projected the elegance and command and easy grace of a master. One of the passages was entitled "Spoils of War, Verses 65–67," and another, "Surah 74, Verse 31," was underlined: *"We have set none but angels as guardians of the Fire. And we have fixed their number as 19 only as a trial for the disbelievers . . ."*

Perhaps, Karima thought, these were Sami's favorite passages, or lines that he had wanted to commit to memory, or verses that his imam had assigned him to copy. By including these passages in his "gift" to her, had he wanted to show her what a diligent student of the Koran he had become, how sincere he was in his faith?

Her eyes fell on a passage marked as Surahs 55–56: "The Most Generous" and "The Event." She recognized it as scripture dealing with paradise, because she and Sami had once discussed the two celestial gardens, redolent with fruit and pomegranates, populated with beautiful, brown-eyed maidens reclining on green cushions, nymphs with whom no man had had *tamth*. She had asked him how he imagined such a place, careful not to make fun of it for fear that he might fly off the handle, even if it caused her a twinge of jealousy. She'd wanted to know whether he really believed in the Koranic portrayal.

Toward the bottom of the pile, there were pages of a different sort. One was a letter to Sami from his father, Farrah, dated June 12, 2001. *Dear, elegant Farrah*, Karima thought, the dedicated public servant. He had been so kind to her, and so generous to Sami. The old man's handwriting was scratchy, the swirly Arabic calligraphy, once so lovely and artistic, now uneven and inexact.

My dear Samir,

Here is your monthly installment of 2000 dollars. I am so proud of you, my son. When you complete your degree, you will be a credit to your name and your clan. You bear our family name, Samir, as your middle name, and this is your bond to our distinguished line, stretching back to the Prophet himself. It may not be too long before you will be asked to take the leadership of our family. Your sisters will help, but as my only son, you must carry on our traditions.

I am sorry to tell you that I have taken a turn for the worse. We are dealing with it as we can and must. I don't want you to worry. I don't want to interfere with your studies there, but I am hoping that you will be able to come home soon for a visit.

Your loving father, Farrah

There was also a clipping from the Sarasota *Times-Herald*, dated the same day, about the execution of Oklahoma bomber Timothy McVeigh.

The last page seemed to come from some kind of aviation manual, printed in bold.

The 757 flight deck is designed with a fully integrated flight management computer system (FMC). The FMC uses flight crew-entered flight plan data, airplane systems data, and data from the navigation database to calculate airplane present position and generate the pitch, roll, and thrust commands necessary to fly an optimum flight profile. Automatic flight functions manage the airplane's lateral flight path (LNAV) and vertical flight path (VNAV) from immediately after takeoff to final approach and landing.

The precision of global positioning satellite system (GPS) navigation is available as part of the FMC. Before each flight the flight crew enters the routing, including all waypoints up to the destination into the FMC. These waypoints are defined by coordinates. Each waypoint is assigned an overfly altitude and speed. Upon engaging the autopilot the aircraft will fly to its destination along the green line in the Navigation Display. <u>The active routing can always be changed during flight.</u>

Sami had underlined the last sentence. Clipped to this page was another, in his handwriting.

My Check List: (Upon gaining control of B757)

- *Check autopilot ON.*

- *On FMC change routing profile by creating new waypoint.*

- *Waypoint 1: US Capitol. enter as: N3853.3W7700.3.*

- *Assign elevation of Waypoint 1 to 60 meters.*

(Row of middle level windows.)

- *On FMC use "direct to" function to navigate to Capitol.*

- *Check autopilot modes LNAV and VNAV are engaged.*

- *Double-check that "green line" on Navigation Display is pointed to desired destination.*

In the event of emergency:

- *Turn off auto pilot, fly manually.*

In event of passenger resistance:

- *Push control column forward as hard as I can. Passengers not strapped in will hit ceiling.*

  WARNING: If control column is pushed forward for more than 15 seconds, dive will be so steep, may be impossible to regain control.

And then the last page.

To abort the mission and land safely

- *Re-engage autopilot for autoland.*

- *Enter IAD as new destination airport (not just as waypoint).*

- *Select instrument approach in FMC capable of autoland.*

- *Position aircraft to fly approach.*

- *Near airport lower landing flaps (speed schedule).*

- *Set approach speed.*

- *After touchdown, disengage autopilot, brake, keep aircraft on runway.*

Why had he included that page? Karima wondered. Was he taunting her? She tried to imagine him in his motel on the last night, writing his love letter to her, gathering these random notes and his journal, and dropping this page in as an afterthought, stuffing the whole of it into the envelope and putting the stamps with the US Capitol on the right corner. Had he really thought of this as an act of love?

***

Sami had known the kind of microcassette player Karima used to record her patient notes. On her couch she slotted in the first cassette, dated June 5, 2001, and pushed play.

"I think it was in the residence hall that I first met Muhammad Atta," Sami began. *"He was wearing this tattered robe and flip-flops. Pretty small guy, not much more than five feet. I think he had a full beard then. Not exactly a commanding figure. Not the leader type. But there was something unusual about him. It was his eyes. Piercing . . . you know, really intense.*

"We exchanged pleasantries. I lent him some toothpaste. When he invited me to the mosque, I said no thanks. But Hamburg was lonely without you, albi. *I had no friends. My courses were hard. I was struggling to get by. I had to call upon Allah and on the goodwill of my professors—'Won't you help this poor, dim-witted Arab?' I wanted to ask them. At night, I felt down. We talked a lot on the phone in those days. We were just two lovers, honest and*

raw, longing to be with one another. In those days I had nothing to hide. But I guess talking with you was not enough.

"I take that back. Because I want to be honest with you. I'm embarrassed to tell you this now. But I did have something to hide. In my loneliness I began to mosey down to the Reeperbahn on a regular basis. On the street called Grosse Freiheit, I would run into Arab girls. At clubs like Café Reese and Thomas Reed I would just stay in a corner and watch the dirty dancing. And yes, I admit it: I did wander over to the other side of the Reeperbahn where the whores lounged in front of their picture windows. Just to look. I had my fantasies, but I never hired one. It would have cost me half the money my father was sending me every month, for one thing.

"Sometimes I went instead to the harbor. I'd walk along the promenade at Landungsbrücken and watch the great container ships leaving for some exotic location. Always a little afraid that I might run into some skinheads. I usually ended up at a club called Pupasch. It was a great flirting place, but I wasn't very good at flirting with strangers. They hand out free condoms there. I came away feeling empty and wondering what I was doing with my life and feeling guilty as if I was cheating on you. I wasn't really cheating though, Karima, just thinking about it.

"The next time I ran into Atta, he invited me to the mosque again. 'Oh, well, okay,' I said. Why not? I didn't know anybody. I had nothing else to do. He said there was free food and a soccer game afterwards. The mosque called Al-Quds was run of the mill, even a little dumpy. The doors on Steindamm were unmarked, no sense of it being a religious place. Atta called it The Box. It was a box, all right, smelly and stuffy.

"I remember that first visit really well. In the small library of the mosque, about eight guys were sitting there, whispering in Arabic. One was dark-skinned, a Sudanese. There was also a Syrian, a Turk, an Algerian, and a big guy from the Emirates. Very international, a mixed group. When I came in, they stopped talking. Atta introduced me and said, 'This is Samir. His friends call him Sami. He's from Lebanon, and he knows a lot about the suffering of Palestinians. He's studying aeronautical engineering.'

"That got their attention. Then he said, 'Technically, he's Sunni, but he admits that he's not a very good Muslim. Isn't that so, Sami?'

"Of course, I didn't really like being introduced that way to these guys, but it was true. One of them said something like, 'God willing, we can show him the light.'

"That was the night I met Omar. Atta called him the defender of the faith, and he's the one who led the instruction. Omar is taller than Atta, broad shoulders, has a full beard. I liked him right away. He pretty much took charge.

"'Stand straight!' he commanded, and everyone stood up. 'May Allah have mercy on you.'

"He spoke very fast. 'Welcome, Brother Sami. My name is Omar. I come from Hadhramaut, the region of Yemen. Today we're continuing our consideration of the Battle of Badr. Do you know about it?'

"Of course I did. Who doesn't know about Muhammad's first decisive battle? This tiny Muslim army attacking the caravan of the superpower, the Quraish, as it came across the desert from Syria to Mecca. The overwhelming odds. The divine intervention. The

battle that made Muhammad and Islam a force to be reckoned with. Even I knew this story, right?

"*The lesson was Surah 3:123–125, which I know a lot better now, believe me. First he read it in Arabic. And then, a German translation. 'Allah helped you when you were a pathetic little force.'*

"*The Syrian guy asked, 'How big was the prophet's army?'*

"'*Three hundred thirteen,' Omar said. 'Three hundred thirteen that brought down a superpower. They were outnumbered at least three to one.' And then he finished reading. 'Remember, faithful, is it not enough for you that Allah should help you with three thousand angels? If you remain firm and act properly, even if the enemy shall rush you in hot haste, your Lord will help you with five thousand angels, and you will make a terrific onslaught.'*

"*People liked this story, and we talked about why it was important.*

"*Someone said, 'He was raiding the caravan of the wealthy and the powerful, and that's like attacking the economic might of the superpower. The caravan was the symbol of Mecca's wealth.'*

"*Of course, Atta had to have his say, so he interrupted the discussion with a quote from a magazine—the* Jihadist.

"'*Listen to what the Sheikh has written. 'Those who kill excellently are they who fight in the front row. They do not withdraw until they are killed. They will sit in the upper ranks of paradise.''*

"*I was a little confused. Were they talking about the Battle of Badr, or something else? Sheikh? What Sheikh? But Omar took over again before I could ask anything.*

"'Allah said in his Glorious Book, Why fear the Infidels? Now Allah hath more right that you should fear Him, if you are believers. Fight them! So that Allah will punish them by your hands and disgrace them and give you victory over them and heal the breasts of a believing people.' Everyone was quiet, and you could tell we were all feeling the power that Omar and Atta were channeling. Then Atta got up, and his eyes were even more intense.

"Looking at each of us, he shouted, 'Are you ready to fight for your belief?' When he got to me, he screamed—seriously, he was screaming at me, yahabibti—'How strong are you, anyway?'

"Then the Turk tried to calm him down. 'Take it easy, Mohamed, for God's sake. They'll hear you in the prayer room.' Atta turned on him viciously. 'You're too weak for this! You're too weak to follow the path. I know wimps like you. I've worked with many of them. You cease to exist for me. You are dismissed. Leave!'

"People looked at one another uncomfortably. I wondered if I was supposed to leave too. So, the Turkish guy, he stood up and shouted at Atta, 'You son of a donkey . . . May you burn in hell' and stalked out of the room.

"It was really embarrassing. I felt bad for the guy who was getting Atta's broadside. And then the other guy, the Syrian . . . he snickered—you know, nervously—and Atta turned on him as well and shouted, 'How can you laugh when people are dying in the intifada!'

"And the guy was like, 'What has Palestine got to do with it?'

"And Atta goes, 'Talk to Samir here. He will tell you. Tell him, Sami. Tell him why Palestine is everything. Tell them about Sabra and Chatila!'

"I didn't say anything. I was not about to get tangled up with these people. I was there for the food and the soccer. It was awful, yahabibti. *But Atta didn't care.*

"'It's obvious. It's obvious,' he said to the Syrian guy finally, seeing that I would be no help. 'You are too small for this matter,' and then he sat down.

Karima switched off the machine. "I don't have the strength to finish this segment," she said to herself. "Perhaps I will in the morning."

3

WHEN KARIMA AWOKE EARLY the next morning, she pulled Sami's package from its hiding place again. Upon glancing at it, her first thought was, *Kommissar Recht would kill to get his hands on this.* Handing the material over might exonerate her of any involvement with the attacks. She would have to listen to all of the tapes to be sure. For now, she couldn't hand them over. Not yet anyway. Not until they'd apprehended Omar. With him, the thought was a little different: *Omar will kill to get hold of his sacred materials.* With Omar and his cohorts still at large, her life was definitely in danger. She was not confident that Kommissar Recht could protect her.

Still in her bathrobe, she sat down on her couch and took out the machine. "I have to finish this segment no matter what," she said to herself. "I have to."

"One day on Mariienstrasse, I ran into Atta again." Sami's voice seemed calm, as if he was enjoying this part of his story. *"He had a big, bespectacled guy with him, a guy I recognized as one of the men from The Box. When they noticed me, the fat guy waved a hasty goodbye and hustled down the street before I could say anything. Atta smiled—I thought he was a little embarrassed—but he greeted me warmly, and we walked along the cobblestone streets together toward the campus, talking about the usual subjects— exams, finances, pizza places. Finally, when we arrived at the town square, Atta turned to go to his building.*

"'Mohamed,' I said, '. . . about that meeting at Al-Quds . . .'

"'I suppose I owe you an apology.'

"'Not at all,' I said.

"'I got a little emotional. I'm sorry,' Atta said. 'Sometimes I get carried away.'

"'You didn't invite me back.'

"Atta gazed at me. 'I sensed you weren't really that interested in religion . . . or in politics.'

"'It's true. Maybe it's just my . . . weakness, as you might say.'

"'I don't think you're weak, Sami,' Atta said.

"When the light changed, Atta seemed impatient to get to class. He looked me up and down, as if he were making some sort of appraisal, and then turned to go.

"'Wait,' I said. 'Would you invite me next time?'

"Atta turned back to me.

"'Look, Samir, I broke the rules by bringing you. I was criticized for it later. The others are on a higher level than you. Except for that idiot I kicked out that day, they have all studied and proven themselves capable. I could tell that you were bored.'

"'No, I found it interesting. I could study too,' I said.

"'Anyone can study,' he replied. 'We're not an academic group.'

"'What kind of group is it, then?'

"He thought for a minute. 'Honestly, Sami. I'm not sure this is right for you.'

"'Or I might not be right for it,' I said.

"'Yes,' he replied, 'if you want to put it that way.'

"'Try me,' I said.

"'Really, I have to go.'

"'No, I mean it; try me,' I insisted.

"'I don't know.'

"'Perhaps you think I'm too small,' I joked, towering over him. The guy doesn't have much of a sense of humor, but he smiled a little.

"'Okay, let's do this,' he said after a pause. 'Let me see if Omar would give you a Koran lesson. One-on-one. He's quite busy, you know, between his private tutorials and his job at the bank.'

"'He works at a bank?'

"'Yes.'

"'I could meet at his convenience,' I said.

"'Okay, I'll see if he can fit you in for a session. It will just be a trial session, no obligations. I can't make any promises.'

"'No promises, no commitments.'

"'Perhaps at the very least, we can make you a better Muslim.'

"I put my hand on his shoulder. 'Mohamed,' I said in mock serious-ness, 'I think you need a good challenge.' Atta recoiled from the touch.

"I stood on the corner and watched the little man limp away. His gait was unsteady. He should see a doctor, I thought to myself.

*** *

When Karima stood before him for their session later that day, Recht gazed at her for a long, judgmental moment before he spoke. Her eyes fell on the huge, unsightly mole that disfigured the left side of his face. *Perhaps that's why he's not married*, she thought. *He should have it removed.* It crossed her mind that he might be trying to decide whether to turn her over to the Americans for more vigorous interrogation.

"Dr. Ilgun," he said finally, "I would like to believe that you have been completely forthcoming in our conversations. I want to believe in your total innocence. I really do. But as you can well imagine, I'm not alone in this investigation. There are many people who are interested in what you have to say about Samir Haddad, especially the Americans. Many people read my reports. I have noted your nervousness in our last few sessions, and this has raised questions."

"Do you expect me to be calm under the circumstances?" Karima snapped. "Think how you feel when you go the dentist."

He was not amused.

She could picture cold-blooded investigators in America complaining to the German authorities about her. They wanted to believe she was an accomplice. At that moment she was all they had. She could imagine tense discussions about who should have access to her, and what interrogation methods to use. She wondered if not only the BKA and Omar's men were watching her, but the CIA too.

"Who wouldn't be nervous in my situation?" she repeated.

"Yes. That, of course, could explain it. Nevertheless, I must inform you that from now on, our conversations will take on a more formal tone. Henceforth, not only my summaries but a complete transcript will be prepared. These will be provided to the American authorities, as well as to our criminal division. You will be placed under oath. I advise you to take this a little more seriously, Fräulein. We are on the verge of bringing charges against the one surviving member of the Hamburg cell."

"Who is that?"

"His name does not matter. He's a foot soldier, not a principal."

"Am I a principal?"

"At present, you are a witness."

"Not a suspect?"

"Let's just say you're a person of high interest."

"What if I just didn't take part in these interrogations?"

He scowled. "I don't think that's in your interest. Uncooperative witnesses often become official suspects automatically and are treated accordingly." He looked at her disapprovingly and added, "You will need to show more respect for our proceedings, Dr. Ilgun. If you are untruthful or deceptive, you will be subject to the full force of the criminal justice system. Do you understand?"

"Yes, I understand."

"Of course, convicting a peripheral figure who may have lied once or twice or provided a little money here and there will scarcely satisfy the American people for the crime of 9/11. They are out for revenge. Such a conviction will provide no satisfaction for them, unless they're able to have a few public hangings."

"Do they want to hang me?" she asked.

Recht frowned.

"For having the wrong boyfriend?" she pressed. "Is that what you want?"

"We want to know what motivated these men," Recht replied, "partly so we can protect ourselves from another attack. The masterminds of the American attacks are still at large—"

"Who are they?" she interrupted.

"Two of them in particular. One calls himself Muktar after some sort of Islamic revolutionary from the 1930s."

"Where is he now?" she asked.

"We think he is in Pakistan."

"And the other?"

"The other calls himself Omar. He took the name of the second caliph from the Prophet Muhammad's time."

"And where is *he* now?"

"Don't you know?"

"I beg your pardon?"

He paused, glancing at her sideways. "I said, don't you know where he is?"

"No, I don't, Kommissar Recht."

He stared at her, appraisingly. Then he said, "Have you ever heard of them?"

She shook her head. "No."

Recht glanced at the mirror and scribbled something on a pad before him. "We're not sure, but we think Omar may still be in Germany. His next target could be German. First the US Capitol and then the Reichstag. It would be a logical progression. The bomb could be ticking right now. We need to know how they dealt with one another. We need to know who's still working with the ones that are still out there. And we need to know it *now*."

"I would want to know that too," she whispered.

"I must tell you this bluntly, doctor. Because Haddad was a loner, because he maintained his intimate relationship with you—in violation of his orders from his al-Qaeda masters—"

"How do you know that?" she snapped.

"It is a reasonable surmise."

She said nothing.

He waited . . . then he said, "As I was about to say, he could well have been our best chance to disrupt the entire plot . . . if you had come forward."

"Come forward about *what*?" she exploded. "I have told you over and over, I knew nothing about his secret life!"

"Calm down, please. I am speaking in hypotheticals here."

"There is nothing hypothetical about this for me! You have no right to imply such things!"

"Perhaps. Perhaps not," he said flatly.

"Samir Haddad used me! He deceived me! He lied to me repeatedly. I was involved in only one half of his double life. I knew nothing of what he was hiding. Why can't you believe me?"

"I have a job to do. Please try to collect yourself."

The kommissar got up, reached in his coat pocket, and drew out a blue pack of Gauloises. He stood at the window, his back to her, inhaling long draws on his foul cigarette, with its stinking Syrian tobacco. Karima fumbled through her purse for a perfumed tissue. She looked at her watch.

When he turned back, he again leveled his gaze at her before speaking.

"As I've said, I'd like to believe that you have done nothing wrong," he said. "If I assume your total ignorance of the plot, we're still on—how should I say?—a journey, a quest together. You are our best witness. We want to know why Haddad persisted with Atta and the others. He had a good relationship with his family and a very satisfying romantic relationship with you, it seems. But there was emptiness somewhere. Otherwise, he would not have been ripe for a religious awakening."

"I'm not sure he *had* a religious awakening."

"Really? . . . We will explore that later."

"Later? I've told you what I know. How much longer is this going to go on?"

"I will decide that."

"Kommissioner Recht, you are a policeman. You have the authority to take me on any journey you want, as you put it. Anything I say . . . I'm just guessing."

"Guessing?"

"Yes, guessing. You wish I had all the answers. And when I do not, you make me out to be a liar and an accomplice."

"That's not true," he said.

"I will not be your scapegoat, Herr Kommissar. For you or the Americans or anyone else."

When she disappeared downstairs, the first kommissar emerged from the mirror room and confronted Recht in the hallway.

"Recht, I did not see much progress in that interrogation. She's uncooperative and defensive and hostile. And she's a good actor. I think she's in cahoots with Omar. Listen here, kommissar, and listen well: I must have that package!"

***

That evening Karima came home exhausted. On the afternoon after her morning interview with Recht, she had a particularly trying extraction at the clinic. The patient had been querulous and rude, insulting her after the procedure. More than rude. The woman was sorry she had put herself in the hands of an amateur, she screamed, just to save a few pennies. "I wish I could cut your fingers off," she hissed. Karima slunk away to find her supervisor and get her to mollify the woman. She resented the way the poorest and most difficult patients were palmed off on junior residents like her. The encounter had taken its toll. Perhaps she had not been at the top of her game that afternoon after her session with Recht. She had to ask her supervisor for a leave, but what could she give as a reason?

At home that evening, she threw her purse on the living room table and then noticed something odd, an odor of some kind. She went to the kitchen. Had she forgotten to take out the garbage? The can was empty. She went to her closet to change into something more comfortable. When she pulled open the top drawer, the rows of socks were amiss. And then she realized what she smelled.

Syrian tobacco.

She reached for her phone to call Recht. Static crackled in her ear, and the receiver seemed to emit the vague smell of an electrical solder, like the smell her own solders made when she had fashioned the metal anchor in her implant procedures. Returning the receiver to its carriage, she turned the device over to spy an additional wire. Her eye followed it to its jack in the wall. She paused for a minute, her eyes darting around the room. And then she dialed him.

"Are you deliberately trying to drive me crazy, Kommissar Recht?" she said in a trembling voice. "You can't get Sami Haddad. So, driving me insane is the next best thing. Is that what you're trying to do?"

There was a long pause on the other end. "We are only trying to protect you, Dr. Ilgun," he said softly. Did he really think she wasn't aware the police had searched her apartment—that his goons had pawed all over her things? She felt dirty and violated. His men had to back off, she shouted. She had to have more space to be alone in her own apartment, she said, without the police breathing down her neck.

He listened without apology or admission. But he did say that her "protection" might be relaxed a little.

"There is a difference between protection and spying," she quipped.

Kommissar Recht had not asked her directly and specifically if she was withholding any letters or tapes. How could he know she had such a thing—or was she imagining things? Only by sheer luck had she shifted Sami's stuff to a new hiding place the morning before. She was no lawyer, but she had some notion about the punishment for withholding evidence. What if she were just to destroy the tapes? But they were all she had left of Sami.

Sami's farewell letter haunted her. She went back to it again and again. "*You should be proud of me,*" he had written. "*This is an honor. You will see the results, and everybody will be happy.*" Happy? Had he really, in his heart, believed that? He was dead. She and his family were tormented. The families of his forty victims in Shanksville were devastated. The families of thousands more were grieving. The world was in upheaval. Christianity and Islam were at war. What was he talking about? Who was this "everyone" who would be happy?

***

June 6, 2001

"A week after my last encounter with Atta, I heard from Omar. He had had a cancellation. He would see me in the library of the Steindamm mosque. But he had only forty minutes, his message said.

"When we were together, he greeted me warmly. I thanked him for making the time in his busy schedule. We sat in the folding chairs, face-to-face. Omar pulled out two cell phones and put them on the adjacent chairs.

"'You never know,' he said. 'The bank might call.'

"Again, his charm and intelligence were captivating, but I was determined not to sound too eager.

"'To the good Muslim, he began, the world is divided into three parts. There is the land of peace, where Islamic law is in force and where peace covenants exist with other Islamic lands. Then there is the gray area: lands where Muslims do not rule, but which have covenants with Muslim lands. And finally, there is the black hole: places that are not Islamic and have no covenants with the lands of peace.'

"'Like Israel?' I said.

"'And America,' he replied. 'In this black hole, the rules of behavior prescribed by Islamic law do not apply.'

"'You mean anything goes there?' I asked.

"'No, not necessarily. In relations with the black hole, a Muslim state cannot engage in hostilities without good cause.'

"'Without good cause?'

"'There are exceptions,' he went on. 'If the enemy violates the norms of war—'

"'Like what?'

"'Well, like a mutilation of bodies of fallen warriors. In such a case, those accused of such crimes must be turned over for justice. The other exception is when Muslims are driven out of their homes . . .'

"'Palestine.'

"'Yes. Your home, Sami. The home of the refugees. Where the Jews occupy the Noble Sanctuary. The believers are obligated to regain their homes and drive out the nonbelievers.' His voice trembled when he said that.

"My education had begun, Karima. Omar was patient with my questions. Not arrogant, like Atta. I had met the spiritual leader of the group. I was curious about the makeup of the study group now . . . who played what role. Finally, I got up the courage to ask about Atta.

"'He's the decision maker,' Omar replied. 'We call him the Emir.'

"I hooted. 'Atta, the emir? Of a study group?' I imagined the little cripple with a rusty crown on his head. 'Why would a study group need an emir?'

"Omar's expression remained blank, inscrutable, suddenly menacing. It's like he was waiting for my amusement to pass.

"'You have the wrong attitude,' he said coldly. 'You have a lot to learn.'

"I was embarrassed and confused. I had caused an offense. We sat in silence for a long while.

"'I think the session is over,' Omar announced.

"'Omar, I'm sorry. I'm new to all this. I know I have a lot to learn. Please excuse my immaturity.'

"The frozen look on Omar's face began to thaw.

"'I like you, Sami,' he said finally. 'You have potential. You might even become a valued member of our study group. But you're in love with the pleasures of this life. Look at you, how well you are dressed. You're vain about your clothes and your appearance.'

"'What's wrong with looking nice?'

"'And we have found out a few things about you. Your girlfriend in Greifswald, for example. Your nights in bars and discotheques . . .'

"Now I was getting angry. 'So what? What's wrong with that?'

"'Nothing,' Omar said calmly. 'Nothing at all.'

"Again there was a long pause, as if he were waiting for me to say something else stupid or juvenile. Finally, he said, 'You love the fact that you're good-looking, don't you?'

'There's always someone better-looking. My mother used to tell me that,' I said.

"'How do you think you would look in a beard?' he asked.

"'I really don't know. I never thought about it before. It itches, right?'

"Omar's hand absentmindedly stroked his beard. 'Not after a while,' he said.

"'How long does it take to grow in?'

"'Two months.'

"'Doesn't it come in unevenly? Patchy? I have an anniversary coming up.'

"'You think it might cover up your good looks?'

"'I don't know. I wouldn't want it to look, you know, scraggly like a hermit. I would have to ask my girlfriend what she thinks about it.'

"'She will probably find it scratchy . . . since she doesn't wear a headscarf.' What else did he know about you? I wondered.

"'Does your girlfriend like it?' I asked.

"'I don't have a girlfriend,' Omar said. He looked sad.

"'I could probably introduce you to a few girls,' I offered.

"'Actually, I'm looking for a wife. The Prophet said, "He is a poor man who has no wife, and she is a poor woman, who has no man." Every weekend I travel away from Hamburg on a search.'

"'To the meat markets? Oh yes, I've heard about them.'

"Omar screwed up his face. 'So far, I haven't found the right woman.'

"'I'm sure you will find someone. There are a lot of attractive women out there. Take it from me.'

"'I'm looking for something more than physical beauty.'

"'Yes, certainly. I agree entirely. What's inside is important, too.'

"Suddenly Omar seemed tired.

"'What do you really love in life, Sami Haddad?' he asked with a sigh.

"It was a fair question, Karima. I had never thought about it before. I'd always just gone along on paths that others had laid out for me.

'I would love to fly airplanes,' I said at last. 'I've wanted to do that ever since I was a boy.'

"'Have you ever dreamed of doing something great in your life?'

"Something great? The question flummoxed me. I'm a college student, I thought. I'm just trying to graduate and get a job—earn enough money, so I can marry a beautiful woman—have a family, and be able to support them. Do something great? What on earth was he talking about?

"Omar changed the subject. 'You know, I'm from Yemen, the land of frankincense. Omar is not my real name. I only took the name of the second caliph recently, when the emir decided that I had earned it.'

"'So, you are now the commander of the faith.'

"'Sub-commander perhaps, in a very small pond. But small ponds can be important too—it was so for the Prophet at first. We all have special names as warriors of God. Someday, you could have one too.'

"'I'm not much of a warrior,' I said.

"'We should stop,' Omar said abruptly. 'Let's end with a reading.' He handed me a Koran, already open to a certain page. He pointed to the verse. 'This is called the Verse of Repentance. Let's read it together.'

"Our words ground together disjointed-like. I stumbled on the unfamiliar phrases, while Omar's voice was lyrical, polished, mesmerizing, as he spoke the words almost from memory. "'Oh ye who believe, what is the matter with you that, when you are asked to march forth in the cause of Allah, you cling heavily to the earth?"

He stopped. 'Read the rest yourself, Sami . . . as if you really believe it. I will listen.'

"I traced the words on the page with my index finger: 'Are you pleased with the life of this world rather than the Hereafter? But little in the enjoyment of this worldly life compares to the Hereafter.'

"'Now,' Omar said with a smile. 'Don't you feel better?'

"'Not really.'

"'Listen to what Anas bin Malik says about that verse.'

"'And who might he be?'

"'He's a prophet of the faith, Sami. Show some respect.'

"'I'm sorry. Am I supposed to apologize?' I asked.

"'Not yet,' he answered. 'Anas bin Malik said about the Verse of Repentance, "Nobody who dies and who believes in Allah would want to come back to this world, even if he were given the whole world and all that is in it . . . except the martyr. For the martyr, on seeing the superiority of martyrdom, would like to come back to the world and get killed again in Allah's cause."'

"'I'm not much of a martyr either,' I told him.

"Honestly, yahabibti, I was glad to get out of there . . . Uh-oh. Gotta go. Atta just drove up.'

***

Early the next morning, Karima went out to get a newspaper. *Perhaps,* she thought, *there will be news from Afghanistan or Pakistan.* At the crowded newspaper shop on the corner, she jostled for a space so she could leaf through some magazines. A story in *Der Spiegel* caught her attention. To its consternation, the BKA was admitting that it had had the apartment at Marienstrasse 54 under surveillance during 1998 and 1999, because it suspected two of its residents, Mohamed Atta and a portly terrorist named Marwan al-Shehhi, had links to Osama bin Laden's terrorist organization. The planning for the 9/11 attack had gone forward right under their eyes. The last known occupant of the apartment, the article said, was a Yemeni scholar named Ramzi Omar—but he had disappeared. Karima wondered if Recht was party to this catastrophic negligence.

Back at her apartment she rummaged in her purse for a tissue—and felt something strange, an envelope. "Sister Karima" was scrawled on the outside. And inside:

Greetings, Karima Ilgun,

I hope that, God willing, you are coping with the pressures the authorities are putting on you. We applaud your behavior so far. We have been observing you from far and near.

Her mind flashed back to the customers at the newspaper store, and then she rushed to the window to see that no police car was parked at her curbside.

We know about the tapes and journal. I am making arrangements for them to be picked up. Heed what the Noble Koran says: Eat up not another's property unjustly or sinfully.

Do not underestimate their importance to us. These are the sacred relics of Abu Tariq al Lubnani's martyrdom, may Allah have mercy on him. Under no circumstances are you to share these things with the police.

If you do not honor this demand, it will go very badly for you and for your invalid mother. We will take her into our care, and we will exact our justice on her for the transgressions of her daughter, according to our reading of the Sharia. For her wrong and for yours, there will be a painful torment.

You will be hearing from me soon. Omar.

***

June 6 (continued)

"Okay, I'm back. Whew. That was close. Atta turns up at the oddest times.

"By the winter of 1999, I began to think that I was not such a hopeless case. I didn't have to call Omar anymore—he'd call me. He was holding public classes. Sometimes with, like, fifty people. But my sessions were private. Special treatment for a special student.

"One time I was late. He sat all alone in the library at the Box, reading the Koran. On the seat beside him as usual were two cell phones. He let me know I was late.

"'Well, hail the Red Baron! Late but flashy!'

"He schooled me that day in the glorious victories of the Arabs. Beyond Badr, the early victories and the early caliphs, the triumph over the Persians at Qadisseyya and over the Byzantines at Yarmou,

how Islam expanded through the Middle East and established the Caliphate. It was all new to me. I told him proudly of my ancestor who fought at Yarmouk, but I never really knew before what the battle was about.

"He talked especially about the role of the second caliph, Omar. Omar was great because of his discipline, his humility, and because he rejected anything showy and ostentatious.

"'And he was always on time,' Omar said mischievously.

"He lectured me about the Battle of Ḥaṭṭīn, which I'd read about in National Geographic *magazine. It had a picture of the Horns of Hattin. So I knew about Saladin's triumph over the Crusaders. But the victory of the Egyptian Mamluks over the Mongols in the thirteenth century? I'd never heard about that.*

"He always came back to Badr, the first big triumph of Muhammad over the rich and powerful empire of the Quraish. He loved to tell about the few hundred raiders ambushing the great caravan. It came about by appointment, he said. God adjudicated the outcome, sent down three thousand angels, led by Gabriel, to slay the infidels. The whole thing struck me as magical thinking. It's a great story, don't you think? It's world history, right?

"One time he said, 'The Sheikh often quotes the Prophet, "I wish I could raid and be slain, and then raid and be slain, and then raid and be slain."' He was so passionate about that kind of stuff, but it always made me kind of uncomfortable.

"When I asked him who he was talking about, he was embarrassed— he averted his eyes, I remember now. Which he never, ever did.

"'Oh, he's just a good Muslim,' he said. 'I'm sorry. I shouldn't have mentioned him. Just a rich man with good intentions who's made some pretty bad mistakes. We're not sure of him, I can tell you.'

"'Who is he?' I asked. And Omar said, 'Never mind, Sami. I shouldn't have brought him up. It's what the Prophet says that's important.'

"'Come on, Omar. What's the big deal? Just tell me his name.'

"And then he told me. 'Sheikh Osama bin Laden.'

"So now you know. I had no clue who this guy was. . . . Anyway, Omar didn't really want to talk about the Sheikh. He turned the conversation back on me. Who was I? What did I stand for? What did I want out of life? I felt queasy every time he started grilling me like that.

"One time he put it to me this way: 'Don't you want to participate in the struggle of your generation?' And another time: 'You grew up in the shadow of Sabra and Chatila. How can you not see that Islam is under attack? Isn't that Palestinian hellhole just a few blocks from your parents' apartment?' I had never really paid attention, I had to admit.

"And the pilot thing, he was very interested in that. 'What is it about flying that so appeals to you? Is it because you think it's so beautiful up there, so clean, not messy like down here on the ground? If you flew over Beirut, I suppose Sabra and Chatila would look just like the rest of it.

"He started calling me 'the Phoenician.' 'You think of yourself as a Phoenician rather than a Palestinian. But Phoenicia is a dead

civilization, and Phoenicians were traders and hustlers and cheaters. We are all Palestinians now.'

"'Phoenicia was a great civilization,' I protested. They founded Carthage and Marseilles and Barcelona, right? I remember that from grade school.'

"He asked me if I knew what the word 'Phoenicia' meant.

"'No.'

"'Come on, Sami. Use your imagination. I bet you can guess, since you're the Phoenician.'

"I couldn't. I didn't guess. So he told me.

"'It's named after the Phoenix, the bird of Arabia.' Which I thought was the falcon. Then he told how the phoenix reached five hundred years of age, set itself on fire, and emerged from the ashes, born again.

"With each session I was becoming less and less sure I wanted to be there. And yet I wanted to prove myself to him. His grasp of history and the Koran was amazing. His passion and commitment were irresistible. When he was moved, I was moved too. I could never doubt his sincerity, even right up to now, even as I am really struggling.

"I felt like a nonentity next to him. Nothing, no dreams, no ambitions. Spoiled rich kid, living off daddy, unable to stand on his own two feet. I stopped trying to joke around with him, and he began to compliment my 'progress.' I was proud.

"Sometimes, Atta would stop by. The first time he limped into the room—he always irritated me, the little shit—I thought about

dropping down to one knee, swirling my hand in a swami salute, and proclaiming my loyalty to the great Emir. But I thought better of it.

"Which was good, because after a while, I came to expect Atta to be there. I liked his attention, even if he acted like a jerk. He'd interrupt Omar to make political points. The religious stuff bored him. Then, one day, Omar and I had been alone for the whole hour, and he'd talked quite a lot about himself. He was ashamed he had never gone on hajj. He had failed a seminal obligation of Islam. Also, he'd never found a suitable wife.

"And then he talked more about jihad. The inner struggle: how the true believer strives for perfection, resists all the temptations that might undermine his quest for betterment. He spoke of the conflicts in men, the conflicts between love and hatred, generosity and greed, compassion and aggression.

"'Take Atta, for example,' Omar said. 'Atta is consumed by hatred.' It was the first time he spoke ill of Atta. It was so weird: that very moment, Atta showed up. He looked terrible, like he'd been up all night. They exchanged this little salute. Atta pointed to Omar with a crooked finger, and Omar pointed back in the same way. And then Atta slumped down into a chair, closed his eyes, leaned his head against the wall. Something was upsetting him. 'Don't mind me. Go on. Don't let me interrupt.' Omar gave me a knowing look, as if to say, 'See?'

"And then Omar suggested Surah 8, 65–66 which I knew, by then, and together we read: 'O Prophet, urge the believers to fight! If there are twenty steadfast persons amongst you, they will overcome two hundred. If there be a hundred steadfast persons they will overcome a thousand of those who disbelieve, because they, the disbelievers, are people who do not understand.'

"Atta sat there, staring at me with those eyes. Then he chimed in from memory. 'It is not for the Prophet to take prisoners of war and free them with ransom, until he has made a great slaughter among his enemies. You desire the lucre of this world, but Allah desires for you the Hereafter.'

"Suddenly I was very tired. I wanted to get out of there. As I rose to leave and was thanking Omar, Atta said, 'Just a minute, Sami. I have something to tell you.'

"I said it better not take long, because I was off to Greifswald for my second anniversary with you. That really threw Atta. Any talk about you, my darling, seemed to upset him. But he said fine, it wouldn't take long. I thought about when he'd dismissed the Syrian. But that was not it at all. He said he wanted me to know that he'd be going away for a while to finish his dissertation. I asked him where, and he said, 'Originally, I thought about going to New York. There's a city planning expert in New Jersey. But I've decided against it.'

"New York sounded pretty good to me. I always wanted to go there.

"'Come on, Sami. America is controlled by Jews. You know how hard that would be on me. New York is their Mecca.'

"I said, 'You know something, Atta? I've never met a Jew in my life. So, I'll just have to take your word for it.'

"'Bosnia, Kosovo, Chechnya . . . the Jews planned all those conflicts, just like they instigated World War II so they could found Israel.'

"There was no arguing with him. I don't know what I would have said anyway. I have no idea who runs New York. He went on

about this idiot Clinton, how the Jews sent their harlot to bring him down. Omar was watching us the whole time, judging me and how I reacted to Atta's rant. I'm thinking I have a totally new perspective on how Omar sees Atta when he goes off like this.

"'Open your eyes, Sami. Get your head out of the clouds. Clinton was getting too friendly with the Arabs. Too pro-Palestinian for the Jews. So, they sent their whore to bring him down. And the dope fell for it.'

"Then Omar said, really softly, but, you know, serious, 'We will have to send something more than a whore. The USA is so powerful, Mohamed.' He was trying to bring Atta down, but Atta went on and on and on about Islamic states regrouping economically to achieve a caliphate. When Omar said he should give it a rest, that the USA was too powerful to take on that way, Atta stood up to him.

"'No! Something can be done! There are ways. Look at how they turned and ran in Beirut, after their barracks were bombed.'

"'That was years ago,' Omar scoffed.

"'The USA is not omnipotent,' Atta insisted. 'They ran away like dogs.'

"Omar and I just stood there, quiet, letting him wind down. Finally, he said he had to go.

"'So where will you be going?' I asked.

"'Malaysia.'

"'Well, have a nice trip,' I said."

4

THE PHONE RANG. Karima grabbed it.

"Kommissar Recht!" But it was a female voice.

"Karima darling, it's Gretchen. Please don't hang up." It was the lilting, soft, sweet, intelligent voice of her old roommate. "Karima. Karima?"

Paralyzed with fright, Karima froze. Finally, she sputtered, "Hello, Gretchen."

"Oh, Karima, I've been thinking about you every day. It's so terrible. Please let me help you."

"I'm okay," Karima whispered.

"But you must let your friends help you. You can't go through all this all alone."

"Thank you for calling, Gretchen." Karima said, trying to catch her breath. "I love you. It's just that I . . ."

"I know. I know. It's natural that you would pull into yourself, shut everyone out, even those like me. It's terrible . . . terrible . . ."

"Yes. They're saying I caused it all."

"That's ridiculous. Totally absurd. Who's saying that?"

"It doesn't matter."

"Listen, have you retained a lawyer?"

"A lawyer? What for?"

"What for? Karima, *liebling*, you can't minimize the danger you're in."

"The danger isn't legal."

"Not legal?"

"Anyway, I haven't done anything wrong. I didn't know anything about all this."

"I know. Of course not. But they may not believe you. They may try to stick something on you, just because they need a scapegoat."

"Maybe. I don't know."

"All the real villains are dead, including him. You know I never liked him."

"I know."

"So they need someone to blame."

"The police say they are protecting me."

"You might need someone to protect you from the police."

"What do you mean?"

"Have you told them everything?"

"Yes."

"That's good . . . Everything?"

"I couldn't be very helpful."

"I know how hard that must have been for you. You'll forgive me for saying so, but he was such a bastard!"

Karima paused. "Worse," she whispered finally.

"Can I come to see you? I mean, we wouldn't have to talk about all this if you didn't want to. Just be together . . . you know, like old times."

"I can't, Gretchen. I'd like to . . . really, but I can't. They won't let me."

"Okay, I get it. But remember, my brother is a lawyer. He'd be glad to help."

"Please, Gretchen, I implore you, please don't talk to anyone about this."

"I really think you should call him."

"Please, my darling, no one else. I'll call him if I think I need to. I promise. Really, it was very nice of you to call."

Karima hung up and then immediately placed a call to her mother.

"Have you had any strange phone calls, Mutti?" she asked, immediately regretting that she had asked so directly.

"Strange phone calls? From whom, *liebchen*?"

"Oh, never mind. If you haven't, you haven't. Everything's fine. My mind's a bit scrambled, that's all."

"I can certainly appreciate that," her mother said. "But please tell me what's going on, Karima. This is about your boyfriend, isn't it?" And then in a whispering voice, "They're saying he was one of that group that attacked America . . . God forbid."

"Yes, Mutti, God forbid."

As if the walls weren't closing in on her enough already, Recht called Karima the next day at work to inform her that that her name had been placed on an international "watch list" and that she had to turn over her passport. "Some things are simply beyond my control," he said.

She gave him no response.

"Karima, are you there?"

"I'm here, Kommissar."

"Okay, I see. Well then, I'll be in touch." And he hung up.

When she got home, she had three voice messages. The first was from a reporter at *Der Spiegel*, requesting an interview. It did not take a genius to guess what they were after. And then the second message came on. She heard static, and then a voice, speaking in a near whisper through the crackle.

"Hello, Sister Karima. Here is Omar. We honor your love and your support for our hero, Sami. I have made an arrangement to pick up his personal effects. One week from today, the Witnessing Day, go to Lades Chicken on Steindamm at 1 p.m. and order Adana kebab. When a waiter asks if you would like wedding soup first, hand Sami's things to him."

***

June 10, 2001

"I'm just back from Las Vegas and a little tired. We stayed at the Luxor Hotel on the famous Strip and played a little blackjack. I wish I could take you there someday. It's really an amazing place. I've never seen anything like it. We flew first class on a Boeing 737.

"But I was telling you about Omar. I started meeting him more and going to class less and less. I felt like I was in a kind of daze, and my professors had noticed. My grades were slipping into dangerous territory. Sometimes, to be honest, I just forgot to take the tests. My professors all gave me second chances. I was their project. But I had run out the string.

"Then, right before leaving to meet you, I was summoned to meet my academic adviser. Professor Strate looked at me straight with pained disappointment. 'You seemed to have such promise when you first came here, Herr Haddad,' he said. The university had so few eligible Arab candidates, and the faculty tried to make allowances. They appreciated that our community faced 'special hurdles,' but things had gone too far.

"'Listen, Samir. I'm sorry, but I'm afraid I can no longer recommend a program that would put you on a path toward flight training. Perhaps you can become an airplane mechanic. But with candidates

in aeronautical engineering, the first thing we look for is reliability. A captain's first job is the safety of his passengers.' And so it went.

"I could scarcely blame them. It was true: something had come over me. I was finding it hard to concentrate. Sure, I wanted to fly airplanes someday, but I was losing interest in academics. I began to worry about what you would think. And my father? I could not expect him to continue sending me money. He would say I had fallen in with a bad crowd. And Omar? All those jokes about me and the Red Baron. Why would such a brilliant person waste time on a C-minus student about to flunk out of school? I was not only a lousy student. I was a lousy brother.

"The train whistled along toward Lübeck, and Atta's rage flitted in and out of my mind. Atta had never been to America. Israel was an abstraction to him. And yet he linked the two places as the same. The mere mention of these evil black holes could send him into a rage. How much contact did he ever have with Jews? I wondered.

"Could it be that he hated himself? When he looked in the mirror, did he only see a short, ugly cripple? Was that why he was so uncomfortable with women? Was his manliness in question? His shouting and bombast, his bullying, his grandiosity: something very deep was tormenting him. I couldn't believe it was Israel or America. Sometimes I pitied rather than despised him.

"And yet, it was true, Atta had gotten into my head. I can't deny it. He's brilliant and dedicated. He's serious and focused. All the things I am not. He knows who he is and what he believes and what he wants. I admire that. I can't help it. Between Atta's aggression and Omar's persuasiveness, I feel constantly offguard. Before, I was just plodding along. Now I'm frequently upset, unsure, longing for something without knowing exactly what it is.

"When the train stopped in Rostock, I pulled out the book that Atta had given me for my 'edification.' It was The Jewish State *by Theodor Herzl, published in 1896.*

"'A little outdated, isn't it?' I said to Atta as I took his gift.

"'Read and learn,' Atta said.

"When the train started to move again, I dipped into its yellowed pages. 'Herzl's goal was nothing less than the regeneration of the Jewish nation as a political entity,' the introduction read. 'There was no Jewish nation in a political sense; only Jewish communities scattered throughout the world.' The idea of a Jewish State had the power to motivate Jewry, for 'all through the long night of their history the Jews have not ceased to dream this royal dream.' My eyes drifted out the window to the passing countryside. This royal dream. It sounded familiar. Like the Caliphate. A world governed by the Sharia. Our royal dream. Isn't it about the same?

"I read a few more pages, and I thought I was beginning to understand Atta better. A diabolical Jewish conspiracy is afoot in the world, and he wants to persuade me of the danger. Herzl is the philosophical underpinning. New York is their Jerusalem, where they control the world economy and the world's media. They're launching their campaign to expunge Islam from the face of the earth. Washington is the 'faculty of black arts,' as he calls it. Their US Capitol is the symbol of their corrupt Western democracy. Politicians there are bribed and pass laws supporting the Jewish state. All the misfortunes of the Islamic world could be traced back to this single evil conspiracy. The tragedy of Palestine is Zionism's ultimate triumph. But the omnipotence of the USA is a myth, he proclaims often. But something can be done about it.

I laid Herzl's book aside. As the small Pomeranian villages went flying by, I returned to my daydreams.

"*Since I could not fathom Atta's anger, I embraced Omar's intelligence. He helped me to see that instead of studying to be a mere engineer or technician, I could be more than a pusher of buttons or manipulator of nuts and bolts. One day I could be a spiritual and a cultured person like him.*

"*You must believe this, Karima. It never crossed my mind that I was being manipulated.*

"*Only later did it dawn on me that Omar's weekend trips, supposedly a search of the German marriage markets, were actually recruiting trips. I was not his only prospect—just the one who had the technical skills he needed.*

"*When the train neared Greifswald, I remembered how much I despised my time there, except the time with you. These gray, rectangular rabbit cages that passed for dormitories are so ugly and depressing. As the train slowly pulled into the Greifswald station, all these morose thoughts disappeared. There you were on the platform. I will always hold that picture of you in my mind. It was the last time we were perfect lovers. Leaning against a lantern in the low light of the evening, plumes of smoke wafting from your cigarette, you watched the cars go by, one by one, scanning the windows for me. I did not immediately throw the window open to greet you. I just feasted my eyes on you, flush with my good fortune.*

"*You were especially gorgeous that evening, your fitted jacket; snug, short, black skirt; and patterned tights. You had pulled your lush hair back with a clasp, and you wore the dangly, chandelier earrings with the tiny emerald studs that I had given you on our first anniversary. Who needs Atta's forty virgins, bringing honey and pomegranates, if you have Karima bringing you falafel and lentil soup?*

"*We had falafel at the Lades Chicken-land, and then went dancing at the Fly-Boy. 'And then?' I asked, and you giggled and jabbed me in the ribs. 'Down, boy, down,' you said.*

I wore rinse Levis, remember? A fitted black T-shirt, and a pullover from Hamburger Hof. You liked me in slim-fitting jeans. You said it made me look like Steve McQueen in The Great Escape. *Before we left your apartment, we admired ourselves in the mirror. We were a handsome couple.*

"*You could tell how I was afraid that night of being noticed, but even more running into skinheads again like we had the year before. There he was, in my face, that pimply Nazi oaf, shaved head, leather, and tattoos, screaming in the strobe lights about a raghead and a camel jockey in the house. His stormtroopers started chanting, 'No A-rabs, no A-rabs.' We got up and hurried out, my arm around you. Never again, I swore to myself. The little maggots are everywhere.*

"*I couldn't tell you that night that I was failing all my courses, every one—not just mathematics, but technical mechanics, fluid dynamics, and macroeconomics as well. I was consciously trying to make my life sound normal, nothing special. I needed to be good at being boring. But it was hard to think of commonplace things I did in Hamburg that didn't involve Omar and Atta. It was getting harder to talk to you without lying.*

"'*You seem tense, Sami,' you said, as we headed toward the club. 'What's wrong?' I just shrugged my shoulders.*

"As usual, there was a long line at the Fly-Boy. The crowd was mainly German, remember? The usual mix of townspeople and university students, with a few gays and Goths and overeager kids waiting to do their lines in the darkness. But there were a fair number of Arabs and Turks as well. You got mad when I ogled a few flirtatious, Palestinian girls in their full-body silk outfits. The only visible flesh was their excited faces. The rest was to imagine, their shimmering, vanilla gowns very tight around their waists, especially their lovely . . .

"'Sami? What are you looking at?' you said tartly. I loved your jealousy.

"'Nothing. Really nothing,' I replied. 'I'm just a guy.'

"'That's what they call Islamic modesty,' you scoffed. 'Head scarves and killer stilettos.'

"Inside, I remember the music was loud and pounding, making it nearly impossible to talk. The strobes and starbursts were blinding. We found a table far away from the dance floor. The Paul van Dyk remix of "For an Angel" was playing. Not long after we sat down, on came my favorite, Madonna's "Ray of Light." Before we knew it, we were dancing right next to the Palestinian girls.

"I had noticed this guy across the room. Kind of skinny, flat face and dull eyes, clean-shaven except for a moustache. Wearing a red bandana, the pirate in a masquerade. Ya'youni, I felt someone was watching me and ogling you. Several times I glanced in his direction. He averted his eyes.

"But then I went to the bathroom. When I came out of the stall, there he was.

"'Salaam,' I said and started to walk past him.

"'Wait,' he said. 'I want to introduce myself. My name is Ahmad.' He spoke in the Hejazi dialect of rural Saudi Arabia. I assumed he probably came from a small, desert village, and I couldn't imagine how he'd found his way to Germany. But I didn't appreciate being spied on, especially not in a place like that. He apologized, made some remark about how pretty you were, and I started to get annoyed.

"He put up his hands. 'Please, I meant nothing. You're just a lucky person, that's all.'

"'I need to get back.'

"'I followed you in here . . . so you would know.'

"'Know what?'

"'That I am a friend of Omar.'

"I slumped against the wall. 'Okay, Ahmad, fine. What can I do for you?'

"He gestured for me to put my ear close to his mouth to hear his secret.

"'I wanted to meet you, Sami, because I've been assigned to your team.'"

***

Within minutes of Omar leaving his demand about Witnessing Day on Karima's answering machine, Braun and a technician named Klingmann gathered in Recht's office at Bruno-Georges-Platz to listen to the wiretap. At the last minute, the first kommissar stormed in.

"That's the second message in a week he's left on her machine," Braun said.

"Do we know where the call came from?" the first kommissar asked.

The technician shook his head.

"Not even whether it originated in Germany?"

"No, sir. The calls come from random pay phones."

"How do we know that this is really Omar?" Braun asked. "The accent doesn't sound Middle Eastern."

"You're right, Braun. It sounds more African than Middle Eastern," the first kommissar said.

"We don't know," Recht said. "Not for sure. What's our latest on Omar's whereabouts?"

"We thought he left the country on September 8," said the first kommissar. "But he could still be in Germany."

"Omar seems awfully eager to get those postcards and dental bills she told us about," Braun said with a smirk.

Recht shot a peeved glance at his assistant.

"We might have seized these sacred relics two months ago," Braun said, rubbing it in.

Recht took another drag on his cigarette. It was true. These gangsters were desperate to get their hands on Haddad's personal effects. What could possibly be so important to them? Recht wondered, so important that they would risk getting caught. Whatever it was, their desperation made Karima's situation that much more dangerous...and potentially more productive. And as long as he was unable to lay his hands on the contents of the package due to the infuriating privacy laws in Germany, Recht's situation was precarious as well with the first kommissar.

"*Danke*, Herr Klingmann," the first kommissar said. "Let me know immediately if there's another message." And he stomped out as rudely as he had stomped in.

***

Karima's thoughts drifted to that terrible spring more than two years before when she had come to the end of her patience with Sami. Her suspicions had been deep, but her evidence was thin. Their relationship had become a roller-coaster ride: spats followed by apologies and tearful reunions and promises, followed by more spats. He had made offhanded references to his friends in Hamburg, and then grown angry when she asked about them. He was often withdrawn, spending hours on the web, even when they were together.

Her attraction to him remained strong, however. He had that beautiful face and that wonderful wide smile. He could still make her laugh. Couldn't her love for him pull him away from all this? As his beard became full, his sanctimoniousness became overbearing. He spoke more frequently about religion, then grew curt when she asked about his interpretation of concepts like jihad.

"I can't discuss that with you," he would say. "Let's just say it means 'holy war.' But I can't discuss that with an unbeliever."

Of course, this insult wounded and angered her. Worse, his mentions of Chechnya and Bosnia and Afghanistan scared her. Unsure of where to turn, she decided to call Sami's parents in Beirut. When she reached Sami's mother, the sweet woman blurted out her concerns in her halting French. Sami was taking his religion far too seriously and hanging out with unsavory people. She had heard that he spoke frequently about jihad and had even mentioned martyrdom. It occurred to her that he might volunteer to go to some dangerous place to fight for Islam. Please, wasn't there something they could do with their son?

It was around this time when Samir Haddad received the news that his powerful uncle, the daunting Assem, was flying from Beirut to Hamburg to see him. He immediately suspected that Karima was behind it. He called to confront her, and she denied it, but she was a bad liar, at least to him. He hung up on her and went silent. After a while, from guilt as much as anything, she tried to reach him to confess and apologize, but he would not pick up. She began calling every day. Nothing.

Finally, she wrote him a letter.

My dear Samir,

Again I haven't been able to reach you, though I have called a number of times. I left messages for you to call me back, but you haven't done so. I want to assume that you're merely busy or that you didn't get my messages. But I couldn't sleep at all last night. I thought for a long, long time about us. What is love for you, Sami? This is what love is to me: to take the other as he is, to share every-thing with him, mentally, physically, materially, in all areas of life, to do things for the other you wouldn't do for yourself, and to be there for the other, especially in bad times. I want to ask of you only one thing. Be honest with me, Sami. Don't just say you love me if you don't really mean it with all you are, all you believe, all you feel. If you can't give me that promise of honesty, it is better to forget about our relationship, even though it would hurt me terribly.

I love you, Karima.

She never knew whether he had even opened her letter.

Perhaps she *should* call Gretchen's lawyer brother and begin to talk about all this.

Then the phone rang, and it was Gretchen again, she saw. Karima let it ring and waited for the message.

"Karima, it's Gretchen. My brother says you haven't called." Her voice trembled with worry. "Please call me back. Let us help you. You don't have to face all this alone." *Dear Gretchen*, Karima thought, *forever watching out for me. I love her so much.*

It had been Gretchen, Karima remembered, who'd really made her see the transformation in Sami during the winter of '99. Not long after they had spent that wild night at the Fly-Boy club in Greifswald, he began to grow his patchy beard. The beard scratched her face when they kissed, and their kisses became less frequent. It annoyed her further how pleased he seemed when Arabs in Greifswald looked at him misty-eyed, interpreting his beard as the mark of a truly spiritual man. It was merely an experiment, he told her. He wanted to know how he would look with a "full growth."

"More manly perhaps," he said with a twinkle.

"More vain," she responded. "Uglier." She tried humor, calling him her "grand mufti" or "muffi" for short. He was not amused. Their conversations turned more often to religion. She sensed that he was going to the mosque occasionally and getting some rudimentary instruction. He parroted lessons that seemed to come from a grade school class in Islam. When they got deep into these discussions and she challenged his premises, his rote recitations broke down. She gave him the benefit of the doubt. It was another experiment in self-discovery, she allowed.

As she groused about his beard and deportment, so he became more critical of her flashy style. Her short shirts, her makeup, her streaked hair, her high heels—these were un-Islamic, he complained. "Good," was her tart reply at first. But to mollify him, she began to dress in a less flashy style and even donned a headscarf occasionally. It pleased her when he said that wearing the headscarf made her sexier. (Of course, as soon as he boarded his train back to Hamburg, those demure dresses and satin headscarves went straight to the bottom of her closet.) He griped as well about her smoking and drinking, though he did not own up to the fact that in Hamburg, especially after an emotional session with Omar, he would sneak away for beer and schnapps at a *Bierstube*. She quit smoking and drinking.

His double life . . . and hers . . . had begun after their second anniversary. In Arabic it was called having two faces, but in effect, they had more than just two. She did not care so much about the face he presented to Omar and Atta. Or how he was lying to his family as the loving son or to his teachers as the earnest but struggling Arab. All she cared about was the false face he presented to her as her lover and as a spiritual seeker. It was an odd form of cheating. Perhaps he derived pleasure in juggling all these roles and, however unconsciously he was doing it, found the variety to be romantic and exciting.

They quarreled more. Their phone conversations became shorter and less frequent. When Karima struggled to read certain passages of the Koran, or to find clothes that would make Sami happy, Gretchen watched with dismay.

"Can you imagine being married to *him*?" she said. "You would have to give up your career. You would have to honor the restrictions of a tyrannical and hypocritical husband. It would be like living in a prison."

"Sami knows how important my career is to me," Karima said.

"Karima, aren't you scared of him?"

"A little," she confessed.

"Don't you see what he's becoming?"

Karima did see what Gretchen saw, but felt she had to defend Sami. She chalked it up to jealous roommate syndrome and tried to laugh about it with Sami. Soon enough, Sami caught wind of Gretchen's efforts to undermine his relationship with Karima, and he was furious.

On one of his visits to Greifswald, Karima had insisted that Gretchen join them for pizza. The meal started out innocently enough, but when the conversation strayed onto the subject of Israel, the familiar passions rose to the surface. Sami seemed to go overboard just to irritate Gretchen, and she turned cold and patronizing. And then he exploded.

"Today we eat together," he said coldly, "but tomorrow I will take you out of the picture."

So searing, so shocking, so repellant had been that remark that Karima never forgot it. It showed a violent side of him she had never seen before. It scared her, and she let him know it.

"I don't ever, *ever* want to hear something like that from you, never, ever again," she told him.

After the ugly exchange with Sami, Gretchen claimed she wanted to move closer to school, found a new roommate, and moved out. She and Karima gradually saw less and less of each other. After that, Sami became more and more controlling, and eventually, Karima capitulated.

On another visit, when they had another spat over the headscarf, they broke up and did not see each other for two long months, until they couldn't stand it any longer and reunited tearfully. Karima asked again about his courses. Sami said they were going fine. She threatened to call his parents. He told her she'd better not.

Through the tears and pouts. she demanded to meet his friends in Hamburg. He refused. It would be too embarrassing, he said.

"Embarrassing to whom?" she replied. "To you? To your friends? To me?" Karima felt herself more and more isolated. "Who is this Mohamed Atta?" she asked him. "And why do you talk about him all the time?" She blamed him for Gretchen's move and felt more and more as if she were existing in a bubble.

And now? In a way, even in death, Sami continued to keep her in isolation. It was true. She did know more than she was telling Recht. There was no way she could call Gretchen's brother for legal assistance now. Omar would regard that as consorting with the enemy. His threatening words about her mother rang in her ears. They terrified her all over again.

All the rage, fear, and guilt were making it impossible for her to sleep. Whenever she nodded off, she'd find herself inside a recurring nightmare: she saw herself huddled over a desk, hands on her earphones, and suddenly notice the pungent smell of Syrian tobacco . . . and turn to see Kommissar Recht, a self-satisfied smirk on his face, standing behind her and holding up handcuffs. Sometimes, the figure behind her was Omar, not Recht, and he was holding up her mother's torn blouse.

It was three days to Witnessing Day. She had to speed up her listening.

***

June 12, 2001

"Yesterday, Timothy McVeigh was executed in Oklahoma. That's a place in the middle of the US. He's the one who bombed a

government building in Oklahoma City. I watched the coverage most of the day. The headline in the Sarasota paper this morning asked the question, 'Can We Forgive a Terrorist?' And listen to this: the editorial reads, 'There is no victory in killing innocent people. McVeigh's crime was an act of cowardice and cruelty. It was pointless.' And on the next page was the poem that he gave to his executioners before they killed him. I underlined these lines: 'Under the bludgeonings of chance/My head is bloody but unbowed . . . I am the master of my fate/I am the captain of my soul.' It was really upsetting. Am I Timothy McVeigh?

"I was telling you about Omar. I had a meeting with him shortly after our anniversary in Greifswald. We usually met in public places. At last I was invited into his inner sanctum, and I was honored. At his door Omar greeted me warmly, ushering me into a bright, modern apartment. He had posters of Formula One cars covering the walls.

"'Well, what did you expect?' Omar said, noticing my surprise. 'Candlelight? The wail of the muezzin? Hamas call to arms?'

"'Certainly not the roar of a Ferrari,' I said.

"'You should have seen the crash at the Belgian Grand Prix. You think my obsession with speed is strange?'

"'I just hadn't expected this.'

"'Speed is exhilarating, Sami. Well, I don't have to tell you that.'

"I sat down on his couch. 'You wanted to see me,' I said nervously. 'I wanted to see you too.'

"'Yes. I know. Ahmad,' Omar replied. 'A very strange fellow. He has a big imagination.'

"'He was following me.'

"'Ahmad has a suspicious, conspiratorial nature. You should forget about him.'

"'But he said—'

"'He says all sorts of things, Sami. Actually I think he needs medical attention.'

"'He mentioned a team. My team. What is that about? I demand to know!'

"'Come on, Sami. We're all on the same team. We're all one big raucous, diverse team, under the Almighty.'

"'How could he have known I was in Greifswald—at that club—at that time?'

"'With your Karima,' Omar said with a smirk.

"My anger welled up. Finally, I said, 'Yes, with my Karima.'

"'Did you know, Sami, that the glorious Islamic Caliphate ended with the Turks? Yes, it's true. It was the Turks who destroyed our religious empire. Muslims have been looking for a caliph ever since.'

"'Don't change the subject,' I snapped. 'How did that guy know where I was?'

"'He knew because I told him.'

"I was shocked, dumbfounded.

"'Look, Sami. I have put myself out for you, way out. So has Atta. We're believers, living in the land of the infidel. We worship a different God. We treasure different things. There are people out there who would do us harm, who want to destroy us or deport us or undermine our faith. We have to be careful, very careful, about who is invited into our circle.'

"'I don't like being spied on. I came here only to learn.'

"'We have shared many confidences with you. We have trusted you, and we have to know that our trust is well-founded. We must be sure that our confidences are protected.'

"'Why did you want to see me? Not to tell me that, or discuss the Belgian Grand Prix.'

"'No.'

"'Why am I here?'

"'It's about Atta.'

"'What about him?'

"'He has written his will.'

"'Is he sick?' I asked.

"'It doesn't matter why he has written it,' Omar replied. 'He just has. And he wants us to witness it.'

"'Us? Atta hates me.'

"'Yes, us. A proper will requires two witnesses, and he wants you and me.'

"'You and ME?'

"'Atta is honoring you by this request. As a good Muslim, it's your duty to oblige. You may not like Atta, and he may not like you. In fact, Atta has no friends, not even me, and that's the way he wants it. He's on a quest, and we must honor that. His quest may be dangerous.'

"'Dangerous,' I scoffed. 'He's an architecture student.'

"'I don't know; maybe the danger he imagines is why he wants to get this done. I'm not sure. Sometimes when a person devotes himself totally to a cause, he takes big risks. You or I may not be so bold or courageous. But we must respect his commitment.'

"He reached behind his head and pulled a document from the bookshelf, handing it to me. It had an elaborate cover and really nice Egyptian calligraphy and an epigraph that read:

My prayers and my sacrifice

And my life and my death

Belong to Allah

Lord of the Worlds.

"Inside, scrawled on parchment as if it was done hurriedly, the will had a preamble. He stated his belief in resurrection. There was a plea that his survivors follow the path of the Prophet and a reference to Abraham, 'a good Muslim, who brought his son to die.' And then instructions about what should be done with his body.

"Let me tell you something, my darling. I had doubts about Atta's manhood before. Now they were confirmed. No woman should beg pardon for him at his grave? Whoever washed his body should wear gloves and not touch his genitals? No woman should attend his burial? No pregnant woman 'or other unclean persons' should be allowed to be present at his burial? It seemed obvious. I had to know.

"'Is Atta a homosexual?' I asked.

"Omar leaned back on the couch and put his hand over his eyes, as if he was suddenly fatigued.

"'Sami, it's true that you're different from the rest of us,' he said finally. 'You come from Lebanon, a land tainted by French sophistication. Unlike Atta and the rest of us, you hail from a well-to-do family. You have read too many French novels.'

"'Well, is he?' I insisted.

"'You have become my project, Samir. But sometimes you try my patience almost to the limit, and I wonder if it's worth it.'

"'I'm sorry, but—'

"'You are projecting your Western values onto him!' he said. His voice was rising now. He sat up and turned on me. I tell you. He scared me. 'Atta is on a spiritual journey. It may be beyond you now to *understand it. He is preparing himself, and his will is part of his purification. This is a ritual for him. What you interpret in your adolescent way is for him an act of cleansing himself.'*

"'But women and genitals—'

"'His manhood is not in question here! You think these references indicate that he hates women. The reverse is true. He worships the woman as pure and noble. Primarily it is his mother he is thinking about in this will. He knows his death would bring grief to his family. He cannot stand the thought of women wailing at his funeral. He does not want his mother weeping at his grave.'

"Again he slouched back, resting his head on the back of the couch, and closed his eyes.

"'But no pregnant woman be allowed to say goodbye?' I persisted, looking at the provisions of the will. 'Associating that with an unclean person?'

"'I'm not sure what he means by that, Sami,' Omar replied, still with his eyes closed. 'It's true that's strange. But it is not for us to comprehend everything that is swirling around in that head. In the name of God the Compassionate, the Merciful, we are mere witnesses here. We are being asked to witness his quest, so that for him, it is official, so that his affairs will be in order. We must do as he asks.'

"'But wait—how can I be associated with this, if he's planning to do something rash?' I said. 'You're asking me to sign something that might get me into trouble.'

"'As always we must look for understanding in the Holy Book.' He reached around him and pulled his Koran from the shelf, handing it to me.

"'Turn to Surah 74, verse 26.'

"'Oh, please, not that. Not now.'

"'I insist, Sami. Surah 74, verse 26.'

"I hated this. But I flipped through the wrinkled pages anyway until I found his passage. It was marked with three long red lines and three exclamation points.

"'Read until I tell you to stop.'

"Flatly, without interest, I read: "'Soon will I cast him into Hell Fire. And what is Hell Fire? It spares no sinner nor leaves anything unburnt. It darkens and burns the skin of man. Over it are the nineteen angels. They are the guardians of the Fire. We have fixed their number as Nineteen only as a trial for the disbelievers.'"

"Omar raised his hand. 'That's enough.'

"I was mystified. 'I don't understand. Nineteen. Why nineteen?'

"'That will be your next assignment, Sami. Let your mind rest on that passage. Now we must do our duty.'

"Again he reached behind him and handed me a pen.

"Pointing to the end of the document, 'There,' he said.

"I signed in my best Arabic calligraphy, Karima. I'm not proud of it. Not now. It seemed like a simple thing to do at the time. Simple and meaningless. The act of signing did have an impact on me. I felt good . . . and proud. It made me downplay Atta's faults.

"When I finished, Omar nodded in satisfaction, and then he signed as well.

"'Now we are brothers,' he said. He raised a crooked finger, and I returned the salute."

***

It was forty-eight hours to the Witnessing Day, and Karima was imagining the scene at the Lades Chicken joint at the busiest time of the day. What would her waiter look like? she wondered. What does a terrorist look like anyway? She rehearsed ordering Adana kebob and asking for wedding soup and then finally unburdening herself of Sami's materials. What would she feel afterwards? Relief? Shame? Terror? The problem was, she would be giving his memoir to the wrong people and destroying her alibi.

Recht called. "I must come to see you tonight."

When he came through the door, his face was grim. By now, she had come to read his moods well: his elation at good news from Afghanistan, his frustration with the overall investigation and with the Americans, most of all, his determined scowl when he was about to get tough with her. She knew immediately that this session would be one of those.

He got right to the point.

"You told me that you know nothing of Omar."

"That's right."

"I do not believe you, Karima."

"I'm sorry."

"Let me make myself clear. You are underestimating the danger."

"The danger to me? Oh, I'm very aware of that. You said you would protect me, Kommissar Recht."

"We are dealing with very desperate people. There's only so much we can do."

"You've never put it like that before. What about my mother?"

"What about her?"

"I'm worried about her, about her safety as well."

"Has something happened?"

"I'm nervous, that's all. You talked about desperate people. Desperate people lash out."

"We're trying to cover all the bases."

"Well, I think you should assign a bodyguard to my mother as well."

"I would need a reason, Karima. I'd need to know what we'd be protecting her from. I'd have to brief my officers on a specific threat if there was one. And I'd have to convince the first kommissar that this is necessary."

"Let's face it, Kommissar Recht: you're not really protecting me at all. Your Sergeant Braun is a clown. You're spying on me."

"Look, if you're so worried about your mother, go see her. Put in some new locks or a new home security system."

"Fine," she said with a note of disgust. "Why have you come here tonight?"

He waited for her ire to cool.

"We know you received a package from Haddad after 9/11," he said.

She looked at him quizzically. After a pause, she said, "I received a letter."

"A letter?" he said with surprise.

"Yes, a farewell letter. A love letter."

"I would like to see it," he said.

She rose from the couch without comment, went to her desk, and thumbed through her voluminous patient files.

"I intended to give it to you all along," she said throwing the letter into his lap, "when the time was right."

She watched him read it slowly, his lips moving as he whispered the words almost aloud. *I do not leave you alone. Allah is with you. . . .*

He put it down on the table and looked at her sternly.

"We believe you received more than this letter."

He reached into his breast pocket and pulled out Braun's photograph of her removing Sami's bulky package from the mail slot.

She took the picture, pondered it, and then burst into tears. At length, she rose again from the couch and went to her chest of drawers and her desk again.

"Yes," she said, swirling around on him defiantly, "there was more. He sent me his Koran and his engagement ring and his *mahr*, his wedding gift. There!" she said throwing the items on the couch beside him. "Do the police want these too for their evidence file!"

He sat still for a moment, an inscrutable expression on his face. Slowly, he picked up the leather-bound, pocket-sized, gold-embossed Koran and leafed to its frontispiece to see the inscription: *"For Karima Ilgun, My love. My beloved lady. My heart."* And his signature, *"Sami Haddad."*

And then he picked up the jewelry case, opening it to see chandelier earrings with emerald studs.

"He bought them for me in Pakistan and kept them until the last day," she blurted out.

He examined the gold coin and then opened the little case with the engagement ring. Closing its lid slowly, he stared at her for a long moment. Then he rose abruptly and turned on her harshly.

"Okay, Dr. Ilgun," he said, his eyes narrowing. "I tell you this formally, as a police warning. Under no circumstances are you to have any contact whatsoever with Haddad's associates. We're going to tighten our surveillance of you to make sure that does not happen."

She started to speak, but he held up his hand for silence. "Good evening," he said sharply and left.

***

June 16, 2001

"*Ahmad arrived today. Omar insists that he stay here with me in this tiny apartment. Need to be careful.*

"*Where was I? Oh, Omar . . .*

"*Soon enough I became a regular at Omar's apartment. One day he announced that we were going to watch a video. 'About Jihad. Atta is coming. And Marwan. Do you know him?' I did not.*

"'*He's a Gulf States romantic,' Omar explained. 'Married. Very straitlaced. His wife wears the niqab. I've never seen her full face, but she has very lovely brown eyes. They live simply, and when he's questioned about his lifestyle, he says, "Well, the Prophet lived very simply too." He's a little overweight.'*

"'*Really.'*

"'*And like you, he's not much of a student. He's nearly flunked out a bunch of times. But he's very good value.'*

"*The concept stuck in my mind, Karima. What did that mean? Good value for what?*

"'*But first you must do your homework,' he said. 'Atta has a present for you.'*

"*He handed me a simple, cardboard-bound book.* The Sayings of Martyr Abdullah Azzam. *'Look at the dedication,' Omar said.*

"In the frontispiece Atta had written in his florid calligraphy: 'For Abu Tariq al Lubnani—'

"'This must be for someone else,' I said, closing it and starting to hand it back.

"'No, my friend. He has conferred upon you a secret name.'

"'My name for the struggle?' I said, half-joking.

"'You may call it that if you wish. This is not a joke, Sami.'

"'I'm sorry.'

"'Figuratively, the name means, "The Lebanese, father of one who knocks on the door."'

"'Am I knocking at a door?'

"'Not yet.'

"'I thought the name Tareq meant "traveler," I said.

"'Traveler—or conqueror. Or both. Atta has honored you with a connection to one of the greatest military leaders of the Umayyad age, Ṭāriq ibn Ziyād.'

"'Ṭāriq ibn Ziyād?' I was confused.

"Omar looked at me, amazed. 'Sami, you confound me. All he did was conquer most of North Africa and then all of Al-Andalus in the eighth century. Glorious Al-Andalus, the highest expression of Islam in Europe. Gibraltar derives its name from Tareq, you know. The Rock of Tareq.'

"I turned again to Atta's dedication.

"'Someday, Sami, you will be our Rock of Gilbraltar,' Omar said.

"I could feel my embarrassment. The inscription read:

> *In the name of Allah the blessed and the merciful.*
>
> *I give you this book, asking God that it may be useful to you, that you understand it and act. That you act according to this book, after you have read the Koran. That you may do good and stay far from evil, that you be true to yourself, even if that should not please the unbelievers or if they should not be afraid as they should be.*

"Omar had turned his back and was looking out the window.

"'This all comes with a price,' he said at last.

"'Oh? How much?'

"He turned back to me with a smile.

"'You need to pull your grades up, Sami,' he said. 'And start attending your lectures again. You're no good to us if you can't stay in school.'"

5

ON THE NIGHT BEFORE her appointment with Omar at the Lades Chicken joint, Karima slept fitfully. It was time to unburden herself from this terrible weight, she concluded. She had to decide in favor of her personal safety, and that of her mother. To be sure, delivering Sami's materials to one party or another had its consequences. They were precious to one side, and crucial evidence to another. Wasn't jail preferable, the safer bet? She had to get rid of them one way or another, even if she didn't yet know his full story.

When she awoke, she knew what she had to do: Let them have their sacred relics. Let them deposit the tapes in some ornate reliquary the way the Christians put the blood or bones of their ancient kings in a vessel of some sort and placed it on a pedestal. She could see the flowing inscription: "The Memoirs of Abu Tariq al Libani, hero of ath-thalatha, Djumade l-akhira 1422." She imagined a dark cave deep in a high mountain like Tora Bora, an al-Qaeda museum lit by candlelight, a place of pilgrimage to those who hated the West and all westerners.

When she awoke, she dressed hurriedly, and when it was close to the time of the appointment, she wrested the tapes from their secret crevice. Spreading them out on her coffee table, she set the last two tapes aside and threw the rest in a tote bag. "Goodbye, Sami," she said for what seemed like the twentieth time. "I'm sorry I don't have time to hear your whole story. But I know how it turns out."

As far away as three blocks from Lades Chicken, she could hear the murmurings of a crowd. The curious seemed to be streaming along the sidewalks of Steindamm in that direction, as the noise became louder, the concatenation of whisperings. Within a hundred yards of the place, the police held back the crowd.

"What's going on?" she asked a man.

"They've arrested a terrorist in there," he said.

Karima craned her neck to see over the people in front of her. By the entrance to the joint, she could see Recht and Braun. They were talking to a burly man who held a bullhorn and seemed to be issuing orders. Within minutes two policemen escorted a slender, diminutive, slumping figure out of the restaurant and placed him in an unmarked van. A towel covered his head. In the crowd there was a smattering of applause.

The man next to her turned to her.

"Well, that's that," he said with a shrug and a smirk. "Our great police force in action." He swiveled to leave, and Karima followed him languidly, deep in thought, clutching her tote bag to her side more tightly than ever. What did this mean?

***

A few days after her missed appointment at Lades Chicken, she received her summons for her first formal investigative session. At first, there would be "executive" sessions with a senior judge, Recht informed her, closed to the public and conducted at BKA headquarters. When the time came, Recht ushered her into her now-familiar interrogation room. This time, the inquisitor was a judge of criminal court, named Gerhard Leicht. As she made her way to her seat, she felt faint and had to be supported. But her first glimpse of Judge Leicht was reassuring. Elderly, kind-faced, and mannerly in a musty, old-fashioned way, he was a senior jurist whose first words to her exuded sympathy.

"You may refuse to answer any questions if you think your answers could endanger yourself or your family," he said in a gravelly voice. "If you should answer falsely, the consequences would be severe. Please do not accuse anyone without evidence, and please do not try to protect any other person from possible punishment."

"Thank you, Your Honor," she whispered.

From many weeks of fear and self-examination, she was exhausted, she told the judge. She knew nothing of the diabolical plot, since Sami Haddad had said nothing to her about it and had shielded her from his friends. With dismay, she had watched her lover change before he went to Afghanistan.

"Then upon his return he seemed to have miraculously recovered his old, carefree self." At this statement members of the court exchanged meaningful glances.

Karima acknowledged that they had had countless phone conversations when he was in Florida for his flight training, but their conversations dealt only with ordinary things, like their future life together after he became an airline pilot. His involvement in the attack had come as a complete shock to her, she professed.

"I'm still trying to come to grips with this, Your Honor," she said. "My life is in a shambles."

The old judge listened attentively. He asked her only a few questions—about the members of the Haddad family with whom she had become acquainted, about a few phone numbers in her address book. Then abruptly, as if he were late and had been held up in traffic, a bald, younger man with a pointed goatee entered the room, apologized

perfunctorily for his tardiness, and introduced himself to the witness/
suspect as Judge Henning Schneider. Judge Leicht deferred immediately
to him, and Judge Schneider took over the questioning. Peering at her
through thin, rimless lenses, he dispensed with the pleasantries.

"There is this extraordinary letter that you have provided to
Kommissar Recht," he said crisply. Karima stiffened. He proceeded
to read lines from it in a stage voice, enunciating the tender parts with
particular scorn. Through his performance she was able to control her
emotions until he came to the line, *You should be very proud of me. It's
an honor, and you will see the results, and everybody will be happy."*

"You remember these words?" he asked.

An answer formed somewhere deep in her throat, but it came out in
an unintelligible gurgle. The judge waited for her to pull herself together,
his eyes down at his desk on the sheaf of papers before him.

"May we proceed?"

She nodded.

"Why did you not immediately hand this letter over to the authorities?" he asked, still looking down at his papers and then up at her.

"I was frightened," Karima said.

"You were frightened, Fräulein?" his question carried a note of
mocksurprise.

"And besides—"she began.

"Besides what?"

"Nothing, Your Honor."

"Now—" he started, but she cut in.

"I'm exhausted. I would like to end this testimony now and continue
at a later time."

As the senior judge, Judge Leicht nodded. A second hearing was
set for days later.

When she got home that night, she paced around her apartment.
She turned on the radio. "Under a clear sky lit by moonlight, a steady
American bombardment of Kabul began Sunday night—" She turned
it off. Omar dominated her thoughts, his specter now even greater and

more terrifying. He would be livid that she had not shown up for Adana kebab and wedding soup. Not only had he not received Sami's materials. He had lost a valued member of his cell. There could be no doubt that Karima was responsible. Omar would be even more dangerous to her now, she realized. Was there any way he would hear that she had surrendered Sami's precious letter to Recht? The vice kommissar had called it an executive session. Supposedly, that meant all testimony was secret. But who could be trusted anymore?

Now she regretted not asking Recht to keep the letter's content secret. It would have been her right under German law. She had only handed it over to gain points with him . . . and with the hope that he would be satisfied. But her long delay in doing so looked bad. Imagine their reaction if they ever learned about the tapes! she thought. And yet nothing Recht or the court could do to her now was as horrifying as her nightmare at what Omar might do, to her or to her mother, if she hung onto the tapes much longer.

She had to get Sami's tapes out of Hamburg. She decided to take them to her mother's place in Stuttgart. Maybe not the last tape or two. That was her ultimate exoneration, she felt. Her trump card. In a pinch she might need it close at hand.

***

June 19, 2001

> "Only a month before we're together, my love. Perhaps I will give you these tapes then, and years later, we will listen to them together and laugh and wonder how I became involved with such a thing.
>
> "Atta preached that we all had a moral duty to jihad. As my father's only son, I'd escaped military service, you know, because Lebanon values the importance of the single male as the head of a family, and I was excused. I'd had never fired a rifle in my life before now. If I was an unlikely holy warrior, Atta was even less so. With his gimpy

leg and spindly arms and unhealthy ways, he would not last long.

"When the American embassies in Kenya and Tanzania were blown up, and the press blamed a Sheikh named Osama bin Laden, there was high excitement in our study group. 'You see,' Atta crowed, 'something can be done!' Two weeks later, the Americans fired seventy-five missiles at the Sheikh's training camps in Afghanistan. The bombs kicked up a lot of dust, hit the camp's kitchen and mosque and a few bathrooms, and killed three Yemenis, an Uzbek, an Egyptian, and a cook. A cook! Can you believe it? The emir of Marienstrasse could scarcely contain himself. He waved an editorial from the English magazine in our faces about how the American attacks had created ten thousand new mujahidin where before there had been none.

"In the months that followed, I felt like a reluctant brother to Atta. I wasn't very interested in studying. I was ashamed of being a lousy son to my ailing father and a bad boyfriend to you. My parents kept calling, beseeching me to return to Lebanon. With each monthly check, my father spoke of his poor health and his hope that I would come home soon. Wouldn't I like to have a car in Germany? Not just any old car, but an Opel coupe that a friend of his in Düsseldorf did not want. If I would only come home to sign the title, the car was mine. But I kept evading them.

"I had grown comfortable in the study group. My ability to hold forth on the subject of holy war grew more polished. When I talked of martyrdom as the highest glory for any Muslim, I watched the heads nod and the smiles form. When I expressed dissatisfaction for the way I had led my life previously and spoke of my desire to leave this world 'not in a natural way,' Omar nodded his pleasure.

"My sessions in Omar's apartment became more frequent; sometimes *there were as many as four a week. During the summer of 1999, I spent fewer weekends with you. He made me feel more connected to a wider world. I derived pleasure at being seen as an activist and a militant. I even started praying occasionally, though I could not manage five times a day.*

I knew I was changing, my darling. Because Omar was funny and soft-spoken and thoughtful, because he could talk of auto racing and football, and politics was not so all-consuming for him, I came to value his friendship. I admired Omar as a man of depth. I began to see Atta as a visionary.

"*And then late in the summer of '99 came that call from Uncle Assem. Of course, I knew you were behind it. After all the lies I told you, I cannot blame you now. You meant well. A visit from the impressive patriarch of our family would be intimidating, I knew.*

"*We met at a pizza joint in the city's center. When Uncle Assem stood up and offered his hand, I lost my nerve. He was dressed in the uniform of his business success, and he towered over me. I could not look at the old veteran without imagining him plying the back alleys of Algiers, in search of Abu Nidal.*

"'*Your father has had a heart attack,' Assem said.*

"*This news genuinely shocked me, Karima. I could not imagine it. My father had always been healthy, always so strong. I always thought of him as invincible. He is a good and generous man. He did not deserve to die.*

"'*Will he survive?' I asked.*

"'*Yes, but he must be very careful.'*

"'How bad is it?'

"'He wants to live. He wants to see you, Samir.'

"I had anticipated this familiar request, not the heart attack perhaps, but certainly a fierce demand to come home. 'You know how much I'd love to jump on a plane right now, uncle,' I said. 'I'm so relieved that he's okay. I will come soon, I promise. But for now I'm stretched thin with upcoming exams and other obligations.'

"'What other obligations?' he asked.

"Just obligations. You know the kind of thing students have. And I have a very demanding girlfriend.'

"Uncle frowned disapprovingly. 'I'll be honest with you, Samir. We have heard reports about the company you are keeping, disturbing reports.'

"'What kind of reports have you heard?' I asked.

"'Well, for instance, that you're becoming very religious.'

"'It's true. And what's wrong with that?'

"'Nothing . . . in moderation,' he replied. 'It's like drinking. Best not to get intoxicated.'

"'It's personal, uncle. Religion is a personal thing. Young men my age struggle to understand what they really believe.'

"'And you are hanging out with dangerous militants.'

"I threw up my hands. 'They're students! Like me. A few of them talk a big game, but they're harmless.'

"'Listen to me, Samir. I've known you all your life. I've watched you develop—with great pleasure, I might add—as a normal, healthy kid, with normal, healthy instincts. A little lazy perhaps, a little lackadaisical in your studies, but with a wonderful sense of fun. You're no religious zealot. Let's face it: you're going through a phase in your life. Ya'youni, you're no longer a kid. You're an adult, and a phase like this can be dangerous and have consequences.'

"I wondered how much longer this would last.

"He leaned forward over the table. 'I want you to come home with me, Samir,' he said.

"'I can't. I just can't.'

"'You need to remember where you came from, my son. You need to rediscover the values you were raised with.'

"He was making me very uncomfortable. 'I honor my family. I have not forgotten where I came from.'

"'You have obligations at home. For the good son, those are primary.'

"'In a few months. I promise.'

"'When exactly? I tell you that your father is dying, and you tell me that sometime later, at your convenience, once your girlfriend approves it, you'll move yourself to come home!'

"'I will come as soon as I am able.' I had to be adamant.

"Assem's exasperation was evident. 'I have brought the title to that car with me,' he said at last. 'Here, take it. It's yours.' He reached for the clasp on his briefcase. I put my hand on Uncle Assem's arm to stop him.

"'Uncle, really. I appreciate the family's generosity. But honestly, I don't need a car. I'm a student. I get around just fine on my bike. But thank you. And please thank Dad.'

Assem rose to leave. 'Remember what I told you.'

"'Remember what?'

"'The obligations of a good son.'"

***

The next day, Karima arrived home from running errands and accidentally kicked a letter at her feet. The return address read, "Boulevard Zeitung." With dread she tore it open.

> *Dear Dr. Ilgun,*
>
> *We will be publishing a story on you and your relationship with the death-pilot, Samir Haddad, in two days. Of course, we would like to offer you the opportunity to comment, or to challenge any facts, as you choose.*

She crumpled up the letter and threw it on the floor. At least it wasn't another missive from Omar—that she dreaded most of all—but the media barrage was about to begin. She picked up the ball of paper, opened it, and read on.

I hope you will be willing to help the German public understand what might have been going on in Mr. Haddad's head and heart, as he became involved with the Hamburg group, and how he could have been so effective in masking his plans when he prepared in Florida for his mission.

We accept entirely and totally that you have absolutely no culpability whatever in his actions.

Spare me your absolution, she thought. Popping an Ambien, she fell onto her bed without undressing. "I have to finish that last segment," she said to herself. She retrieved the machine and hit play.

"I have to make it brief tonight, yahabibti. I just had a close call. Ahmad found a handkerchief of yours. I had put in my duffel and forgot about it. They are questioning my commitment. I must be very careful now. He has gone out for a while. I think it is safe to record.

"Oh, my love, I have been thinking about you all day. Only four weeks until we're together! I am wondering if I will have the courage to share these stories with you. I want so much to tell you about this secret life. I imagine you, your love, your smile, and I feel the strength to say no. I'm counting on you to make me strong. I need you desperately, yahayati. Next month could be our last time together, or it could be just a beginning. I will have to make my final decision. From that point forward there will be no turning back.

"That's why I'm telling you the whole story now. I want you to know, but I don't know if I can tell you when I see you face-to-face. I feel like such a coward. I don't know if I can take your one-way ticket back to Germany. If I did . . . if I did . . . we could just fly off to Beirut and lose ourselves in the love and protection of my family, my clan, away from Germany and the US, from Atta and Omar and Abu Musad and Muktar and . . . all of it.

"In a way, the easier path is to carry forward, to join the struggle of the Prophet. I have made a solemn oath to the Sheikh—Ahmad reminds me of it all the time, and of the many people who have placed their trust in me. He speaks of the glorious path we're walking together, fighting in the cause of Allah.

"I hope you will be able to forgive me, whether we are together in the years ahead or not."

***

Afterwards, she slept, dead to the world, for twelve hours. When she awoke, she packed her bag, retrieved the tapes from their secret hiding place, and left her apartment quickly through a back door in the basement to catch the train to Stuttgart. She wanted to be with her mother when the hurricane hit.

When she opened the door to her mother's apartment, there sat the sweet lady, dressed in her finest robe, her upper body stiff and upright in her wheelchair. Karima leaned down to give her a big kiss and hug, careful not to push against her tender, swollen legs.

"Greetings, my darling," her mother said. "I'm so glad you have come, especially now."

They ate döner kebabs and tabbouleh and talked of everything except what was on their minds.

"You haven't had any strange phone calls, have you, Mutti?" Karima asked.

"Why do you keep asking me that?" she wondered with a note of irritation. "No, I haven't. Should I be getting strange phone calls?"

"No, of course not. I'm sorry. I'd forgotten I'd asked that before."

That night, after her mother went to bed, Karima checked that all the doors and windows were locked. Then she drifted into the room where she had grown up. Her mother had kept it as a kind of shrine. On the wall were rough paintings she had made in kindergarten and a photograph of her in a grade school production of *Rotkäppchen* when she starred as Little Red Riding Hood. Her mother kept her childhood poetry books and her high school yearbooks just as they were ten years ago. On her schoolgirl desk was an album with pressed flowers and valentines and photographs with her favorite friends. Next to it was a Hello Kitty change purse and a pencil holder. Her eye fell on two letter boxes on the bookshelf. She opened one to see several sixth-grade notebooks and a bundle of letters from friends.

Karima slipped into her bed, surrounded by stuffed animals, retrieved a tape from her briefcase, and wondered: *Is Mutti safe here?*

***

June 23, 2001

> *"For Atta the time for study is over, and the moment of action has arrived. He gathered us together in Omar's apartment with an air of urgency. By now I am accustomed to his rants. His lesson for the day was the inspirational history of the Chechen struggle. 'Look how the greatly outmanned and outgunned mujahideen prevailed in Afghanistan in the 1980s,' he said. 'See how in the First Chechen War, again believers had humiliated that drunken pig, Boris Yeltsin. Now it's Putin's turn.'*

> *"The drift of the discussion made me nervous. But I knew I had to be careful. Before I could speak up about the practical difficulties of Chechnya, I needed to demonstrate my commitment to the cause. Atta had asked me to contribute something uplifting and motivational to the meeting. So, I composed a little poem to appeal to the Jihadist in Atta.*

> *"'I'm not much of a poet,' I told the group. 'But I wrote this for you last night.' I fished out a crumpled piece of paper and read with gusto.*

'We will return to him (Allah)

But the spring of my country has been murdered

The red shining sunrise will come

The morning will come.

The victors will come, will come

We will search, we will find you, and we will defeat you

The earth will shake underneath your feet.

I came to you with men

Who loved death as much as you loved life.

The mujahideen give their money for weapons,

Food, and travel, with the goal

To succeed and to die for the cause of Allah.

But the unfortunate will perish.

Arise, Oh sweet smell of Paradise.

"They clapped boisterously and I gave them a long, sweeping stage bow.

"After I read my poem, I thought it might be safe to raise some objections about the Chechnya mission. How could we join such a *faraway fight? How would we be trained? Who would provide us the money for the travel and the training?*

"Atta had the answers. There was this agent in Duisburg near Düsseldorf, a Mauritanian he knew only by a code name, Abu Musab. He might be willing to help us. Within a few days, the four of us were on the train southwest to the province of North Rhine-Westphalia. I was not sure what to expect. A bearded, one-eyed fanatic, wearing a lace white skullcap, peering out through round, Coke-bottle glasses.

"In Duisburg we made our way to Hochfeld, a working-class neighborhood of rundown three-story houses and the pervasive stink of garbage. At Eigenstrasse 92, Atta rang the bell. The door opened, and before us stood a short, dark-skinned, smiling man of about forty, dressed casually in a floor-length blue Dra'a and slippers. He was the perfect image of an elegant junior professor. 'Guten Tag, meine Herren,' he said with a twinkle, 'or should I say—' And he made a clicking sound that is the Mauritanian greeting: 'I wish you no evil.' Then he ushered us into a bright, modern flat. Large abstract paintings dominated the walls, Andalusian shag rugs covered the floor, and a coffee table was piled high with oversized art books. The book on top was about ancient North African ruins. A side door was open a crack, and I glimpsed Musab's study, with a large computer at the center and various computer manuals stacked around it.

"Nervously, Atta blurted out why we had come. 'We're all graduate students,' he said, 'all in various technical fields. I'm in urban design, Marwan in shipbuilding, Omar is a banker, and Sami is a future pilot, studying aeronautical engineering. We've all been in the West for more than three years.' He went on to describe how we had grounded ourselves in the Koran, in the history of the Prophet, and in conflicts between the West and Islam over the centuries.

"'Now we wanted to put our beliefs into action by fulfilling our obligations as Muslims.'

"As Atta proclaimed our desire to fight in Chechnya, the Mauritanian listened patiently, a look of worldly empathy fixed on his handsome face.

"When Atta finished, Abu Musab offered tea in small cups. The first cup, he explained, was unsweetened, to represent the struggles of life. The next cup, he promised, would be sweetened and minted, to signify that life would get better when one married. I shot a glance at Omar. Through the door to the next room, opened just a crack, I noticed a coffee-skinned beauty about our age, wrapped in a colorful sari, preparing our sweets.

"Abu Musab gazed at each of us, as if he were gauging our worth. He expressed his gratitude for these heartfelt sentiments.

"'Do you have an email address?' he asked.

"'Yes, everyone has at least one gmx account and a Hotmail account,' Atta replied.

"'Very good,' he said. 'We can stay in touch, then. Be careful of those Hotmail chats. They can be traced, you know.'

"'Yes, we know,' Atta said.

"'Send me your MSN names, and I'll add you to my contact list. You'll get an invitation from mauritanian01.'

"'I always use a combination of el emir for my accounts,' Atta said.

"'Fine. I appreciate your trouble to come all this way—just to be disappointed.'

"Disappointed? What had we done wrong? Surely the ranks of Allah's army could always use more warriors.

"'It's true,' he was saying. 'The fight in Chechnya is important. Local commanders need young, idealistic men like you who are ready to fight and even die for Islam. Before this villain Putin is finished, he will level Grozny flatter than the Americans flattened Hiroshima in World War II. Mark my words.'

"He paused, again picking up his ornate curved tea pot and refilling our cups with an elegant sweep of his hand. This time he offered lumps of sugar with it.

"'You asked about training. That is a subject I know something about. For this battle, training is taking place in a city called Urus-Marten. Have you heard of it?'

"'Is it in Mongolia?' Fatfat asked.

"Abu Musab smiled. 'It's a town of about one hundred thousand, the third-largest city in Chechnya,' he said. 'But how would you get there? And how would you pay for that privilege?'

"'Couldn't we just fly there?' Fatfat piped up.

"'The airplanes landing there are mostly Russian military jets. You could fly there—and then you could spend the rest of your life in a dungeon. And how would you pay for that?'

"'Sami's daddy could send us a check,' Fatfat said, and they all laughed, except me.

"After this lighthearted moment at my expense, Abu Musab made clear that most Arab fighters trying to make their way to Chechnya were being detained in Georgia. Only a few were getting through; most never had the chance to train.

"The professor pondered our crestfallen faces, as if we were schoolchildren who had just watched their ball bounce away down a hill. 'That's the way it is,' he said, shrugging his shoulders. 'I'm sorry.'

"Atta rose to leave, and we followed suit. Omar expressed thanks on behalf of the group.

"'Thank you for coming,' Abu Musab responded.

"'Let us know if anything else occurs to you,' Atta said.

"The Mauritanian nodded. 'Go in peace,' he said, 'and may God's mercy and blessing be with you.'

"Our letdown was evident. As Atta started through the door, the Mauritanian put his hand warmly on Atta's head.

"'Of course, there may be another way,' he said."

6

THE FRONT PAGE of the tabloid carried pictures of Karima Ilgun and Samir Haddad side by side against a black background with huge block letters for the headline: "THE DEATH PILOT AND HIS LADY." His grinning image came from his martyrdom video. The headshot of Karima seemed to have been taken by a security camera as she passed by the hospital guards. Inside, there were more side-by-side photos, of her entering the hospital while he entered the plane in Newark airport, and a picture of them together, smiling, in a flight simulator in Florida. Teaser headlines were embedded in the text: "IN BED WITH A TERRORIST," and "IS THIS WOMAN ONE OF OSAMA BIN LADEN'S VIRGINS?" Most wounding of all: "SHE WANTED CHILDREN FROM THE TERROR-PILOT."

In the article itself, they reported lurid details. She and Sami had been together for four years. She was Turkish and sharp-tongued, a non-practicing Muslim who had handled financial transactions and travel arrangements for him. They had been married in a religious ceremony unrecognized by the state. And most incriminating of all, they had spoken by phone nearly every day during the nine months before 9/11 when he was training in Florida, and she was "training" in Germany. Indeed, he had called her from the Newark airport on September 11 as he waited to board the plane.

And in a sidebar, there was this item: from a postal package that Sami Haddad sent to his female friend, investigators have secured a farewell love letter, which they regard as incriminating. So Recht had leaked her letter to the press!

At nine o'clock on the morning the article appeared, Karima's frantic landlady called from Hamburg to say that there were four television trucks outside her apartment, their antennae spooled to the sky, waiting for her to return. A newspaper reporter had barged into her landlady's house, was sitting on her living room couch, and refused to leave until she told him about the "9/11 babe" who lived downstairs. An uncle called her mother to say that reporters approached, trying to arrange a meeting with Karima and had been offered serious money for the favor. "How much?" she heard her mother ask, and then whistle. "Two thousand marks!" When she hung up the phone, Mutti pointed out how much pay Karima was going to lose over this mess. A little later Karima checked her answering machine remotely, and the flat digital voice announced thirty messages.

When she got home, late at night two days later, a copy of the newspaper lay at her front door. Scrawled across the headline in bold, felt-tipped, red letters were the words:

YOU ARE A CELEBRITY!—OMAR.
GOD WILLING, YOU WILL NOT BE IN THE
NEWSPAPERS AGAIN.

Karima's second day of interrogation loomed, and she was dreading it. She dressed with the radio blaring. The news reported that al-Qaeda's military chief, Mohammad Atef, had been killed in an airstrike, along with seven other terrorists, but Osama bin Laden was not among them. The killings had been accomplished with a new weapon called a drone, the announcer said, fired from a pilotless aircraft. Karima shrugged. *Good riddance*, she thought.

When she was called to the witness chair, the younger judge, Dr. Schneider, nodded to her as she took the stand.

"Is Judge Leicht ill today?" she asked.

"Judge Leicht has been removed from this case," he said tartly. "I am taking over. Would you like to swear to tell the truth with your hand on a Koran, Fräulein Ilgun?"

"Do I have to?"

"You merely have to say, 'I swear.'"

After she swore to tell the truth, he began by showing her a number of photographs of various Arab men. She knew none of them, she responded. And then he mentioned more than a dozen Arabic names. One by one, she denied any knowledge.

"But of course," he said with a smirk, "each of those names shows up in your computer's sent mail file." He paused to let her respond. She said nothing.

"You have no response?"

"No, Your Honor."

He turned to Sami's sixteen months in Florida. He showed her a map of Miami with various markings in the margins and a circle around the Four Seasons Hotel.

"Can you explain these markings?" Schneider asked.

"I don't remember," Karima said.

"Are you aware that the Four Seasons Hotel is seventy stories high and the tallest building in Miami?"

"No, I wasn't aware of that."

"Are the marginal notes in your handwriting?"

"No . . . I mean, I don't remember writing them."

The judge put the map away. Was it true that Samir Haddad wanted his residence in the United States kept secret from his friends in Germany? he asked.

"He told me never to share his address with anyone. That's all."

"But you testified that you didn't know his friends in Germany." Again he paused to allow her to answer.

"I didn't know his friends."

"Now then, Dr. Ilgun, did you ever visit a mosque with Mr. Haddad in Hamburg?"

"Yes, once. It was not his regular mosque. We went somewhere different, so he wouldn't encounter his friends. He was ashamed to be seen with me because I refused to wear the veil. I thought, better he be religious than someone who constantly picked up girls."

A court reporter snickered, and the judge shot her a disapproving glance.

"Dr. Ilgun, we have information that you married Samir Haddad under Islamic law."

"I don't wish to comment on this."

"From correspondence between yourself and Mr. Haddad, which we have in our files, one can ascertain that you were pregnant once."

She remained silent for a minute. Finally, she whispered, "I do not believe that is the business of the court. I refuse to respond."

"Have you ever undergone psychiatric treatment?" he persisted.

"Yes."

"For what condition?"

"For suicidal tendencies."

"Go on."

"I was eighteen, and I tried to commit suicide in Turkey. I took thirty antidepressants."

"What led you to this act?"

"I was in conflict between my Turkish roots and my German upbringing. That is all I wish to say. I only went to a psychiatrist twice."

"Have you sought psychiatric help since the events of September 11?"

"I do not wish to answer."

He asked her about Haddad's summer work in a VW factory. He focused on her many bank transactions on his behalf and about being his unofficial travel agent. He held up a copy of *Boulevard Zeitung* and asked if the picture of her and Sami in the flight simulator in Florida was authentic.

"Yes," she answered. "He was very happy during that time, constantly joking around."

The judge was not laughing. "You provided quite a little support system for him, didn't you?" he said without looking at her.

He shuffled some papers for a minute to let his accusation sink in. Then he turned to the story about Haddad's losing his passport after he returned from Afghanistan. "Did you know that Mr. Haddad reported to the authorities that he lost his passport?"

"Yes, I knew."

"Did he lose his passport?"

"I'm not sure he really lost it."

"Actually, you are sure. You know that he didn't lose his passport, isn't that so?"

"Yes."

"But you didn't object to his false statements to the authorities."

"No."

And then he got to the contents of her computer.

"The browser on your computer shows that someone visited the US Pentagon website, 'pentagon.afis.osd.mil.' Did you visit this website?"

"No."

"You have never, ever been on a Pentagon website?"

"No, never. I never searched such a site."

"You never *searched* it?"

"I mean, it's true that after Sami visited one time . . . maybe a few weeks after . . . I was looking for one of my research files in my computer's history file, and I saw something like that. But I didn't look at it."

"You assumed Haddad had searched it?"

"Yes."

"Weren't you curious to know what he was looking at?"

"No. I assume he was just surfing. If it had been called periodontics.com, I would have looked at it. The Pentagon did not interest me."

"But Haddad's metamorphosis interested you." He did not let her respond. "Now, in July 2001, your computer visited a site called Products Caravan. It links to a website called 'Az Publications for jihad and mujahideen.' And a book called *Join the Caravan*."

"I did not visit such a website."

"Did you notice that one as well in your history file?"

"I may have. I can't remember. He wasted a lot of time on the computer when he was with me."

"Is it not true, Dr. Ilgun, that you had left Florida in late July?"

"Yes."

"Don't you think it's possible that Mr. Haddad wanted you to see the websites he was visiting?"

"I don't understand."

"I think you do, Dr. Ilgun. You have told Kommissar Recht of his family worry that he was becoming a fanatic. You saw these sites, and now you say you were not curious enough to look at them?"

"Perhaps I should have. I see your point now, judge. Yes, I should have paid more attention."

"I agree. Maybe you should have paid a lot more attention. Or maybe you did pay a lot more attention that you are telling us." Again he shuffled papers. Then he looked up at her sternly. "It's hard to believe that Samir Haddad was so sloppy—he was a terrorist in training, after all—that he was so sloppy as to leave such incriminating files on your computer . . . unless he *wanted* you to stumble on them."

"Perhaps he did. I don't know. There is so much about all of this I don't understand."

"A trained terrorist, especially one who is sophisticated with computers, would know to clear his history of compromising material, unless suspect files were left there deliberately, don't you agree?

"I don't know what to say."

"Wouldn't Haddad know that you could check the browser history?"

"I guess so. I never thought about it before."

"Is this something that you ever did together?"

"Sometimes he showed me things online. I don't remember ever looking at the browser history with him." She paused. "Judge Schneider, I am a junior dentist. My fascination is with molars and bicuspids, and I'm very busy. I don't spend much time on random websites."

"In that case you are quite an unusual member of your generation," he said sardonically. "Now, in mid-July, only five weeks before the attacks on September 11, you visited Mr. Haddad in Florida, correct?"

"Yes."

"You stayed with him for nearly two weeks. Isn't that so?"

"Yes. I was quite ill with a throat infection."

"On July 22, your computer visited a music site, Napster. You accessed a musical group called I Am the World Trade Center."

"No!" she exploded. "No. No. No. That is not true!" she shouted. "I don't listen to that kind of music! In fact, I hate it. I like only Turkish music."

The judge peered up at her, his bald head glistening with perspiration in the overhead light, his lenses slipping down on his nose. He waited as Karima glowered at him and then averted her eyes, rummaging for a tissue, sitting down in embarrassment.

His next words dripped with sarcasm.

"Dr. Ilgun, if you don't listen to *that* kind of music, how do you know what kind of music I Am the World Trade Center is?"

The question hung in the air like bad odor. She sat whimpering in the chair.

The judge began to gather the papers in front of him.

"Let me tell you something, Dr. Ilgun," he said finally, glancing at Recht. "Our investigators believe the hijacker, Samir Haddad, offered them their best chance to thwart the 9/11 attack. And that you offered them the best chance to thwart Sami Haddad. I am inclined to agree with them."

When she finally got home that night, drained and exhausted, she still seethed with anger. The nerve of that devil to trample on her personal life so viciously! What right did he have to question her about her most closely guarded secrets, when they had nothing to do with any of this! A bald-headed, stone-hearted, squirrelly-eyed infidel like him could never understand a secret Islamic marriage that was never really a marriage anyway. And her pregnancy and her psychological problems! Her schoolgirl religious studies flashed through her mind. *Let not Satan hinder you. Verily he is to you a plain enemy.*

Lying awake that night, Karima wondered if she had ever really been in love with Sami Haddad. How can anyone be in love with half a man? Yes, it was true that she knew about his other life. Not the full dimensions of it. She was just learning those from his tapes. She had tried to ferret it out. She had confronted him. She remembered the exchanges vividly.

"Sami, I want to meet your friends."

"Sami, why on earth are you growing that ugly beard?"

"Come off it, Sami. You're not really the religious type."

"Tell me something, Sami. What do you mean by this word *jihad*?"

What more could she have done? What more *should* she have done? She rolled her memories back through her mind, as if they too were on tape, and she could stop the tape at random and insert something she should have said. But she had only sniped at him. Potshots—that's all she had taken. When he grew angry or deflective, she had always pulled back, afraid that pursuing the issue would cause another breakup. She had never confronted him full bore with her suspicions. Now she imagined what she should have said.

"Sami, sit down and stop your posturing! We've got to get to the bottom of this, even if it takes all night."

Perhaps that was her crime. All too willingly, she had been swayed by her feelings for him. He had corrupted her and made her an accomplice in his crime. If he was a master criminal, she was the supreme victim. How could she reconcile the side of Sami she had loved with Sami Haddad the mass murderer?

Moreover, as she listened to his story, she wondered if Sami was ever a willing participant. Could he have been forced somehow? She had never really believed his conversion to radical Islam. She regarded his professions of faith as a pose. When she had been with him in Florida, a time when he was happily reveling in his independence, he had expressed no interest in Islam, and they had done many un-Islamic things. Nor did she think he had had a genuine political conversion. Florida was too much fun. Whatever happened to that picture of them sunbathing on the white sands of Siesta Key? she wondered.

Sami Haddad, ready to die for some spurious cause of Allah? Sami Haddad, a hero of some Arabian Night, stepping forward to wound corrupt America, this idol of the age, in behalf of all Arab peoples? Nonsense. Not the Sami she knew. None of that made sense.

Perhaps he was blackmailed. Yes! That was it! She embraced the notion. These ogres, Atta and Atef, the Sheikh, or this terrible Omar, must have blackmailed him. He was forced, she was sure of it.

***

June 27, 2001

"I have been thinking of the many lies I've told you, my love. When I said I was going to Beirut to see my father in November 1999, I told you I might remain in Lebanon through Ramadan. I actually went to Afghanistan. I'm sorry for the lie.

"It had been decided that I would be the first to leave Hamburg. The plan was for Atta and Fatfat to fly five days later, and Omar would follow a week or so after that. I believed at the time I was chosen to go first because I was the most westernized of the group, and, as Atta had always said, I 'had the prettiest smile.' But maybe it was

also because I was the least committed and the most expendable. If there was trouble, it would be the signal to the other three to delay or rethink the plan.

"*In Istanbul, I changed planes for Karachi and then took a rickety Tata bus to Quetta. As I grabbed a seat, about twenty men clambered on top of the bus. It was a slow, dusty trip across the Sind to Hyderabad on the Indus River. The bus was very crowded, and the smell was strong, but I didn't mind. After Hyderabad, we kept along with the river, heading north to Sukkur, and then northwest, away from the Ganges Plain toward the mountains and the Bolan Pass. I arrived at Sibi, an ancient town, and boarded an ancient train, left over from the British colonials, for the ride over the high ridge to Quetta.*

"*In Quetta, women in blue burkas shuffled along the streets. At a bazaar, I tried on an embroidered jacket, a black waistcoat, a Chitrali hat, and I stuck a curved dagger in my belt. In a mirror I looked like a fierce Pashtun warrior.*

"*The Mauritanian had given me only an address and a name, Umar al Masri. At the Taliban headquarters, no one there answered to that name. I explained why I was there, and who had sent me, and that I was the first of four graduate students coming from Germany for jihad. They showed me where I could sleep and gave me food but left me largely alone. It was all so strange, Karima. I wondered if I had made a mistake. Atta and Fatfat arrived three days later, a bit worse for wear. Atta knocked the dust from his clothes, shot me a dirty look, and collapsed on the nearest couch.*

"*Our Taliban hosts gave us only a day to rest before we were escorted to a battered minivan, where we joined a group of twelve for the next leg of the trip. Two hundred bumpy miles later, we arrived at the guest house in Kandahar. Over the door was an inscription in Arabic: Dar al Ansar, or House of Victors. Atta had called his apartment in Marienstrasse the same thing. As we passed through the door, tired and hungry, there was a prominent sign on the wall, listing the rules: 'My brother the mujahidin, my brother the visitor, please keep the house clean.'*

"We were processed quickly, photographed, and relieved of our personal effects. Then we were asked to fill out an application as if we were matriculating in college. What brought 'the candidate' to Afghanistan? How did he get here? How did he hear about them? How did he want to fulfill his obligation to jihad? I wrote 'Chechnya.' After being given new clothes, a scrawny little Algerian with a pug nose and bad teeth introduced himself.*

"'I am al-Sahrawi,' he lisped. 'I am the emir of this guest house. I see that you want to fight in Chechnya.' I could smell his stink. 'Be careful what you ask for. When I was there, huddled in a foxhole, it was too cold to piss.'*

"He told me he was a former handball champion in southern France. When I explained why I was there, al-Sahrawi took notes with precise little scribbles of his pencil, his face close to the paper, only rarely glancing up.*

"'We don't get many like you,' he said.*

"Within a day we were deployed to a training camp called Khalden, near a village called Khost, in an abandoned copper mine. They told us that the year before, US cruise missiles had destroyed a camp closer to the city.*

"*The instructor explained that our first days in camp would be 'days of experimentation.' We would be tested and vetted for 'worthiness.' The day began with an hour's exercise after first prayer before dawn, yogurt and gruel for breakfast, long hikes, map reading, and little sleep. I rode a horse at full gallop. Gradually they increased the intensity. They taught us hand-to-hand combat—and I hadn't been in a fistfight in my life. I was forced to crawl under barbed wire as real machine gun bullets flew overhead. We wore brown tunics and black pantaloons, and our heads were covered with black cloth with holes slit for only the eyes and mouth. On night maneuvers, a trainer gave speeches, usually ending with the invocation, 'O Land of Revelation. Be Patient!' before real bombs exploded nearby. We had to jump through burning hoops. We learned how to disassemble and reassemble a rifle. In training exercises, we broke into buildings and shot at targets painted with Christian crosses and Jewish stars. All the targets on the firing range were dressed in American uniforms.*

"*All around were teenage men from humble backgrounds and with limited education. I could tell they had been drawn to jihad because of all the glorious things they had heard about the Sheikh. Some bragged about having memorized large portions of the Koran.*

"*We slept on straw mats on the floor in mud huts and were told the Sheikh did likewise, for he wished to live simply and be alert and ready like the Prophet himself. The rules were posted on the walls of the barracks: 'Follow Islamic Principles/ Pray Five Times a Day / Be Punctual for Food / Clean Beds and Tents Once a Week / No Arguments / No Insults / No Drugs / Go to Bed Early.' On the wall of one classroom was a sign that read, 'Two illegitimate reasons for leaving jihad: love of the world and hatred of death. If you leave jihad, then God will take away mercy from you.'*

*"A number of recruits left during these 'days of experimentation.'
Fatfat was faltering. At the end of each training day, he dragged
himself into the hut and collapsed on his straw bed. At night as
he rubbed his feet, he began to talk more and more about his wife
and child.*

*"And then we were taught to kill. In earlier drills we had practiced
thrusting a knife into a straw man, as we shouted out,* 'Mout ya
Kafir! *Die, unbeliever! Die! Kill! Kill! Kill!' Then one day, the
instructor handed out long knives and took us to a sheep barn,
where there was a pen with some thirty newborn lambs. He grabbed
one by the scruff of its neck. As its high-pitched wail filled the rafters,
he handed it to Atta.*

"'Okay, slit its throat,' he said.

*"Atta stared at him blankly for a second and then did the deed with
dispatch. Fatfat followed, and then Omar. By the time he came
down the line to me, there was blood everywhere. I was handed a
lamb, I raised my knife, and then fainted dead away on the straw.*

*"Moral guidance infused every aspect of the training. 'Without a sign
from the leader, do not retreat,' one instructor shouted, 'because the
Koran says, "Do not retreat, but stay steady. The only power is the
power of Allah."' In a session on ambush, we were told that, when
lying in wait for the enemy, we should save ourselves from melan-
choly and self-indulgence and confusion by prayer and meditation
on Allah. In the common building, where we gathered before bed,
the literature of jihad was everywhere, including messages and
statements by the Sheikh himself. The cover of one magazine, called
the* Window, *featured a woman, cowering and weeping, as a huge
cobra, festooned with a Star of David, hovered over her.*

"Martyrdom was mentioned often. Two weeks into the 'days of experimentation,' we were given a list of Muslim martyrs and had to write a short essay on one of them. Just to please Omar, I wrote about Omar, the second caliph, waxing eloquent about how the caliph had expanded the dominion of Islam over Palestine, Syria, and Mesopotamia before he was stabbed by an Iraqi from Kufa in 644 CE. I got a very high mark.

"Posters listing the goals and objectives of jihad hung in the mess hall: (1) establishing the rule of God on earth; (2) purifying the ranks of Islam from the depraved elements, and finally and most importantly; (3) attaining martyrdom in the cause of God. The struggle is global, our drill instructors told us, and the only way to deliver the world from the atheists of the East and the infidels of the West is the establishment of an Islamic Caliphate. Even the soldier who is killed by his own forces would still be considered a martyr, and would be granted immediate entry into heaven.

"On the night before the final 'experiment,' a forty-kilometer hike in the mountains, I fell into conversation with my bunkmate, a young, diminutive Yemeni named al-Khatani. He had been in camp a few weeks longer than me and was in good physical shape. He hailed from a large Bedouin family of thirteen children, and his father was a policeman. With some self-importance, he announced that he was a businessman and an artist.

"'What kind of art do you do?' I asked.

"'Mainly animals. I love to paint baby lambs.'

"I could tell al-Khatani was lonely and homesick. That night, after lights out, he whispered about a recent dream.

"'I saw the Prophet Muhammad,' he said. 'I looked to his left and there stood Fahd, king of Saudi Arabia. Muhammad pointed to him and said, "Those are not from me, and I am not from them." And then Muhammad walked farther down a path, where he encountered Sheikh Osama bin Laden and the martyrs, and the Prophet said, "Those are from me, and I am of them."'"

"The next morning, we rose early, ate our normal ration of bread and yogurt, and then mustered near an old bus that would take us to the trailhead. This was to be the climax of our training. Atta looked uncomfortable in the cold, rocking from one foot to another, his flat-topped Chitrali hat slightly cockeyed on his head. Fatfat seemed really worried. And there I stood, not knowing what to expect. None of us was looking forward to the day.

"Just before the order was given to load up, a young Syrian rushed up and called my name. 'Sami Haddad, you will not be making the hike today. Come with me.'

"As I fell out of the line, I turned to Atta and Fatfat and said, 'Sorry, brother. God give you strength.'

"'Kuss immak,' Fatfat hissed. 'Shove it up your mother's cunt.'

"'Please,' I said, holding up my hand in objection. 'Remember. No insults.'

***

For once Karima reached Recht directly.
    "I really need to see you," she said.
    "We're very busy here right now, Dr. Ilgun."
    "I insist. I must see you."
    "I'm sorry. We're preoccupied. There are developments."

"Developments?"

He paused. "Okay, I'm going to read you something because it will be in the papers tomorrow."

"Are you leaking something else to me?"

There was a pause. "You must believe me, Dr. Ilgun," he said finally. "I did not leak your letter to the press. I'm sorry that happened, and I did what I could to prevent it. But this place can be a sieve."

"I trusted you," she said and then, as there was nothing further to say on that subject, "What's your news?"

He cleared his throat. "Okay, this comes from the FBI," and he read haltingly: "'Certain information, while not specific as to target, gives the government reason to believe that there may be additional terrorist attacks within the United States and against US interests overseas over the next several days.' See what I mean?"

"Kommissar Recht . . . You mentioned the ringleaders once, Mudor or something. . . ."

"Muktar."

"And an Omar, I think."

"Yes, Omar."

"Are you close to arresting them?"

The silence on the line seemed like an eternity to her.

"Kommissar Recht?"

"That is confidential police business."

"I'm frightened, Herr Recht."

"You have reason to be."

They made an appointment to meet three days later.

***

"The Syrian led me through the huts and across a dusty parade ground until we arrived at the administration building. Inside, the escort knocked on a door. A commanding voice inside called out his permission to enter. 'Rely on God,' the Syrian whispered in my ear

as he nudged me forward and closed the door behind me.

"There before me sat Mohammad Atef. I recognized him immediately from pictures I had seen in Hamburg in Omar's apartment, and from the descriptions of him in camp gossip. He was referred to as the 'emir of all emirs.' I understood that long ago he had been an Egyptian policeman and air force officer and a founding father of the organization and a veteran of the Russian jihad. As chief of military operations to the Sheikh, they said, he had planned the attacks on the African embassies. Once he had even been a professional volleyball player. I had heard that he was an excellent equestrian, though not as good as the Sheikh himself. He was seated cross-legged on a cushion behind a low coffee table before me. His head was erect, shoulders held back, chin high. He wore a white turban. His deep-set eyes were hooded beneath thick eyebrows, and even though his beard was dark and full, extending down below his shoulder bone, his face was brown and smooth. The collar of his white robe was open, and over it was a dark, sleeveless vest. Resting against the wall beside him was a Kalashnikov.

"'Salaam, Abu Tariq al Lubnani,' he said and motioned for me to take a seat on the floor opposite him. 'I am Mohamed Atef.'

"'Yes, yasayyidi, na'am,' I said. 'I have heard many things about you.'

"My eyes flickered upward to a poem framed in gold above his head. It read:

> *Our listeners gave us their ears and heard us—let the sword occupy the pulpit*
>
> *Whoever seeks his rights must eventually find the sword to be his best guide.*

When they refused to respond to our demands, we turned our saber rattling into songs.

"'I welcome you to the Emirate of the Faithful,' he said. 'You have nearly finished the first phase of your training, I understand.'

"'I wish to apologize for my performance, eminence,' I said. 'I am not much of a fighter. I would understand entirely if the organization deems me unqualified.'

"'What did you expect when you came here, Abu Tariq, rose water and lovely ladies?'

"'I expected the training would be hard. I did not realize how soft I am. I am a graduate student.'

"'But you expressed a wish to fight in Chechnya.'

"'We decided that as a group in Hamburg.'

"'And you went along.'

"'Yes, na'amyasayyidi.'

"'We send only our toughest brothers to Chechnya.'

"'I would hope there might also be less strenuous assignments.'

"'All our assignments are strenuous,' he said sharply. 'Here in Afghanistan, we operate under the authority of the Taliban. They rule the country. We are their Arabian section, and our fighters are the most disciplined, best trained, the most heroic in battles against the American puppets.'

"He glanced at me, looking amused. 'If you are interested in laughter and entertainment and beautiful women, you should volunteer for Bosnia.'

"'I would follow your guidance, sayyidina'amya. I would like to satisfy my duty to jihad in a manner that best suits my talents.'

"'Remember what God said: "Those who strive in our cause, we will guide them along our path."'"

"He reached for a paper in front of him. 'I was impressed by your essay on Caliph Omar. You have a sense of history, Abu Tariq. That is good. And your qualifications are good . . . on paper. You seem to have special talents. You see, our organization has evolved in recent years. Once we needed only muscular, tough fighters, schooled in the Koran, dedicated and disciplined, ready to die in the cause of Allah if need be.'

"'Like those who could make a forty-kilometer hike without complaint,' I said eagerly.

"Atef cast a sidelong glance at me. 'We pride ourselves in inspiring young men toward jihad. But after we triumphed over the Russians in Afghanistan, our mission widened. Now our struggle extends far beyond these borders. Now we need young men who are just as tough, but who can do more than look down the barrel of a rifle.'

"'I'm pretty good with computers,' I said.

"Again, Atef's gaze drifted out the window to the comings and goings on the parade ground outside. After a long pause, he turned back to me.

"'We have known about you for some time, Abu Tariq al Lubnani,'
he said at last."

***

The Botanical Garden was Karima's favorite place in all of Hamburg. She and Sami had strolled the grounds there together many times. It was a cold day, with the wind whipping up in the North Sea, cold enough to keep the crowds down. As she made her way down the path toward her meeting place with Recht, she suddenly had the feeling that she was being followed. She swirled around to see a slightly swarthy man abruptly turn down a separate path.

When she saw the kommissar ambling toward her far down the path, her anxiety dissipated. She decided that she had to get over her anger about the leak of her letter. Perhaps it was not his doing, as he professed. In any event, it had happened, and there was nothing to be done about it. More important problems faced her now. Even at a distance she could tell he was in good spirits. His happy moods were easy to identify, since his normal expression was almost always dour.

"Why are you feeling so good today, Kommissar Recht?" she said.

He looked at her appraisingly, uncertain how much he could share. "They have killed an important al-Qaeda figure," he said at last.

She prayed silently that he would say the name Omar.

"Osama bin Laden's military commander, Atef."

"Oh yes, I heard about that on the radio. By one of those new weapons. I can see why that would make you happy."

"Yes, and the Americans have offered $25 million for the head of bin Laden. The noose is tightening around him in the mountains of Afghanistan."

"Who says?"

"My counterpart in the FBI."

"*Sehr gut. Bravo!* I'm glad for you. I'm not really following it, you know."

"You should, Karima. You should."

It was the first time he had used the familiar form of *you*, and the second time she could remember he called her Karima instead of Dr. Ilgun.

When they found a bench near the crocuses, she changed the subject abruptly.

"That judge taunted me with personal questions," she said. "I said more than I should have."

"That is his job," the kommissar replied stoically, lighting up the first of his cigarettes.

"He had no right to bring up my marriage or my abortion."

"It is his courtroom. He does what he wants to."

"Those things have nothing to do with 9/11. He was just taunting me, trying to make me angry."

"And succeeded, it seems."

"And to make me lose my composure."

Recht frowned and said nothing.

"But our marriage was never registered with the state. Sami used it as a pretext to bully me and to force me into a display of piety. I never considered myself to be married. Neither did he . . . toward the end."

"I suppose, in the wake of possibly the greatest crime in history, you expect to be treated like a lady?"

She turned on him angrily, started to say something, and then remembered herself.

"Look, Karima. It's no good trying to underplay your attachment to that man. We have your emails."

"What emails?"

He reached in his coat pocket and handed her a folded piece of paper. She read:"I just wanted to write you that I'll always love you. Your Karima."And: "I love you, your yearning wife, Karima Haddad."

"There were other emails," she said softly. "They were not all like that."

"Yes, that's true. There was this one as well." And he pulled another paper from his pocket.

"I had to think about our baby today. I am sorry about everything I did to you."

She started to speak, caught herself as words choked in her throat. She rummaged in her purse for a tissue. "I didn't want to be left behind with a child of a husband gone off to a fanatic's war."

His expression became stern. "So, you were aware that he was going off to a fanatic's war."

"I didn't mean that. You know what I mean."

"Whatever your awareness was or is, the point is this, Karima: At the very least, you are suspected of giving substantial material support to a terrorist. Maybe it was innocent material support. I happen to believe it was. But it was support nonetheless. He needed it. He couldn't do without it. He was needy, and he depended on you. You were the successful one, not him."

"On the surface he was so confident."

"But inside, I think he was timid and terrified. You were on your way to a fine career. He was struggling with his courses. He had always struggled, going back to his childhood. He was the kid who always needed extra help just to get by, while you just sailed through."

"Sailed through?" she scoffed. "That's not the phrase I would use."

"Did he ever tell you that he needed an extra year to finish high school?"

"An extra year?"

"He never told you that?"

"No."

"It's true. His parents, with considerable difficulty, paid for a full year of private lessons in math and physics before he went to Germany."

"They were so generous."

"What was he going back to in Lebanon? A house in a dusty village in the Bekaa? A fancy car provided by his sugar daddy? The confinement of a family compound? The empty life on the family dole where everyone looked upon his wife as a dynamo and looked at him as a dunce?"

She was not listening. "I think he was blackmailed."

"Why do you say that?"

"He was no fanatic. It was just words. He had nothing against America."

"How do you know that?"

"Because he told me."

"He told you that?"

"Yes."

"When?"

"When? Well, a bunch of times."

"A bunch of times!"

"Well, yes," she stammered."Not in so many words."

"When?"

"In Florida, I guess. Yes, that was it. When I visited him Florida. And when he came to see me here."

"He told you that he had nothing against America? Only six weeks before 9/11?"

"I think so. I mean, I don't remember exactly. He loved his time in Florida. But yes, in Florida, I suppose."

He looked at her coldly. "I thought you never talked to him about the operation."

"No. No, of course not. But what I wanted to say—"

"Wait a minute, Karima. Did you ever talk to Sami Haddad about the operation, yes or no?"

"No, I never did. I've told you that over and over."

"Well, it sounded just then as if you had."

"I'm just getting confused. I've heard so much in the press—and from you. I dream about him all the time. He lives in my head. I even see his face in my apartment sometimes. I can't seem to get rid of him. If it sounds like I talked to him about his crime, I have, yes. I talk to him all the time in my thoughts. I imagine things I might have said, and things I might have done to turn him away from his course."

"Okay," he said, softening. "I get it."

"I'm sorry. I get confused between what I know and what I imagine."

He took a long drag on his cigarette. "It has also occurred to me that he might have been blackmailed."

"You see!"

"But not in the normal way. I'm sure they threatened him with dire consequences if he faltered."

"He was tormented by doubts; I'm sure of it."

"You're just hoping he was."

"No, I know it."

"How do you know that?"

"I know it in my heart."

"Oh, I see. In your heart. Well, in the end, he made up his mind."

"Yes."

"He made it up when he was with you."

"Yes. Don't you think I understand that? What do you think haunts me every minute of every day?"

He took another long draught on his cigarette. They sat without speaking for a while.

"Well, come on, then," he said finally. "I'll buy you an ice cream."

She rose and looked at his lumpy face. "Kommissar Recht," she said, "do you mind if I call you Günther?"

7

AS SHE HAD LISTENED TO HIS TAPES almost nightly, Karima thought she was beginning to understand Sami's dilemma. He had been so vulnerable to it all: the spoiled kid from the well-off family, the below-average student who always needed extra help, the bumbler who could never seem to complete any large task, the charmer who covered up his deficiencies with his pretty smile, the dreamer who was always waiting for the chance to show everyone there was more to him than they had come to expect and who was so easily impressed by his betters. The only hitch was that he had to die, disgrace his family and his clan, and ruin the one person he truly loved. At last she was coming to realize what she had been up against in July 2001 when he faced his choice.

Was that the blackmail of an unusual sort that Recht was talking about? First comes the appeal to his manhood, then the overlay of noble religion and politics, next the promise of eternal bliss in Paradise (but never, ever a mention of hellfire if you're wrong), then the excitement of being a player in history, next the flattery on how unique and vital you were to the success of the group, then the fear of Mohammad Atef's retribution for any disobedience, and finally the solemn loyalty oath to the Sheikh.

Why did she still feel the instinct to protect him? He had betrayed and disgraced her, leaving her with a shattered life and an unbearable burden of guilt. She should hate him with a hatred so incandescent it would burn away that guilt with a molten, white-hot anger. If he was blackmailed, he had blackmailed her most of all. Perhaps that was why he had recorded these reminiscences. It was an act of contempt, not love. Had he just done his deed and left no explanation, it would have been easier. He was a liar, a cheater, a manipulator, purely, pristinely, a monster. So why was she feeling sorrow and pity instead of hate and need for some sort of revenge?

At last, she felt herself withdrawing from him emotionally. With her exacting scientist's brain, she had known the importance of this for a long time. Now, her heart was finally following her brain. After the shock and the denial, the fear and the nightmares, the conflicts over her love, the anger at his betrayal, the faulting of herself, her brutal inter-rogations, she had opened herself up at last to the enormity of his crime.

Karima had taken to watching Al Jazeera at night. She felt compelled to get news "from the other side." Despite professing to be apolitical, she found herself feeling more sympathetic to the victims in the Middle East, especially now that the television was carrying pictures of American B-52s pounding the outskirts of Kandahar. The media had exhausted nearly everything there was to say about New York and Washington and Mohamed Atta, and now they were moving to softer stories.

The phone rang.

"Karima darling. It's Gretchen again. Please don't hang up . . . Listen, you should turn on your TV right away. Al Jazeera is just starting a show called 'The Reluctant Hijacker.'"

"The reluctant hijacker?"

"Yes. Brace yourself. It's about Sami."

"Okay," Karima answered flatly. She was the reluctant one.

"And Karima, I read about your court appearance in the paper. Don't forget about my brother. He's there for you."

"I won't."

When she switched on to a program series called *Your Eyes Only*, a shadowy, grainy, menacing image of Sami was background for the reporter's intro. As the reporter droned on, the sequence morphed into a shot of the dark underbelly of a plane flying noiselessly overhead, then to a sequence of Sami gleefully dancing the *dabke* . . . with her! . . . at a wedding a year before. Hands held high, snapping his fingers to the rhythm and stamping his feet, he moved with such grace and joy.

She remembered that night vividly. It was a night of ecstasy, when lovers had called out to the darkness as their refuge, *YaLayl, YaLayl*, without fear that anyone would hear or see them. Full of life and longing and expectation, they had lost themselves in the music and in each other. If only in that moment of spiritual union, she had been able to see her lover's agony. Through the night he had been tender and playful. And the sweetness and the gentleness afterward.

And then the program cut away to an interview with his parents.

"What is your strongest memory of Sami as a boy?" the reporter was asking.

His father sat rigid in his chair. Dressed elegantly in a light tan suit, he held himself with enormous dignity, his handsome, chiseled face ruddy and ravaged, his eyes hooded by grief and disgrace. Karima could almost hear him ask himself why he had agreed to do this. Sami's mother, the French teacher, sat dutifully beside him, her hands demurely folded in her lap, perspiring under the hot light. Karima loved them. They had been so courteous and welcoming and generous to her. And they had loved their son—at least, the son they knew.

"He was our middle child, our only son," he was having trouble using the past tense. "He was a lovely boy, very caring for his sisters and for us. He was quite normal, really. We sent him to the best schools in Lebanon. He was a happy boy."

"Did politics interest him?"

"He never cared about politics."

"Religion?"

"No."

"He wasn't interested in religion?" The reporter's skepticism took on an edge.

"No, he was never religious. He liked to go out or play volleyball. He was a person who loved life."

"He liked beer?

"Sometimes."

Why, thought Karima, *are these Westerners so fascinated in the drinking habits of Muslims?* And then she answered her own question: because they want to believe all Muslims were hypocrites.

The reporter turned to his mother. "When was the last time you saw your son, madam?"

"It was in February last year. He came to be beside his father after his open-heart surgery. We told him that his father's condition was quite critical. He stayed several weeks."

"Was he different?"

"No."

"Same old Sami?"

"Yes."

The camera cut away to the dusty main street of the village of Al-Marj in the Bekaa Valley, where the Haddad family was local gentry. Slowly, the camera panned over the billboards of the main street: Haddad electronics, Haddad furniture, and Haddad bridal gowns with a huge poster of a radiant bride, holding a white dove aloft, about to release it. *Peace*, Karima thought, and then remembered that in an Arab wedding, the symbolism of the dove was the loss of virginity—the formal wedding she would never have. The camera followed a side street to a trendy neighborhood of graceful, granite houses with balustraded balconies and elegant, oriental windows. Then the video zoomed in on a vacant lot where a lone black Mercedes was parked and idling. The patriarch sat in the driver's seat, the reporter next to him.

"And when did you hear from him last?"

"Two days before . . . ," and the next word choked in his throat.

"Before September 11?"

"Yes. He called as usual on that Sunday and confirmed that he was coming to Lebanon on September 22. He would stop in Hamburg and pick up Karima—"

"His girlfriend."

"Yes, and then they would come with a big announcement. We knew it would be their formal engagement. And we were prepared for it. I had bought this lot where I planned to build a home for them after they were married. And I would give him this 300 series Mercedes."

"Was he pleased with your offer?"

"Not entirely. He said, 'No, give the car to my sister. I would prefer you to give me one from the 400 series.'"

"He wanted the fancier car."

"Yes."

"What did he say in that last call?"

"He confirmed that he had received the extra money he had asked for."

"Extra money?"

"Yes, I was sending him $2,000 a month to support his studies. He had asked for another $3,000."

"Wait a minute, he wanted $3,000 more, only a few days before 9/11?"

"Yes."

"What for?"

The old gentleman paused. "He said it was for fun."

"For fun." Karima whispered the words. For fun? Was it possible? Was it just remotely possible that in the sickness of his last days, he was actually enjoying his deception, his duplicity, betraying even his own father and mother? For fun. And then she caught herself. Of course! Money for his escape. Why had she been so stupid? Oh Sami, why am I always doubting you! You were planning to bail out! And you needed money!

The camera moved in for a close-up, and she looked again at the wreckage of his father's face. "We were not able to talk to Karima for many days after the event."

"Nobody is able to talk to her," the reporter groused.

"When we finally did speak, I asked her a very direct question. Did Sami know Mohamed Atta and this other portly fellow who is suspected?"

"What did she say?"

"Absolutely not. Sami did not know those men."

"She was absolutely sure."

"Yes."

She *had* told them that just to reassure them, that's all. They were all in shock and denial and pain in the first few weeks. It was an act of kindness. No one can be held responsible for anything they say at a time like that, can they?

"We are quite sure that Sami had nothing to do with the terrorist plot," his father was saying. "He's not that kind of person. Besides, he was not that brave."

"Not that brave." Again, Karima whispered the words. What did bravery have to do with it? The words of Bush from the television rang her in ears, condemning the "cowardly act" of the hijackers. Not that brave? Whatever else his act may have been, there was bravery there, she thought.

"How can you be so sure?" the reporter was saying.

"We know him well. He was raised well, with good values, in a good family."

"You mean, by nature, he was not a risk-taker?"

"No, never. He was a cautious boy. He must have been just one of the passengers, off on some pleasure trip. Perhaps he was kidnapped."

"He did not fit the profile of the terrorist?"

"No way. We have heard the voice from the cockpit on Flight 93, the voice that told the passengers that they had a bomb on board. It is not Sami's voice! He had a very distinctive voice. He was French-educated, after all."

"By Christian teachers."

"Yes. And besides, he was not qualified to fly a 767. Only a Cessna Piper Cub. I have talked with his Florida instructor."

"The $3,000? How do you explain that?"

"Why would Sami ask for money just days before, just days before . . ." His voice trailed off.

The reporter let these rationalizations roll out unchallenged.

"Do you think he is in Paradise?" he asked.

The old man's gaze drifted to the horizon as he struggled to control himself.

"Like us all, he must face the Apostle of Allah. We have prayed for forgiveness of sin, as we do for all who die."

"But do you consider him a martyr?"

"I think he was a victim. He was merely a passenger in a doomed plane. We're sure of it. The Prophet did not offer forgiveness to the martyrs of the Battle of Uhud."

"The Battle of Uhud was a setback for Muslims."

"Yes."

"What if he *was* a suicide? . . . and he was a terrorist?"

The old man's eyes dropped to his hands, folded in his lap. His next words came slowly, his sentences modulated. "Whatever he was or whatever he did, we honor his rest. If he is really dead, we hope for his entrance into heaven. We pray that he may be protected from hell-fire. We pray that he be cleansed with water and snow and hail, and that he be cleansed of sin, like the prayer says, as a white garment is cleansed of dirt."

The reporter paused and glanced at his notes. After a moment, he dropped his sympathetic look.

"I have just one final question," he said. "According to FBI records that *Eyes Only* has obtained, between February 28 and September 8, 2001, you, Mr. Haddad, talked by phone to your son, Sami, seventy-eight times. How do you explain this?"

The accusation hung in the air, stark and unanswerable. Surprise froze the stricken patriarch's face as he stammered to repeat the question, but the audience never heard the answer as the program cut to a commercial.

When the show resumed, the reporter was blathering on with his wrap-up, now the mantra of the entire press corps: Sami Haddad was a puzzle, an enigma, a mystery. He was a young man with many opportunities. His mind was beyond knowing. Karima had heard it all before. She reached to turn the set off, and then she saw herself on the screen.

"Next week, the girlfriend," and another picture of her flashed up on the screen. "What is this woman hiding?" the reporter said dramatically. "And why are the police hiding her?"

***

June 30, 2001

> "My meeting with Mohammad Atef was a milestone. Everything that had happened before reeked of fantasy. I never believed until recently that 'this thing,' whatever it is, could really happen. In Hamburg we were a bunch of puffed-up graduate students. When the four of us strode down the streets of Hamburg, bluffing other students, daring them to challenge our rants, I felt like a genuine mujahin, bent on the destruction of the depraved West, and it made me feel important. Then the trip to see the Mauritanian was like a spy movie, replete with codes and whispers and fictitious names. Even the first weeks in camp in Afghanistan, despite the deprivations, I was becoming fit, climbing over walls, fording streams, shooting a rifle, and crawling through barbed wire. I felt good.

"What was I thinking?! Did I really think that, when my training was over, I would say, thank you very much, Mohammad Atef . . . Good luck to you, Sheikh . . . Give Atta the what-for and just walk away? You don't know these men, Karima. If I walk away now, so late in the game, I know what they would do to my family . . . and maybe to you.

"Atta has nothing to live for. His path is easy compared to mine. I am blessed with you, my life, my love. I am so honored by your love. And so ashamed for how I have mistreated you. I want to make it up to you. How many men would cry out for joy for such good fortune? They want me to think I'll be a hero for this act. I'm supposed to think I'll go to paradise as a martyr. I worry instead that I'll burn forever in hellfire, taunted by snakes and scorpions.

"I don't know if I have any decency left. I am Sami Haddad, the one who could not kill a lamb . . . I have to go now. I hear Atta and Ahmad coming.

Later that evening, June 30, 2001

"My love, my beloved lady, my heart. You are my life and my hope. It's safe to talk to you some more now.

"It became clear to me that Atta was in Afghanistan before. From the beginning they saw me as an asset that the organization lacked. For two years they have imagined some sort of operation with airplanes, but they didn't have the people to pull it off. Atta was an urban planner; Fatfat a ship builder; Omar a banker and philosopher. And then suddenly, I meandered into Atta's circle, a budding airplane engineer. Westernized, an innocent, pining for my girlfriend. Omar was probably in on it from the beginning . . . and the Mauritanian. Chechnya was a ruse, and the trip to

Duisburgwas a charade, staged for my benefit. I realize that now.

"And so, they ignored my sarcasm, my disinterest in jihad, my ignorance of the Koran, my indifference toward America. They brought me along slowly, deliberately. Now, Mohammad Atef has taken it to the next step. I can no longer hide on the fringe of the group.

"'You have finished your basic training,' Atef said in our next meeting. 'We can send you right away to the front lines. Or we can put you into elite training. It's up to you.'

"'What's involved in elite training?' I asked.

"'The usual,' the general replied. 'Motorcycles, machine guns, shoulder-borne missiles, bow guns, techniques of guerrilla warfare. It's training, Abu Tariq, like in the best military colleges in the world. But we must be sure of your commitment.'

"'Of course.'

"'We are investing a great deal in you.'

"'I understand, yasayyidi.'

"'We mean to give you a new identity as a true mujahid. And you could be selected for command.'

"I must have bobbed my head up and down like some African bird, because Atef looked at me with disapproval, as if he thought my acquiescence was coming a little too easily.

"'Let me ask you something, Abu Tariq. Do you know what the word Islam means?'

"'Not exactly. "Faith," I guess.'

"'It means "surrender to the will of God." God has a plan for you, Abu Tariq. You should never question God's plan. And that's what we're talking about here. Surrender to the will of God, and surrender to the goals of this organization.'

"'Surrender,' I repeated.

"'Yes. You will need to swear a solemn oath.'

"'What kind of oath?'

"'An oath of loyalty and obedience to the Sheikh himself.'

"'Would I get to meet the Sheikh?'

"'Yes, and swear a personal oath to him.'

"I had sworn oaths before, Karima, to my parents, as a schoolboy to my country, and to you, my darling, as my Muslim wife. But this was different.

"'The Sheikh,' Atef went on, 'has a grand vision for the Islamic world.'

"'What is that vision, yasayyidi?' I asked.

"'To draw the United States into a life-and-death confrontation with all Muslims.'

"That night, as I waited for the other three to return from their forced march, I read the Sheikh's 1998 fatwa carefully. I had only

glanced at it before, as much for show as anything. Now seemed the time to read and consider it more deeply. Then I heard the old bus sputter up to our hut. I put the fatwa down and eagerly awaited the return of my comrades from their all-day hike. When the door opened, Fatfat entered with Atta's arm draped over his shoulder. Wincing in pain, Atta hopped painfully and gingerly on his good leg, as his bad leg dragged behind him. He was in bad shape.

"'Ah,' I said with a big grin. 'Behold the mujahidin!'

"In the succeeding weeks, I threw myself into my elite training. We learned how to use bigger and more lethal weapons, SAM and Stinger missiles, recoilless and antiaircraft guns, and were given training in explosives and poisons, even sabotage and kidnapping. Our instructor stood behind us, proclaiming verses from the Koran: "'When the forbidden months are past, then fight and slay the pagans wherever you find them. Seize them! Beleaguer them! Lie in wait for them with every stratagem of war!'"

"The hikes through the desert became more frequent and longer, and we had the bad luck to endure these physical tests during Ramadan. At night we were ravenous after a strenuous day without food. Others in our cadre of twenty had greater strength and stamina. I suppose I was the most athletic. Atta struggled, and although I taunted him, I secretly admired his grit. I longed to love the cause just as totally, without reservation.

"In the training, America was an obsession. Not only were all the targets American, but they were given American names. As we took aim on the firing range, the instructor stood behind us and screamed about hitting the American soldier or the American tank. There was more to it than merely target practice; symbolism was important. What would be the point of killing an American soldier

in the darkest jungle of Africa? And then he answered his own question: 'It would have no impact whatever.' Targets were chosen for their publicity value.

"In the classroom, we three were quicker than the rest. The reading load was heavy. Of course, it began with the life of the Prophet and the early caliphs. The triumphs of Saladin over the crusaders in the twelfth century followed, probably because the Sheikh had a son named Saladin. The defense of the Arab world against the Mongols was mentioned, as was the push of the Ottoman sultan, Suleyman the Magnificent, into the heart of Europe. We heard lectures about the Iraqi holy sites of Karbala and Najaf, coveted by the Americans just as they occupied the land of the holiest sites of Mecca and Medina. The glories of ancient Al-Andalus were highlighted.

"One day, an instructor told us, Islam will again be the flower of European culture as it was once in Grenada and Cordoba in the ninth century. We were exposed to Arab poetry, connecting a poetic sensibility to bravery on the battlefield. One instructor told us about the story in Arabian Nights called 'Ali with the Great Member' and quoted the line from an Arab African poet named Al Jahiz: 'If the length of the penis were a sign of strength and honor, then the mule would belong to the honorable clan of the Quraish.' We all howled at this.

"We were also assigned excerpts from books by American generals on military tactics and by Western diplomats on strategic bottle necks. One excerpt dealt with a report by an American official named Henry Kissinger on his saber-rattling with King Faisal of Saudi Arabia after the 1973 war. When Faisal threatened to reclaim Jerusalem in a holy war, this Kissinger counter-threatened to bomb the oil fields. Go ahead, Faisal told him. 'We will blow them up ourselves, and we will lose nothing. Because our camels *are still here, and our milk, and our dates. We will survive. You will be the big loser.' This heroic response elicited cheers when the instructor read it out in class.*

"But of all the instruction in the elite course, I remembered best the warning about personal relationships. If we were truly committed to jihad, if we were truly ready to surrender ourselves to God and to the Sheikh, if we were truly brothers in the pure Islamic state, we were to sever all ties with family and loved ones. Our past identity was past. Sami Haddad had ceased to exist. Abu Tariq al Libnani was married to al-Qaeda now. Henceforth, our comrades were our brothers, and our father was the Sheikh. Our devotion was to our one true God, to our glorious culture and civilization, and to the painful history of Islam and the Arab peoples.

"I listened, but knew in my heart that I could never, would never, discard my past, because of my love for you.

"As the end of Ramadan approached, we counted the days until we could break our fast. As a reward for our sacrifice and hard work, it was announced that the Sheikh would be coming to mark Eid al Fitr. He would lead our prayers, beseeching Allah to accept our fasting. Having no money, we would pay our Zakat-al-Fitr as a charity in the form of dates and barley, to make Eid more joyful for the poor and alleviate their suffering.

"It was hinted that the Sheikh would also tell us about the 'big operation' that was coming."

***

For her listening she decided it was time for her to make a ritual out of the séance. She gathered a few aromatic candles in glass cups, put them on her coffee table next to her recording machine, and lit a stick of incense. As she went about her arrangements, she switched on the television to Al Jazeera, absent-mindedly.

The channel interrupted its normal programming for a news flash. Osama bin Laden's top aide, Abdel Muaz the doctor, had been killed, and bin Laden himself was thought to be trapped in a mountain cave at a place called Tora Bora. And then the station was promoting an end-of-the-year exclusive: a secret interview with the two masterminds of 9/11, Omar and Muktar.

Omar interviewed with Muktar! Could that mean Omar was not in Germany but somewhere in the Middle East! Or could it be the other way around, with both of these dangerous characters in Germany? Of course, Omar didn't have to be in Germany to pull these strings. The program said nothing about the venue of the interview or when it had been conducted. She made a note to ask Recht. She hoped the television would carry pictures. *What do these two really look like?* she wondered. By now, she almost felt she knew them. But there was only audio with a translation of their disjointed comments scrolling down the screen, as if it were all scripted.

"We began to plan for the conquest of New York and Washington two and one half years earlier," the voice of this Muktar was saying. "We had plenty of brothers filled with the desire to be martyrs."

"With our brother Abu Tariq, there was a passport problem with his picture. Before he had a beard," Omar said. "But when he came out of Afghanistan, he was clean shaven. It caused him a problem in Dubai on his way home to Germany. Thankfully, policemen are stupid. With God's help, our brother accomplished his mission. May God accept and honor his martyrdom." His voice sounded different, Karima thought, different from his phone messages to her.

The audio cut to Muktar. "Each brother looked into what cover he could take to mislead the intelligence services and blind them." The voice had a guttural tone. "This whole triumph was accomplished without even the closest friends of Abu Tariq having any information about him. These were spectacular hours. You're entering a military battle, against the strongest power on earth. And you are confronting them with a group of only nineteen men."

"Smile and be comfortable," Omar said.

It was call and response, as Muktar said, "For God is with the faithful, and his angels are with you."

Karima hit the mute button as a wave of revulsion passed over her. "May God accept his martyrdom," she repeated in a whisper. How could Sami have been so taken with these maniacs? Their contempt for him was evident. The interview underscored the violence these men could do. Hearing their boasting made her shiver. Her peril seemed greater.

She switched channels. A small man with flashing eyes and a tight-fitting skull cap was being interviewed. The graphic identified him as the grand imam of the al-Azhar mosque in Cairo—the highest moral authority of Sunni Islam. Around him sat a clutch of lesser imams and muftis. What about the fatwa of this Sheikh Osama bin Laden to kill all Americans and plunder their property?

The grand imam grunted derisively. "Osama bin Laden is no specialist in religious affairs," he scoffed. The imams around him giggled. "Islamic law banishes anyone who issues an untrue fatwa."

And what about the notion that the hijackers are martyrs and will achieve heaven?

Again the little man spat out his contempt. "They are not martyrs, but aggressors. They will not achieve paradise, but will receive severe punishment for their aggression," he said. "Whoever shall kill a man or a believer without right, the punishment is hell forever. Allah will be angry with him and give him a great punishment."

This was too much. Karima began to surf the channels for something more bearable and settled on a travel program. The images portrayed a soothing, lovely scene of low hills and rolling farmland with just a hint of late fall color. By contrast with the brash reporters of the other programs, this host had a soft, cultured voice, narrating as the camera languorously panned across the bucolic scene. *He must be a poet*, Karima thought.

"Outside Somerset, you pass down a two-lane road through these rolling hills of western Pennsylvania and turn off on Stutzmantown Road, past fields of corn and goldenrod," the narrator's voice intoned. "And you finally come to this sleepy little town that has now become a household word. And then a few miles down the road, you come over the brow of this hill, and spreading before you is this extraordinary caldera, an open windswept bowl with only a few trees dotting the hillside in the far distance. In the bottomland a pond, and then the famous line of hemlock trees where the thing came down."

The thing?

"This is a man-made landscape. When the massive coal shovels came in years ago, they removed three hundred feet of topsoil to get to the three veins of rich anthracite coal beneath. They left behind acid ponds and befouled wetlands in need of purification. The ground is soft now, and that's why, when the plane came in traveling at 550 miles per hour, the ground literally swallowed it up."

Karima felt faint. She closed her eyes and tried to breathe. She realized she could not even hear them speaking anymore. She opened her eyes and saw that she had unconsciously hit the mute button. A collection of locals were parading across the screen, simple, rural folk who looked German except for their overalls . . . various politicians . . . Then there was an attractive, stylish blonde, and Karima turned the sound on again. It was the widow of the pilot of Flight 93, saying something about tears falling like rain upon the fields of Pennsylvania. Karima felt a certain ghastly connection to this woman. The lady looked out to the line of hemlock trees. "Rich, Rich, if you can see me or hear me, give me a sign," she said.

And then another woman came on, a local notable who had organized the volunteers who greeted the thousands of visitors to this morose landmark. She was talking about the brave passengers who had rebelled against the vicious Islamic fanatics high over the Allegheny Mountains.

"Today is not just a tribute to their heroism, but a source of inspiration," she was saying. "What happened here addresses the age-old question: When you are confronted with a crisis, even in a life-threatening situation, do you act? Or do you wait for someone else to solve the problem?"

Karima could bear it no longer and switched off the television. She knew more than any television program could tell her about the "villain of Shanksville." With a great effort of will, she lit the candles, sat down on her couch, and switched on the recording device.

***

July 3, 2001

> *"When we finally saw the crescent moon rise over the dunes in the east, we rejoiced in the breaking of our fast. For the first time in many nights, I slept soundly, even as little al-Khatani tossed and turned with excitement in anticipation of the Sheikh's visit. The next morning, we gathered with the instructors outside the administration building, its mud walls still pockmarked from the American attacks a year and a half earlier. In white and black turbans, we sat cross-legged in rows to await the Sheikh. The morning was gray and cold, and I shivered under my Pashtun turban and the white Saudi thobe. Atta sat next to me, scowling under his crochet prayer cap. As we waited, I surveyed my fellow fighters. They were mainly Afghans, with a sprinkling of Saudis and Yemenis, Bedouins and a few Berbers. The Africans, in their woolen burnooses, were the best prepared for the morning chill.*
>
> *"Eventually, a small caravan of white Mitsubishi minivans pulled up, and the Sheikh emerged. It was as if he were a modern-day Saladin coming to greet his warriors before the climactic battle for Jerusalem. He cut an impressive figure against the bleak landscape, with the elegant bearing of a royal and the charisma of a true leader. He was tall, taller by far than most of the men gathered there. He wore a tan camel-hair* bisht abaya *over his dishdasha and a long white shawl over his prayer cap. A line from the Koran popped*

into my head. 'When Allah has blessed you with His bounty, your appearance should reflect it.' His beard was long and untrimmed, with a white streak down the middle. It was longer than it needed to be, if the Sheikh was really emulating the Prophet, for it was said that the Prophet's beard was only four fingers in length. As the prince strode by, I noticed the jeweled jambiya stuck in his belt and squinted to see if the dagger's handle was made of rhinoceros horn, as I had heard.

"Mohammad Atef conducted him to the simple podium and microphone that had been set up, and he began to speak against the backdrop of the dreary Kandahar plain, an emptiness interrupted only by camel thorn bushes and mulberry trees. His text that day was Verse 9:120: that it was not becoming for the Bedouins and the people of Medina to remain behind Allah's messenger when fighting, and it was not becoming for them to prefer their own lives to his life. 'For they will suffer neither thirst nor fatigue nor hunger in the Cause of Allah. Surely Allah wastes not the reward for the Doers of Good.'

"His cadence was slow and deliberate, tinged with sadness. Occasionally he raised his long, bony finger to emphasize a point. He never raised his voice in a harangue nor lowered it in a whisper. I found myself drifting in a dreamlike state.

"'Do the people have no imam?' I heard him say. 'Do they have no sense of honor?'

"He dwelt on the tragedies of Palestine and Chechnya and finally, as if he were directing his harangue to me personally, on the massacre at Qana in Lebanon. And then he turned to his fighters who sat dutifully at his feet. 'We must search in the Book of Allah for the reasons and the diseases that have led us to betray the sacred house.

It is clear to us that a dislike of fighting and a love of the worldly life have captured the hearts of many. This is the main reason for our humiliation and our degradation. Some say, "O Lord, why have you ordained fighting for us? Grant us respite for a short period!" And I reply, "Short is the enjoyment of this world. The Hereafter is far better for him who fears Allah."'

"Two days after the Sheikh's al-Fitr speech, I was on the firing range, getting instruction in rocket-propelled grenades, when a minivan pulled up. I turned to see a familiar, unwelcome face. Ahmad. The little shit flashed a big grin and a hearty Salaam.

"'The general wants to see you,' he said in a self-important voice.

"He drove me to the camp's center in silence, past the administration building to a small structure that was set apart from the others. A Pashtun with a bandolier crisscrossing his chest and holding a Kalashnikov by its barrel guarded the door. He nodded as Ahmad led me inside and then through a door into a room where Atef was bent over a map with a magnifying glass. When he looked up, he greeted me warmly and motioned for everyone else to leave the room. I glanced at the map and saw that it was a city map with place names in English. Miami.

"'Abu Tariq, in these weeks you have been watched closely, and you have impressed your instructors with your intelligence and determination. You are being considered for major responsibility in the organization. I congratulate you.' I stood wide-eyed, ramrod straight, like a true warrior of God. 'For that to happen, you must formally embrace the program of al-Qaeda and swear your allegiance to the emir.'

"'I expected that I would have to do this, yasayyidi.'

"'You have heard of the bayah?'

"'Yes, yasayyidi.'

"'In your oath to the Sheikh, you promise not only to obey his instructions to you personally, but also the instructions of any person whom he puts in a position of superior authority over you. Is that clear?'

"'Perfectly, yasayyidi.'

"Atef cocked his head slightly, as if he was measuring my sincerity. 'Once you have sworn allegiance to the Sheikh and have sworn to obey all whom he puts in authority over you, you will be required to put your affairs in order.'

"'With a will.'

"'Yes. Now, Abu Tariq al Lubnani, let me impress upon you the profound importance of this act. In the first place, it is sanctioned by the Holy Book.' He reached for a dog-eared copy of the Koran, put on his half-glasses, and flipped through its pages. 'I refer you to Surah 4:59. Please read it to me.'

"I took the Holy Book and read: "'O you who believe! Obey Allah and obey the Messenger and those who are in authority among you.'"

"Atef took my measure over his glasses. 'Did you know this verse before?'

"I shook my head.

"'Read on.'

"I continued. "'If you differ in anything amongst yourselves, refer it to Allah and His Messenger, if you believe in God and in the Last Day.'"

"'You read well, Abu Tariq.'

"Before I could stop myself, the words tumbled out of my mouth. 'What if I were not to swear the oath?' I asked.

"Atef's face darkened. For a time—it seemed like an eternity—he remained silent, looking down at his hands, folded in his lap. 'That would be most unwelcome,' he said at last.

"'But I have heard of senior members of our group who have not sworn the oath.'

"'That is a lie!' he shouted, his face suddenly contorted in anger. He moved to stand.

"'I'm sorry, then, Mohammad Atef. I was misinformed.'

"Atef paused to collect himself, embarrassed by his outburst, and slumped back into his chair. 'Your question is a good one,' he said, quietly. 'And I will answer it. If you were to refuse to swear the oath, we could not regard you as worthy of an important mission.'

"'Would I be dismissed from the organization?'

"'That would be your choice. We had such a case recently. We helped the wayward brother return to his home without difficulty. We even altered his passport to remove the Pakistani entry stamp so he would have no trouble with the authorities. We would do the same for you.'

"Now it was my turn to collect myself. 'That will not be necessary.'

"'There is another part to my answer,' Atef continued. 'If you do not swear the oath, we can give you a lowly mission. We have a need for tough, smart fighters, and a few who are both tough and clever with computers. But if you were to die without an oath to the Imam, you would die the death of Jahiliyyah.*'*

"'I'm sorry, but I—'

*"*Jahiliyyah *refers to the time of evil and barbarism and ignorance and unbelief, before Islam came to enlighten the world.'*

"'And what if I were to swear the oath and change my mind?'

"Again, that cruel smile crossed his face. 'Abu Tariq al Lubnani, I applaud your spirit! You have great promise. You ask the right questions, and if you accept my answers, you will be all the tougher for it.' The smile disappeared, and a glower replaced it.

"'If you violate your oath, that will be a matter between you and your God.'

"He rapped two times on the table, and Ahmad entered. Atef waved his hand for my dismissal.

"I followed Ahmad silently through the darkness toward a part of the camp I'd never been in before. At one point, as we walked, Ahmad said without looking at me, 'Why do you not respect me, Abu Tariq? I am a fearless man. I am an imam and an orator for jihad. I am a lion from the Ghamedclan of southern Arabia!'

"'Why do I not respect you?' I said dryly. 'Because you're everyone's toady, Ahmad, that's why.'

"At the door of an isolated building, Ahmad knocked twice, then knocked a single time. The door opened, and I found myself in an anteroom lit only by candlelight. A group of brothers were playing backgammon. Ahmad mumbled something to one of them in Pashtun, and the guard nodded back, motioning to a side door. At this, Ahmad knocked again, and I was ushered into the presence of the Sheikh."

***

Karima switched off the machine. And so, Sami had actually met Bin Laden! It was a question she had long wondered about. And now he was actually going to describe the meeting! She got up and walked to the window. Peeking through the curtain, she saw the patrol car in the dim light of the street lamp. She wandered into the kitchen, opened a cabinet, and pulled out the bottle of arak that Sami had brought her from Lebanon. Lebanese heroes fighting the French in the hills above Beirut called the liqueur the "milk of lions," Sami had told her. She would need the milk of a lioness now.

***

"Osama bin Laden sat before me on a bank of pillows. He wore a splendid silk robe, and his white prayer cap made his beard appear ever larger than before. In his arms he held a small boy, maybe six years old, who was obviously quite ill. The Sheikh barely acknowledged my presence. He was chewing dates and then putting the mush into the mouth of the sick child.

"He said my name. 'Abu Tariq al Lubnani. Do you play volleyball?'

"I was dumbfounded, speechless. He asked me again if I played volleyball.

"'Yes,' I stuttered.

"'Volleyball is a wonderful game, especially if you live in the desert. They won't let me and Atef play on the same side, because we're taller than everyone else. So, we have to be on opposing sides. It has become quite a rivalry.'

"His team had lost to his cousin's, he said, and they were playing again the next day. A grudge match.

"'We're going to play at dawn, at the first glimmer of light,' he said, and then chortled. 'In case the Americans are watching. They are big sports fans, you know.'

I didn't know what to say.

"'You are a new talent in our camp,' he said. 'And you're tall! God willing, you will agree to join my side.'

"'Of course,' I said, "Most happily, yasayyidi.'

"'You are most welcome—on my volleyball side and on my caravan.'

"'Thank you, yasayyidi.'

"'In fact, we are most pleased to welcome all four of you from Hamburg. You are a talented group, and I believe you will be a great credit to the organization. Your generation will be our hope. The future glory of our faith lies in your hands.'

"'We will try not to disappoint you, yasayyidi.'

"'Have you met the German?'

"'Christian Zimmerman?' I asked.

"'We don't use that name. We have named him Ibrahim,' he said. The sick boy, he explained, was Ibrahim's son, that he had a severe kidney disease. They needed to find a way to get him to Germany for treatment or he would die. I said I was very sorry to hear that.

"'Let us not grieve,' he responded. 'If he should die, the Holy Book tells us that he will live through eternity as a lovable and much-loved boy in paradise. And his father will receive an extra reward in the Hereafter for his suffering on earth.'

"We sat there in silence for a while. Occasionally, as he kept feeding the boy in his arms, he glanced up at me and leveled me with a stare.

"Finally, he said, 'Why have you come here tonight?'

"I told him I was brought at his command.

"'Did you come of your own free will?'

"'I did,' I said.

"And then he asked, 'For what purpose?'

"And I said, 'To swear my oath to you.' But I said I had a question. At that he was totally silent. I wasn't sure he had heard me, so I repeated, 'May I ask you a question about it?'

"He nodded. 'I've heard you were inquisitive, Abu Tariq.'

"'There is a phrase at the end, "not to disobey my commanders." What is the significance of that?'

"'That is not complicated,' he answered softly. 'If I ask you to do something, you will heed and obey me. If I ask someone else to do it, you will not object. You will not ask, "Why did you assign this task to this individual?" We must remember the holy text: "Obey God and all those who are put in authority over you."'

"I started to interrupt, but he raised his hand for silence. 'You do not like your companion Mohamed Atta, I understand.'

"'No, yasayyidi.'

"I had to put that feeling aside, he said, and I had to put the Cause above personal likes and dislikes. But then he told me he had named Omar as the emir of our group. Omar! Our emir! That made me really happy, and I said, 'Good. Wonderful,' and then I caught myself. 'Atta will be disappointed,' I said. Because I wanted him to know I understood—we were a team.

"He kept looking at me, searching my face. And he said, 'Mohamed Atta has spoken well for your group. He has said that you four came to us needing money to satisfy your duty to jihad. You expressed an interest in the Chechyna struggle. You wanted accomplices and training. He spoke to us of you personally, of your love of airplanes and flying. We welcomed his ideas, and we welcome your presence. We will give you money. We will provide you brothers to help. And for you, we will train you to fly airplanes. In return, we demand loyalty and obedience.'

"It was time for him to get the boy back to his father.

"'Is there anything else?' he said.

"'Yes,' I replied and stood straight, and looked at him.

"'I pledge before God my obedience to you, Osama bin Laden, to listen and to obey, to carry out both pleasant and unpleasant orders, at good and bad times, and to work selflessly, to obey my commanders, and if necessary, to die in the Cause of God.'

"He seemed pleased, and he offered me blessings, and then said, 'I will see you tomorrow at dawn at the volleyball pitch. Your first assignment will be in the front line as a net man. Remember what the Holy Book says, "Those in the front lines of the battle will achieve the upper ranks of Paradise."'

"And then he laid the child aside and reached for the bowl of dates across the table.

"'Would you like a sweet?'"

8

AS CHRISTMAS APPROACHED, Karima received her formal summons to be a witness in the trial of the prisoner from the Lades Chicken arrest. It turns out that he was the only surviving member of the Hamburg cell in police custody. Karima had been dreading this moment for a long time. The trial of the defendant named Mounir had been going on for a few weeks, but *her appearance*, the press wrote with wry understatement, was "much anticipated."

The venue would be different this time. The imposing Criminal Justice Building was a venerable old pile near her beloved botanical garden, and Recht had told her of its notorious past. During the Nazi period, he said, many Jews had been tried there for their supposed "racial dishonor" under the Blood Protection Act. In modern times the building's baroque façade had been painted orange to make it appear more welcoming. There was an irony about this trial, he said.

"This ugly, little Jew-hating Moroccan forged many ties with neo-Nazis."

On the appointed morning she dressed carefully, intent to look more German than Turkish. As she was putting on the finishing touches, her mother called. She was holding a copy of *Boulevard Zeitung*. Karima's picture, she said, took up the entire front page.

"And the headline reads, 'SHANKSVILLE SIREN TO TESTIFY TODAY!'"

Karima groaned.

"Do be careful, my darling. They'll all be gunning for you today."

"Don't worry, Mutti. Are you okay? Anything unusual?"

"Things always seem to be about the same for me, *mein Schatz*," her mother replied.

When Kommissar Recht arrived to collect her, he was his usual laconic self. Karima wondered why she found his fumbling ways comforting. He presented the spitting image of a fussy old bachelor, gauche and rumpled. *Perhaps he feels a tinge of the paternal*, she thought, *and is trying to protect his wayward daughter in distress*. No. She discarded the thought. Her vanity was running away with her.

As they made their way toward the downtown, she broke the ice.

"Günther, you said once that the Americans felt their best chance to foil the 9/11 plot was with Sami."

"Yes."

"What did you mean?"

"Everyone is pointing the finger at somebody else," he said finally. "No one wants to be held responsible. There's a frantic effort to shift blame away from wherever or upon whomever it belongs."

"Yes, but why Sami? How could anyone have known about him? You said yourself he was the perfect sleeper."

"Do you really want to know?"

"Yes."

Again, his eyes wandered to the passing buildings. His stock in trade was asking questions, not answering them, but he knew sometimes you had to give a little in order to get a lot. Occasionally, she said something that seemed to suggest greater knowledge than she had ever admitted before.

"There was a chance, just an off chance, of catching him as he came out of Afghanistan. He was detained in the Dubai airport."

"Oh, yes, he brought me jewelry from there . . . and two lovely dresses from Pakistan. Why was he detained?"

"Because his passport appeared to have been tampered with."

"How?"

"His picture was not affixed to the page correctly, and the entry stamp for Pakistan had been touched with a chemical of some sort. Such defects always raise suspicions. There is evidence that his name was on a watch list, but the Americans deny it. Probably someone is covering up."

"Arabs sticking together?"

"Not necessarily. The Emiratis insist that they interrogated Sami for four hours."

"For four hours! Didn't they coordinate with the CIA or your people?"

Recht shot a sidelong glance at her. "Yes," he said finally.

"Who gave the order to release him?"

"I can't get into that," he said curtly.

As they approached the downtown, she glanced over at him. "Whoever it was must be cowering in a corner somewhere," she said distantly.

Recht said nothing.

"If they had broken Sami, that would lead them to Atta. Is that what you're saying?"

"They didn't have anything on Sami," he responded.

"But you mentioned his doctored passport."

Recht exploded. "*Verdammte scheisse*, Karima! I am not going to sit here and criticize my own colleagues! If you really want to know the truth, you're the one who represented the best chance to stop him. You could have spoken up, but you didn't!"

The fury of his outburst frightened her. She turned away.

"That's just not fair," she said softly.

As the courthouse came into view, she could see the TV antennas spooled to the sky, like the Zaqqum tree of Islamic hell, she thought. She saw the round apparatus at the top of the spools. "*The shoots of its fruit-stalks,*" she remembered from her childhood Koran, "*are like the heads of Devils.*"

"They're going to shout some terrible things at you, Karima," Recht was saying, protective again. "Just keep your shoulders back and your chin high."

"Like the red carpet in Hollywood?"

"Yes, that's a good way to think about it. Today, you're the star of the show."

When they pulled up, reporters swarmed around the car. She could hear the hum of cameras as loud questions were hurled her way. She heard only individual words, like *Atta* or *terrorist* or *Shanksville* or *passenger revolt*. She could sense their pent-up frustration over being unable to reach her until now. It was spilling out as anger. As Kommissar Recht whisked her down the cordon, the animated faces of the reporters whizzed by her as an amorphous mass, except one face she had seen before, a dusky man. He was shouting nothing, just smiling broadly at her. She had a sudden start of recognition. Wasn't that the man she had seen in the Botanical Garden? She turned away for an instant. When she looked back, he was gone. She heard only one full question. A tiny, middle-aged, overweight woman, dressed in a loose-fitting shift, with big lips plastered in red like some garish, overly made-up Cabaret figure, and black hair streaked in gray, leaned over the rope and said in a stage whisper,

"Was he good in bed?"

Entering a courtroom, specially outfitted for this trial of a terrorist, she found the scene daunting. The dark wood paneling was carved in gothic designs, and a massive iron sculpture of the double-eagle symbol of the state hung behind the judge's high dais. Karima glanced to her right to see the press and the eager spectators arrayed in their seats behind a thick bulletproof plexiglass barrier. The ugly little defendant slouched in his seat between his lawyers. The growth on his chin was spotty and his mustache skimpy as he squinted at her with his squirrel's eyes. She noticed his overbite as he scowled. She could hear the audience rustle with excitement as she took her seat. The femme fatale had finally been forced from her secret lair.

When the bailiff asked everyone to rise, the door opened, and Judge Schneider entered in his black robe, velvet vest, white shirt, and tie. He climbed the stairs importantly to his high perch. After some formalities, Karima took the stand.

"As you know, Dr. Ilgun, the defendant in this trial is accused of providing material support to the hijackers on September 11 in the commission of their crime against humanity. Specifically, he is accused of lying about the whereabouts of one of the hijackers. And he is accused of sending money to a hijacker. This is the first public trial on the issue of material support for terrorists. But there may be more such trials in the future."

It was as if he were talking not to her, but playing to the crowd. More trials? What was he talking about? Who else had they captured?

"Did you ever have contact with Mr. Mounir, the defendant here present?" he began.

"Yes. He called me once."

"Go on."

"In the fall of 1999 when my boyfriend—"

"Your boyfriend?" the judge said maliciously.

Karima was determined not to be intimidated. "Yes, when *my boyfriend*, Sami Haddad, left Hamburg and did not turn up at his parents' house in Lebanon, I was very concerned. This man called to allay my concerns. He said he was calling at Sami's request and assured me that he was fine and would be returning soon."

"Are you sure it was Mr. Mounir?"

She hesitated. "It's possible it was someone else."

"Try to be precise, Dr. Ilgun," the judge scolded her. "Were you on the verge of calling the police about your missing lover?"

"Yes."

"But you did not do that."

"No."

"Of course, had you done so, the course of history might have changed."

The judge let his comment hang in the air. His menace was palpable. It was not Mounir who was on trial, she realized, but she. With the press obsessed with her, the judge was making the most of it.

"In fact, Sami Haddad went to Afghanistan to train as an al-Qaeda operative," he continued.

"Yes. I know that now."

"When he went to Afghanistan, did he tell you where he was going?"

"He said he was going to Lebanon to visit his parents."

"When did you know differently?"

"I received a card from him in Yemen. And when he got back, he said he'd been in Pakistan."

"Not Afghanistan?"

"He never mentioned Afghanistan."

"Didn't you ask him why he went to Pakistan?"

"Yes, he didn't want to talk about what he had done there. He said it would be better for me if I didn't know."

"Did that not raise your suspicions?"

"It certainly did, but I couldn't pry anything further out of him."

"Did you know Mohamed Atta?"

"No."

"How about an operative called Omar?"

"No."

"Or someone called Muktar?"

"These names have been in the news. But I never heard of Muktar before the attacks."

"Did he ever mention meeting a Sheikh Osama bin Laden?"

"No."

"Did he discuss jihad?"

"Yes, he did. But I didn't know what it meant."

"Are you not a person of the Islamist faith?"

"Yes."

"And you didn't know what jihad means?"

"In a general sense, yes. I meant I wasn't sure how he understood the concept."

"Did he ever talk to you about his training in Afghanistan?"

"No."

"In a deposition you said you had noticed a change in him in 1999 to 2000. Do you have any notion about how he became radicalized?"

"Only what I have read or heard in the media. I am not sure what 'radicalization' means. He began to pray more frequently, but that was not alien to me. I grew up in such circles. I suppose I did find it a little disturbing. But I preferred him praying rather than hanging around discos and getting drunk."

Titters filled the court room, and the judge sternly gaveled for silence. Karima gained confidence from the gallery reaction.

"Did he ever tell you what his target was in this 9/11 plot?" he asked.

She paused to reflect on this absurd question, as people in the audience leaned forward to hear what she would say. The judge was grandstanding. *Let him*, she thought. It was time to push back.

"I think he put that plane down deliberately in Pennsylvania."

A few gasps came from the gallery. "He what?"

"Yes, so he would not reach his target, whatever it was."

More utterances came from the audience. The judge demanded silence.

"Why do you think a thing like that?"

Again she paused. "It is merely a woman's intuition," she said.

"I thought you knew nothing about his mission."

She realized she was entering dangerous waters. "Well, I just know it in my heart," she said.

"You have no other basis for thinking that?"

"No."

"Dr. Ilgun, we are engaged here in a criminal investigation. We are concerned about the state of your knowledge in your brain, not the hopes and fantasies of your heart."

"I'm sorry. That's just what I feel."

From his perch high above the proceedings, Judge Schneider shuffled his papers. Was it for dramatic effect, Karima wondered? "Dr. Ilgun, did you know in advance that Mr. Mournir would be arrested that day at the Lades Chicken restaurant?"

"No, I didn't."

"Weren't you going there that day to meet him?"

"No, I wasn't, Your Honor."

The judge's frustration showed on his face, as he glanced between his papers and her. She waited for his next salvo, sitting up even straighter and primly adjusting her suit coat. Finally, as if he had come to a revelation about the next phase of his questioning, he spoke.

"Dr. Ilgun, were you in love with Sami Haddad?"

"Yes, I suppose I was once."

"Isn't it possible that your love is blinding you from the truth?"

"Yes, I suppose it is."

"And that this love, even now, is clouding your memory?"

"I have nothing further to say."

"He was your husband, was he not?"

"Well, no, not really. Yes and no."

"He was your husband, yes and no?"

Again the gallery tittered.

"We were married in an Islamic ceremony, but the German state never sanctioned or recognized it as legal."

He nodded. The question had been for the benefit of the audience. "Are you proud of your husband?"

"I don't know what to say, Your Honor."

"When was the last time you spoke to him?"

"At 8:30 a.m. on September 11, last year."

"And what did he say to you."

"It was very brief, and he hung up abruptly."

"But what did he say to you?"

"He said it three times. He said, 'I love you. I love you. I love you.'"

The judge let the words hang for a long time in the furtive air, savoring the moment.

"That, of course," he said finally, "is a terrible thing for a man to say to a woman before he sets out to commit mass murder."

At home that night, Karima replayed her testimony in her mind. As much as she resented Judge Schneider's bullying, she thought she had probably scraped through without damage. She remembered his threats and innuendoes. She reminded herself again not to volunteer anything that might have come from the tapes. But it was becoming difficult to distinguish between what she knew before the tapes had arrived in her mailbox and what she knew afterward. Her mention of Sami's conflict over the mission had been a slip. She hoped it would not be noticed.

But who was that man from the botanical garden?

***

July 5, 2001

"Ten days after Eid al Fitr, I was promised an easy day. No long hike. No pounding on my right shoulder from the recoil of an oversized weapon, no deafening explosions. No long hours. It was a special day.

"I put on a clean, white dishdasha and joined Atta at the 'media relations' building. When we entered, we were directed to a room in the back where a brother was fiddling with a large television camera. The set was simple: a Kalashnikov rifle resting next to oversized pillows. Against the wall hung the familiar green banner about one God and his Messenger.

"Atta and I sat down together as comrades-in-arms. From beneath his thobe, Atta brought out a sheaf of papers and handed them to me.

"'What's this about?' I asked.

"'Today we speak to posterity,' Atta replied.

"Certain portions were typed, I noticed, and other portions were scrawled in Atta's calligraphy.

"'What is this?' I asked more insistently.

"'You'll see,' he said. 'I'll go first. Watch how I do it. Then you do the same.'

"I started to object, and then the quiet voice of the Sheikh echoed in my brain. 'Obey God, the Prophet, and those in authority among you.' Praise God, I thought, Omar has replaced Atta as our emir.

"'Okay, ready to roll,' the technician said.

"'Wait,' Atta said. 'What do you think about the prayer cap? On or off?'

"'I don't know,' the cameraman said. 'Is it your signature?'

"Atta pulled the skull cap down tighter and mugged for the camera.

"'Let's leave it off,' the camera guy said.

"I moved into the shadows to watch.

"For the next twenty minutes, Atta read his testimony in a monotone.

He read fast, his words flat, lifeless, with no inflection given to the emotive parts. His head bobbed up and down between his text and the camera lens. The set pieces, the messages to the scholars, to the poor, to Muslims, to the people of the Arabian Peninsula, folded one on top of another without variety. Because the performance was so boring, my mind wandered to the staging. The lighting failed to highlight his best feature, his amazing eyes, I thought. I made a mental note to suggest that for my performance, the left side of my face, my better side, be highlighted and the right side backlit in low shadow. I would have to decide whether or not to wear my glasses.

"At last—praise God—Atta finished. 'Well?' he said, looking to me for approval.

"'That was great,' I said.

"'Okay, let's go over your testament.'

"'Oh, I almost forgot,' the cameraman interrupted. 'The Sheikh has recorded introductions for your testimonies. Would you like to hear yours, Abu Tariq?'

"I nodded.

"The color bars came on first and then the Sheikh's blurry image filled the screen of the small television set on the floor. When he got his cue, he began speaking to camera.

"'And not the least, Abu Tariq al Lubnani, known to us now for his purity and clarity and beauty. From Lebanon, part of Bilad al Sham, the ancient homeland of the Arab and the believer, the dominion that embraces Syria, Lebanon, Palestine, Jordan, and Iraq, descendant of Abi-Ubaydah Bin al Jarrah, one of the Prophet's ten companions,

famous for his modesty and bravery, who was promised paradise, commander of armies under the Caliph Omar. May God be pleased with Abu Tariq, and accept his gift of good deed.'

"I frowned and looked at Atta, as if to say, 'What's this all about?' But he averted his glance and kept his eyes fixed on the text in front of him.

"'Abu Tariq's presentation is much shorter,' Atta called out to the cameraman.

"'Okay, what have you got here?' I said, testy-like, reaching for his papers.

"I read the first part slowly, whispering each word as I went, trying to act as if I was rehearsing.

"'I spent my adolescence cheap,' the script read. 'I did not do that because I was running away from the hardships of life, as they allege, may God lead them astray. I ate the best food and drank the best drinks. I lived in a fancy house and rode around in fancy cars. I had lovely women as my companions. My parents supported me with money for the best schools. With my parents' intercession, I also had the special advantage to take a tempting job. But I asked myself, Now what? I ran away from the tyrants and their easy jobs and left for the jihad at the height of my manhood and in the name of God. When we have this duty on our shoulders and the duty is in our conscience and God Almighty says, "Whoever wants life on earth and covets its attractions, then his deeds will be rewarded on earth. But those same people will be condemned to hellfire in the Hereafter, for what they did and the chaos they created."'

"I looked up. 'Who wrote this stuff?' I asked.

"'Omar,' Atta answered.

"'Did he write all of it?'

"'No, not all,' Atta replied. 'It was a collaborative effort. Okay, let's get the eighth message out of the way.'

"'Can I do several takes?' I asked.

As the camera was focused, I mouthed the words of the eighth message slowly. And then I read it again. In the second reading, I thought of my father, forever generous and dying now, and of my mother, hardworking and long-suffering, and my two sisters, struggling to find themselves as nurses and social workers in service to humanity. And you, my love.

"'Okay, let's try it.'

"I read, looking into the lens of the camera, serious and sincere. 'O father and mother, I am joining the jihad so that I can meet the face of God. Maybe you are hurting. But I will rejoice with you tomorrow. To my father, I say, consider your son's deed in the service of God and his pledge to follow the example of the prophet Suleyman, who said, "I will visit tonight ninety women and each one of them will bear a child for the sake of God." And to you, Mother, be like al-Kahnsaa, the poet and friend of the Prophet, whose four sons were killed at the Battle of Qadisiyah and who did not grieve, but said, "Praise be to Allah who honored me with their martyrdom."'

"'Good,' Atta said. 'See, you didn't miss a word. Now the ninth message.'

"'How do I look in the glasses?'" I said, to buy time.

"'Let's try this one without,' the camera guy said.

"I read flatly this time, trying to imitate Atta, not looking at the camera, just reading what had been given to me: 'To the wife of the mujahidin. Who has loved her husband, I say: Go, my love, for I will count on you to take care of my children and my wealth. If I return safely, you will be in my care. And if I am lost, then be patient. Our children are in my care. Your secrets are safe with me.'

"Atta grunted his disapproval. 'You're so cold, Sami.' he said. 'Can't you read that with a little more feeling?'

"'Can I mention my girlfriend, Karima, in the second take?'

"'No,' Atta said curtly.

"'But we have no children.'

"'Never mind,' Atta replied. 'No one will care later. Let's move on. Sami, if you liked Omar's contribution, wait till the next part.'

"'Who wrote it?'

"'I did, with a little help from Ahmad the imam.'

"'Ahmad the imam?' I repeated.

"'What do you mean?'

"'I mean, I didn't know he could write.'

"I turned back to the script and read, 'I do what I do because the grandchildren of the monkeys and pigs among the Jews and

Christians committed outrages against Muslim women. Have you not seen with your own eyes how the dirty Jews beat our women in the Holy Land? It tears one's heart out. I embraced jihad when I saw the crusaders among the Jews and Christians wage war against our religion and spill our blood in Palestine and in Chechnya, in Iraq and Afghanistan, Sudan and Somalia. And I do what I do because those who came before me have failed to drive the infidels from the Arabian Peninsula. The great idol of the modern age, America, has suppressed us and humiliated our pride and ridiculed our religion and desecrated our honor. I do what I do to let America know that the soldiers of God are coming. Its demise is near. Let us not be fooled by the state of false grandeur it is in. For God is our ally, and there is no ally for us but God.'

"Atta looked at me, waiting for my praise. 'I like the part about the grandchildren of monkeys and pigs,' I said.

"He scowled. 'Okay, let's do the obligatory.'

"I read the last typed paragraph mechanically. I had become a machine, Karima.

"'Finally,' I said, full-throated now, peering deep into the camera lens, and seeing only your face, disapproving and stricken with grief. 'I wish to praise the mujahidin leader, Sheikh Osama bin Laden. May God preserve him from the plots of plotters, protect him from the envy of envious ones, and defend him from the rancor of rancorous ones. May God add my deeds to the glory of his good deeds.'

"Late that night, Karima, as I lay on my bunk, staring at the ceiling in the darkness and pondering the events of the day, I realized it was now official. I was certified . . . unless I can find a way to avoid it."

***

"Karima Ilgun!"

Through the scratchy connection, the shrill tone of her mother's voice warned of trouble.

"Mama. Is something wrong?" Karima said sweetly.

The words were muffled, as if through suppressed tears. "There most certainly is something wrong. *Verdammtnochmal*, Karima. Very wrong, very wrong."

"What is it, Mama? Tell me."

"What on earth are you hiding, my child?"

"Get control of yourself, Mutti. What are you talking about?" Karima could hear mother clearing her throat. "Mutti?"

"Today, Lailani was here to clean. When she was straightening up your room, she found a tiny cassette tape . . ."

"Mama—"

"It's marked in your handwriting as the proceedings of a dental conference."

"Well, you know what I'm studying, Mama."

"Yes, about gums and smiles. That's what the label says. But, Karima, it is not about gums."

"I know."

"*Mein Gott*, you know?!"

"Yes, I know."

"I thought I might learn something, *canim*. I would be able to talk to you better about your work. And so—"

"Mama, you had no right!"

After a pause, her mother said, "I know. It's true. But how could I have known?!"

"You had no business going into my things."

Her mother cut her off. "How long have you had these things?" she said sternly. "Before September 11?"

The dead space on the phone between them lasted some seconds. Instinctively, Karima knew that her next words had to register.

"No, Mama, not before September 11. After."

"After?" her mother wailed. "After!"

"Mama, try to control yourself. This changes nothing."

"Why haven't you gone to the police?"

Again, Karima paused. She did not want to lie. "I intend to do that."

"*Um Gotteswillen,*" she heard her mother whisper.

There was another long pause. Finally, her mother said, "There is something else."

"Something else?"

"Yes, the doorbell rang today. It was a very nice-looking African man. Very black but nice-looking. He was well dressed and seemed to have very good manners. He said he was a friend of yours, so I let him in."

"You let him in!"

"Yes. He was from somewhere in Central Africa, I believe—"

"Mauritania?"

"Yes, that's right. I believe it was Mauritania. I didn't know you had any friends from that part of the world."

"I don't."

"You don't know this African? He seemed to know all about you."

"What did he say, Mutti?"

"He said he was trying to get in touch with you after the tragedy—"

"Tragedy? He used that word?"

"Yes. Well, of course, I wouldn't tell a stranger where you were without checking with you first. Certainly not someone like him. But he was gracious about it. Said he understood and that he would be checking back with me. He bowed in a very elegant way and made a strange sound as he was leaving." She started to whimper again. "He said . . . he said, 'Tell her that Omar says hello.'"

Karima felt herself choking.

"Karima?"

"Yes, I'm here, Mama," Karima answered, finally collecting herself. "Okay, don't worry. I think I know who that was. But listen to me carefully . . . very carefully, Mutti."

"I'm listening."

"I don't want you to open the door to any more strangers. Is that clear?"

"Yes, I understand."

"If that man—or anyone like him—comes to your door again, I want you to call the police immediately. Do you understand?"

"Yes, I understand," she whimpered. "I'm frightened, Karima."

"Okay, I'll catch a train in a few hours and come down to see you."

When she hung up, Karima knew her situation had changed. To the first person she saw, her mother would blab the whole thing as if she was only asking for help or advice or comfort. And that person would gossip to the next, and on and on, until it inevitably reached the ears of the police. Soon enough, Kommissar Recht would be knocking on her door, furious that she had kept the existence of the Haddad recollections secret. The facts were indisputable: she was withholding vital evidence from a frenzied global investigation. It was her final act of material support for terrorists . . . that's what they would think.

Why hadn't she called the police the very moment she received the package? Judge Schneider had pilloried her on that point, but he didn't know the half of it. To herself at first, she justified her behavior as a crime against history rather than a crime against justice. The Americans would not see it that way, she realized now, and they would blame Recht. And, Omar's gang was demanding that she turn them over as holy relics of their glorious, failed mission.

Her mother's safety had to be her first concern. She had put the old lady in immediate danger by hiding the tapes in her apartment. How could she have been so stupid?! What if the Mauritanian turned up again? Omar's people seemed to know everything!

She had to decide what to do.

Wait a minute! The police had surely heard the conversation on their wiretap. How fast would they act?

Fast. The phone rang.

"*Gruß Gott*, Karima. Here is Günther."

His tone was friendly, almost too friendly, she thought, and intimate—he was never intimate—and it put her on guard. He never called this early in the morning. She braced herself for some reference to her just-concluded conversation with her mother.

"Good morning, Günther," she tried to reply cheerily. "You're calling early. I was just flying out the door to an appointment."

"Karima, I must come to see you."

"All right," she answered. "But it will have to wait several days."

"No actually, I must see you today."

"I'm sorry, Günther. That's impossible. My mother is not well. In fact, I think she's going crazy. I must go down to Stuttgart to see her."

"I thought you said you were going to an appointment."

"Yes, before I catch the train."

"To meet a friend of Sami's, perhaps."

She frowned. "Günther, really, I must go. You're being ridiculous."

There was silence on the line.

"Günther, are you there?"

"I'm here. Your mother is sick, you say?"

"Yes, I absolutely must go down overnight."

"All right, then. If it's really a medical emergency."

"A medical necessity, yes, it most certainly is."

"Tomorrow night, then. But I must tell you, Karima. Something new has come up. Something important."

"Good," she said. "I'm eager to hear what it is."

Recht had told her often about the pressure he was under—the BKA alone had six hundred agents working on the case—as if it might induce her to help him out. With the warming of their relationship, he still could not let her in on the full scope of the massive investigation. Even with the huge mobilization of manpower, things had not been going so well recently . . . for the whole operation and not for him personally. Weeks before, the noose was tightening around Osama bin Laden in the caves of Tora Bora. Now reports of his escape were filtering in.

Before, it was thought that Omar had left Germany before 9/11. Now the police were not so sure. A shift away from law enforcement to large-scale military action in Afghanistan was underway, and the Americans were throwing their weight around. They wanted everything the BKA had, and they could be quite high-handed in their requests. But they weren't sharing their own intelligence. Relationships were fraying, and conversations were tense. A bull-faced FBI man had had the temerity to march into Recht's office and announce, "I just wanted to meet the guy who had been in charge of the surveillance of Marienstrasse."

Lamely, Recht had replied, "We pay a little more attention to privacy rights over here than you do."

But in his conversation with Karima, he had been correct. Something else new had come up. He had received a formal communiqué from the first kommissar.

Recht:

I believe there has been a lapse of professionalism on your part. You have allowed yourself to become too friendly with Suspect 21. I remind you of our professional code of conduct. Basic to that code is the admonition never to become emotionally entangled with any witness or suspect, especially one who is attractive.

Despite your reports to the contrary, I am far from convinced that this woman is an innocent in the 9/11 plot. You still have not discovered what was in that damn package. It was most certainly not just gold coins and earrings.

You are to carry on your investigation as you must. But I am assigning new agents to the case, and they will operate independently under my direct supervision.

First Kommissar Wolfgang Schuh

***

Karima went flying into the clinic, dropped a few things in her locker, and then hurried down a few floors to the medical library. The place had always felt like a sanctuary: the musty smell of old paper mixed with the fresh odor of unopened pamphlets on the latest research. In this provincial all-purpose hospital, the new pamphlets usually went unread. Frau Schenk sat behind the reference desk, glued glassy-eyed to the computer screen. Was she really looking at dental materials? Karima always wondered.

Politely, as always—for reference librarians were her favorite people—she inquired about references concerning the Fourth Annual Conference on Dental Hygienists. Frau Schenk leapt to the challenge eagerly. Yes, the library had some holdings. In fact, Frau Schenk said with evident pride, pointing to a line on her computer monitor, the library had just received some tape recordings of the entire proceedings. How about the paper by a Dr. Meyer on the gummy smile? Karima asked. Frau Schenk hit a few keys and traced her finger down the screen.

"Yes, here it is, I believe. May 4, 2001. Dr. Wilhelm Meyer. 'Optimizing the Aesthetic Results.'"

"That's the one," Karima said.

"What is a gummy smile, Dr. Ilgun?"

"What?" Karima's mind was far away.

"What is a gummy smile?"

"Oh. A gummy smile is when a patient has small teeth and shows a lot of gum when they smile. Some patients think such a smile is unattractive and want to have it fixed."

"How do you do that?"

"Well, either you enlarge the teeth or reduce the size of the gums."

Frau Schenk recoiled. "*Aua.*"

"Yes, it's a complicated procedure," Karima said perfunctorily.

"And painful, I would imagine."

Karima nodded. "How many cassettes are there for the entire conference?" she asked.

"Oh, your conference."Again the finger went to the screen. "Nine cassettes. But Dr. Ilgun, I'm afraid they are those microcassettes."

"Excellent . . . I mean, that's no problem. I use a micro-recorder for my work," Karima said. "I would like to check out the cassettes, please."

The librarian's prissy face clouded. "Oh, Dr. Ilgun, I'm afraid, we don't let audio materials out of the library."

Karima leveled a stare at her. "Frau Schenk, I must go down to see my infirmed mother. She's confined to a wheelchair."

"Oh, I'm very sorry to hear that, Dr. Ilgun."

"Yes," Karima said, and then adopting a confidential tone, "I wouldn't want you to repeat this, but I'm afraid she had spinal difficulty a few years ago, and the doctors botched her operation."

"Oh, my goodness," the librarian said, with genuine shock, manifestly uncomfortable to hear personal details. The subject of medical malpractice obviously upset her.

"Yes, she filed suit against that doctor two years ago. And finally, her case will be heard this summer. If she wins, she will be able to pay some of her considerable medical bills and do something about the disarray of her house."

"That would certainly be a good thing," the librarian said solicitously. "What an awful ordeal. I'm terribly sorry."

"Yes, it's a burden, all right, or should I say, big responsibility, caring for her at a distance like this."

"Oh, I cannot even begin—"

"It means more time away from the clinic than I would like. Herr Doktor Hildebrand is none too pleased."

"He can be a bit of a prig sometimes," the librarian whispered naughtily, and then put her hand to her mouth in embarrassment.

"How true." Karima pulled herself up in a formal pose. "I would greatly appreciate it, Frau Schenk, if you would make an exception in this case. I'm getting behind in my work. I'm new here, and on probation. A long train trip will give me the chance to concentrate."

"Rules are rules."

"Frau Schenk, I'm surprised at you. We have developed a friendly and much-appreciated relationship over these weeks. I'm no ordinary borrower, after all, slipping in here to get out of the cold like some homeless person."

"Well, I really should ask the head librarian—"

"He's even more of a prig than Dr. Hildebrand."

Frau Schenk snickered.

"I won't tell the head librarian if you won't," Karima said.

***

July 7, 2001

"On January 27, 2000, I packed up and prepared to leave the camp. Atta and Fatfat were off somewhere on a bomb-making excursion at the al Farouq camp, and I had not seen Omar for more than a week. As in the departure from Hamburg, it seemed as if once again, I was to serve as the advance guard.

"The mood surrounding my departure was strangely different. The brothers who helped me with my luggage looked at me with a new-found respect. I wondered if they knew something I didn't know.

"At the processing building, that same smelly little Algerian with the bad breath and haughty ways returned my clothes and passport. 'Say hello to Muktar for me,' he said. 'Muktar the Brain! Tell him that Abu Khaled al Sahrawi sends his regards.' He gave me a mobile phone, programmed with a single number in Pakistan to call if I ran into any difficulties.

"And then I was surprised to be taken to say farewell to the Sheikh. With those same sad, sleepy, world-weary eyes, he looked at me with a trace of gratitude.

"'We are preparing to strike the idol of the age, the Great Pagan,' he said slowly in that distinctive near-whisper. 'And it is your honor to be part of that historic operation.'

"He stuck out his huge hand with those long, sticky, date-sweetened fingers. His palms were soft, the hands of one who had never done manual labor.

"'If we hit the head, the wings will fall off,' he said. I nodded, as if I understood his metaphor. I glanced at the enormous ruby ring on his fourth finger. We shook hands, and the Sheikh encased the clasp almost affectionately with his left hand. 'Safe travels,' he said softly, with a slight squeeze. "'You are living a great story, my son.' And then he handed me a little scroll tied with a ribbon. I unrolled it appreciatively. It contained a poem, beautifully printed and embossed.

> *They swore by Allah that their jihad*
>
> *Should go on no matter what Caesar said.*
>
> *Our raids shall never end*
>
> *Until they leave our lands.*

"On the bottom I saw the Sheikh's flowing calligraphy. 'To Abu Tariq al Lubnani, Allah Wastes Not the Rewards for the Doers of Good (9:120). May Allah Smile on His Sacrifice.'

"It was the last time I saw him, Karima.

"When I climbed into a waiting minivan and the weather-beaten driver started up the motor, I asked if we weren't going to wait for others.

"'There are no others, brother,' the fellow said. 'Only you. Special instructions.'

"We drove through the clogged streets of Kandahar and on to the border at Chaman without exchanging more than a few words. As we came into the thriving town and neared the border, the throng of humanity increased. Men and boys rolled huge suitcases or pulled their women in small carts, nestled among taped packages. Angry policemen from the Frontier Constabulary prodded and pushed the border crossers with sticks, funneling them toward a long queue. I noticed that one brandished a whip. And in the opposite direction, young boys, not more than about ten years old, pushed their way back through the crowd hurriedly, rushing against the flow of the horde back into Afghanistan, carrying heavy backpacks and casting backward glances.

"'What are they carrying?' I asked the driver.

"'Fertilizer.'

"'Fertilizer? For what crops?' I asked.

"The driver turned and looked at me. 'Fertilizer for the protection of Islam,' he said in irritation. 'You should know. The Americans are coming.'

"'Where are they getting the stuff?' I asked.

"'You will see,' the driver answered.

"He veered off the main road and wove through a massive parking lot, populated by weather-beaten trucks and duty-free Mercedes Benzes. We passed by a bustling market and into a mud-caked sidestreet.

Far up a hill in the distance, I could just make out the Friendship Gate, which marked the actual border.

"'We get out here,' the driver announced. 'We walk across.'

"'What if we are stopped?' I asked.

"'We are going the back way,' the driver said. 'I don't think we will be stopped.'

"'But what if we are?'

"'Do not worry, brother. I have a cousin who is a commander in the Frontier Constabulary.'

"'What about the Taliban?' I said.

"'I have a cousin who is a commander in the Taliban too.'

We walked through a network of back streets, perhaps a mile, until we came to another minivan. The driver unlocked it, gesturing me into the back seat. As we climbed the hill to reach the main highway to Quetta, safely now in Pakistan, we passed one transport truck after another. Alongside the lorries, young boys waved to the drivers for attention, waiting their turn with empty knapsacks.

"Two days later, late in the evening, we reached the great Indus River. At a guesthouse in Hyderabad, I was finally able to take a shower and change clothes.

"The next morning, we were underway before dawn. At last the highway was smooth, and I was able to stretch out in the back seat. Close to nine that evening, we entered the outskirts of Karachi. For the next hour the driver fought through the noise and chaos, and then, close to a petrol station, he pulled off the road near a car that was stuck on the shoulder. A small man in a Pakistani floor-length robe and sandals was hunched down by the tire. As we got out of the minivan, the man rose.

"'Salaam-u-alaikom, Brother Tariq,' Ahmad said with a big grin. 'Thank God you have arrived safely.' At my frown, he said, 'Aren't you happy to see me?'

"'Flat tire, Ahmad?' I said. 'Bad luck.'

"'Not all is as you see it,' he said cheerily.

"'I missed my evening prayers,' I said gruffly.

"'Allah will forgive you,' Ahmad replied.

"'Who says?'

"'I say, in my capacity as a holy man,' he said, putting his hand to his heart. 'And as a representative of the Sheikh. Get in.'

"Ahmad took the driver aside, and they exchanged quiet words out of earshot, before the peasant sped off without a word.

"'Now,' Ahmad announced. 'I must follow instructions to the letter.' He pulled a long cotton bandage and two large cotton balls from under his robe.

"'If you don't mind,' he said, holding up the cotton. 'It is for your own protection—and ours.'

"Carefully, he placed the two cotton balls over my eyes and then wrapped the blindfold around my head. I could feel him place sunglasses over the blindfold as a final touch. Through the din of honking horns and shouted oaths, we drove for perhaps another half hour before Ahmad slowed and parked. He held me by the elbow as if I were blind, and we stood at curbside for a short time. Then I heard the screech of wheels, and abruptly found myself seated in a bicycle rickshaw. As we came careening around a corner, I could hear young men chanting slogans for a cricket team. Finally, the rickshaw stopped, and Ahmad removed the blindfold. We stood in front of a nondescript apartment building.

"'Okay, here we are, my brother.' Ahmad knocked. The door opened, and I was jerked inside, the door slamming behind me. Ahmad was gone.

"'Salaam, brother Tariq,' said my rough handler. 'Please excuse my bad manners. I am Muktar.'

***

Karima got to the cavernous, open-air Hamburg train station with plenty of time before her 12:05 train. Dawdling in the news kiosk, she leafed through the latest women's magazines and peered over the display cases at the passing travelers. At last, she snatched a copy of the *Boulevard* newspaper, overcoming her loathing; paid; and strode out. With twenty minutes still before her train was to depart, she wandered into a women's lingerie outlet, one with lots of mirrors and changing rooms. At a rack of blouses, she pulled down a silk apricot pullover and made her way to the changing room.

After a few minutes a sales clerk knocked on the door.

"Can I be of any assistance?" she said solicitously.

"No, thank you," Karima chirped. "I'll just be a minute." After a rustle of papers, she emerged glowing.

She looked at herself in a full-length mirror and scanned the reflection for others in the store. The place was empty, except for a dowdy, middle-aged woman in a proper wool suit. Karima wondered why such an ordinary woman would be in a stylish store like this. Then the clerk interrupted her reverie, complimenting Karima on how nice she looked in the pullover. Karima feigned indecision.

Her train rolled in at 12:02. She found her first-class compartment without difficulty and exhaled in finding it empty. "Anya. Anya. Anya," she whispered to herself . . . the name Recht had told her to use when she traveled. She repeated it to herself so it would become rote and instinctive. Throwing her bag on the rack above, she put her briefcase beside her. Through the window she noticed the dowdy lady from the lingerie shop hurry along below her and board. A minute later, the door to the compartment slid open, and the same woman entered, nodding shyly and taking her seat catty-corner, next to the sliding door. Karima noticed that she carried only a purse.

The whistle sounded, and precisely as the hand of the platform clock clicked spastically to 12: 05, the train moved off smoothly. Soon they were through the city and zipping along the open countryside. Her companion pulled out a knitting magazine.

From her briefcase, Karima removed the large program folder for the Fourth Annual Conference and laid it down on the seat beside her, placing it at an angle, so that the woman across from her could read the bold letters on the cover. She pulled her earphones and cassette player from the side pocket and then with thumb and forefinger she took out the cassette, marked "Dr. Meyer." Throwing a quick, apologetic smile to the frumpy woman, she slotted in a cassette and hit the play button.

"So this was the famous Muktar. To the Algerian he was the brains of the organization, the force who came up with the plans and the targets and the methods. In camp, little al-Khatani had told me that Muktar had been involved with the 1993 bombing of the World Trade Center in New York City and with the African

operations, and that he had proposed wild schemes to blow up a dozen American commercial aircraft over the Pacific Ocean. He had been educated, al-Khatani said, in a place called North Carolina in the USA.

"No one knew his real name, Karima, only that he had grown up in Baluchistan, a region of country bumpkins, and was embarrassed by it. He had taken the name Muktar partly because muktar meant 'mayor' and muk itself meant 'brain.' And it had been the name of a famous North African desert guerrilla of the 1930s who had led the rebellion against the Italian colonialists. The real Muktar, I was informed, had been captured on September 11, 1931, and hanged five days later.

"Perhaps after all this gossip, I expected a giant. But there stood before me a small, beefy man, no more than five foot two, with disheveled hair, a thin moustache, and large, almond eyes. The day was hot, a typical ninety-degree day in February on the Arabian Sea. Muktar's shirt was open to a very hairy chest.

"He opened his arms in welcome. 'I have been eager to meet you for a very long time,' he said warmly.

"'Abu Khaled al Sahrawi sends his regards,' I said.

"'Ah, the slippery Algerian.' He rolled his eyes. 'He thinks he is the smartest of all the brothers,' he said with a smirk. 'In fact, he is the dumbest.'

"'He tried to discourage me from volunteering for Chechnya. He said when he was there, it was too cold to piss.'

"'Him? In Chechnya?' Muktar let out a big guffaw. 'In his dreams.'

"'Is it true that he was a handball champion in France?'

"'Rubbish. If I were you, I would give him a wide berth. He's very untrustworthy. I can tell you some stories.'

"The entryway was virtually empty except for a prayer rug and a few pillows thrown to one side. 'Come. We have been waiting for you.' He motioned toward the next room, and we passed through an archway into a large reception room. It too was devoid of furniture, but against the far wall was a pile of telephone books and computer manuals. Two rifles stood upright next to a lumpy cloth bag. I was pretty sure that the bag didn't contain cricket balls. Travel brochures, airline timetables, and videos were scattered around.

"Amid this clutter sat Omar, surrounded by three open laptops, five cell phones, and a stack of blank CDs.

"'Hello, Sami,' he said coolly. 'Good trip?'

"I suppose, Karima, that by this time I should have ceased to be surprised. For so long, I had been in the dark, knowing only partially what was happening around me. What was Omar doing here? He and Muktar acted like old pals, as if they had worked together for a long time.

"'Have you eaten, Abu Tariq?' Muktar said. 'We have lentil soup and chicken sandwiches.'

"I nodded gratefully. I was famished. I stood by Muktar as he heated the soup on a rusty stove. Suddenly, in the next room, Omar exploded in frustration.

"'Saudi fools! Muktar, didn't you tell them over and over to find a place in a regular apartment block? These idiots have moved right into a Muslim neighborhood with a mosque next door and a halal restaurant down the street!'

"'Here, you watch this,' Muktar said, nodding to the soup and sauntering into the next room. He bent over Omar's shoulder.

"'Look at this email.' Omar traced the lines on the screen as he read.

Dear Brother,

Praise Allah, for He has supporters even in this land of the infidels. A fellow Saudi I met at the mosque here in San Diego is helping us with our living situation. And other Muslim brothers have registered us for English classes. I hear they give flight lessons in Arabic as well. So, praise God, there are plenty of brothers here to help us in our mission and who sympathize with our cause.

"'Never mind. We didn't tell them much about their mission,' Muktar said.

"'They were not supposed to mention any mission at all,' Omar fumed. 'And look at this! They sent it from their own computer. They've been downloading videos and text from our website on the same computer. And suddenly, we receive more hits on our sites from San Diego!'

"'Let them know that I am displeased,' Muktar said, 'and that they are to read the manual again. They can read, can't they?'

"Through the doorway, I watched Omar begin to type furiously.

"'Boneheads! Goatherds! . . . Muktar, I told you that we could not rely on those imbeciles. They will never learn English, I promise you. Flight school in Arabic? In San Diego? Ha! They have no experience in Western culture. If you think they can learn to fly an airplane, then . . .' He glanced at me, and his voice trailed off.

"Muktar went to the window and looked down on the noisy mayhem below as Omar continued to pound the keys. After a time, he turned back to Omar. 'They know nothing about the nature of their mission.'

"'It will not work, Muktar. You must get them out of there immediately. They will compromise the entire operation with their flapping tongues. Those American mosques are crawling with spies.'

"Muktar patted Omar on the head. 'Smile and be comfortable,' he said softly. 'God is with the faithful, and his angels are with you.'

"Omar grunted. 'Don't tell me later that I didn't warn you.'

"'They are devoted to the Sheikh, my friend,' Muktar said. 'He has chosen them for their dedication. It is not so easy to insert people with clean skins into the States. Instruct them wisely about security. Berate them sternly for their breach . . . And remember, Omar, Muktar does not like to be yelled at.'

"Omar snorted.

"'You may be right that they will never learn English,' Muktar continued. 'Perhaps they will never go to flight school. I can't say. But we will need their muscle later.' And then he looked at me with a flicker of amusement. 'Idiots and boneheads have their place in the world.'

"'They can never use that same IP address again!' I blurted out.

"Omar and Muktar exchanged glances.

"'Of course, I don't know what you're talking about,' I blundered on, 'but the best way to stay anonymous is to use the computers at internet cafés.'

"'We told them that,' Omar said curtly.

"'Those places don't keep records of who use their machines or when,' I persisted. 'You'll be able to communicate with them through chat rooms instantaneously. Just make sure they don't use the same café too often."

"Again the two exchanged meaningful glances. 'That's an excellent suggestion,' Omar said finally.

"Muktar smiled. 'I'm very happy that our brother from Lebanon is so able,' he said.

After twenty minutes Karima switched the machine off and gazed out the window at the precise, demarcated fields of yellow mustard seed. *The Germans are so precise in everything they do*, she thought. For a moment she wondered if she would be a good farmer. If they sent her to a rural prison, perhaps she would be assigned to the fields. Idly, she opened her tabloid and flipped past the celebrity and crime news to the real news, deep in the middle in a single column of shorts. She scanned it quickly, and her eye fell on the last item.

"US SENDS FIRST TERRORISTS TO GUANTÁNAMO BAY, CUBA"

"I see that you are in dentistry," her traveling companion said, breaking the silence. "Forgive me for noticing."

Karima nodded, not looking up from her paper.

"Do you clean people's teeth?"

"No, we have technicians for that," she said with a trace of annoyance. "I am a dentist. We're the ones who pull the teeth rather than clean them."

"Oh, I see," the woman said. She seemed embarrassed at her faux pas.

"I'm sorry," Karima said. "You must forgive me. I'm a bit edgy and behind in my work. I didn't mean to be rude."

"It's nothing, nothing really. I understand completely. I used to be that way."

"Oh?"

"Yes, when I was in the wool trade. We had a shop in Mannheim. Imported fine wool from Ireland. Ladies are quite particular about their wool, you know."

"I can imagine," Karima said distantly.

She averted her gaze again to the countryside, hoping to cut short any further chitchat. She thought about the contents of the first tape: Sami's upbringing in Beirut, their happy times together in Greifswald, his involvement with Atta and Omar in Hamburg and now Muktar in Karachi. She shuddered at the thought of the police listening to Sami talking about their love affair. Then with a start, she glanced up at the busybody when she heard, "Are you traveling to a conference?"

"Yes," Karima answered. "I mean, no. I'm sorry. My mind is elsewhere. These materials are from an old conference. There's so much to take in when you're a young dentist, and so little time."

"I felt that way too when I was in business," the spinster said. "New products, new techniques. I suppose we might have diversified."

"Into dental floss, perhaps."

The woman did not seem to get Karima's joke.

"My mother is not well," she explained. "I have to come down often, and sometimes it causes problems at the clinic."

"I'm sorry," the woman replied. "I didn't mean to upset you. That was the good thing about being in business for yourself."

"The good thing?"

"Yes, I only had to answer to my late husband."

"I'm sorry, Frau . . . Frau . . ."

"Weiner."

"I'm pleased to meet you, Frau Weiner."

"And your name?"

"I am Anita."

"Oh, you must be Italian," Frau Weiner said.

Karima raised her hand. "I'm afraid I have to get back to this."

And whom did she have to answer to? Karima wondered. A pop song came into her head about being true to yourself. True to myself? True to Sami? True to Germany or to the United States, still reeling from 9/11? Anita? Had she said her name was Anita? Anya. Anya. The train slowed as they approached Mannheim station. Her spinster rose to gather her things.

"I do hope you find your mother in better health," she said politely. "It was very nice meeting you, Anya."

Karima nodded. "Goodbye," she said.

There is a wider question now, she thought, as her eyes followed Frau Weiner through the station crowd. What impact was Sami's story having on her? How should she go on with life? Surely not just as before. Only she had been so close to this enormous evil . . . and this evildoer. Only she had this private knowledge. She caught a glimpse of Frau Weiner's bonnet disappearing into the station.

Wait a minute! Anya? Had that woman said *Anya*?!

The door slid back again, and a man in his thirties with a leather jacket and a leather briefcase entered, nodded formally, and took Frau Weiner's seat. Karima gave him an appraising look. He looked ordinary enough. She adjusted her earphones and switched the machine on.

July 4, 2001

"Late in February, I stayed in Karachi for Muktar's crash course in the peculiarities of American culture. I had been slated for a mission in the United States, probably in Florida. After morning prayers, we worked through the day into the late evening. During the occasional breaks, Omar and Muktar were eager to hear my impressions of the training. I told them of my last meeting with Osama bin Laden, and about the Sheikh's last comment, 'If we hit the head, the wings will fall off.' What did that mean? They chortled without answering, and we went back to work.

"At first, Muktar concentrated on practical things: how to apply for a driver's license and how to make plane reservations. There was instruction on how to beat airport security. In passing through a checkpoint with contraband, put it in the bottom of the backpack and put batteries on top. When the alarm goes off, security will remove the batteries and, God willing, will pass the backpack through unnoticed. Always assume you're being watched. If you put on an immigration form that you'll be staying at a Sheraton, be sure to stay there for one night before moving on. Always use the airport shuttle from the airport to the city center, so your trip appears legitimate. Do not contact associates until you've been at your destination for several days. As an exercise, look in the blue pages of a phone book to identify government buildings by address.

"In the interest of operational security, it was advisable to have as little contact as possible among brothers. When talking with brothers, conversations should be short, and filled with trivialities and pleas- antries and vulgar language in which one short operational message could be inserted. Standard code words. Meat and water *meant money; the word* soheil *meant money exchange; the Sheikh was known as 'the teacher.' For my edification Muktar handed me a*

communiqué from an operative in Bangkok. I'm sorry, Karima. It contains profanity, and I apologize to you in advance. But I want you to know how they operate. I mean, how we operate:

Listen to me man, ain't got time for this shit no more. Anyway man, stop playing with me, dude. Thanks for emailing me, man. I also misund U. I'll send U another email soon. Telling U what's going on. I think code thing now making sense. Yaa sohailbahi only gave me thirty documents so I may need 20 more from him 2morrow. Cuz I think 2 more even. Plztrry to be fair. Don't hold ur water, man. In making SEX with chiks around u, DON'T go INTO HER THIGHS UNLESSU GET CONDOMS, ok, dude? Plz tell me if u have any prob. Plz. Fuck all this shit, man. don't worry who I'm fucking with, ok? Just do the shit right first. Take care. Friends of ours are cool pretty looking but I think I can handle them. Ok shitty babe. I'll talk to you later u know I love you bitch.

PS u enjoy urxmass yeah! And say merry to the teacher!

"'If the CIA sees that,' Muktar snickered, 'they'll probably think it comes from some pimply faced skateboarder. But it contains the hidden message that the brother had received $30,000 and needs $20,000 more from the money exchange.

"Omar gave me my operational internet address: xbigbrother99@ yahoo.com. We looked over brochures for American flight schools and watched a video called 'City Bird: The Flying Dream' about the workings of the Boeing 757-300 jet. I had no idea what they had in mind for me then, but I was glad it had something to do with flying.

"Ahmad showed up periodically with provisions, and sometimes he led us in sunset prayers. Once he came with two fat telephone books he had purchased in a nearby bazaar, one for San Diego, one for downtown Los Angeles.

"For my benefit Muktar painted a glamorous picture of the delights of Florida. Its Gold Coast and Space Coast and Gulf Coast. Miami, Naples, Sarasota, Venice, Disneyland. He became especially animated as he talked about the idioms of American speech, as if he were reliving his days in North Carolina. In greeting someone, I was to say, 'What's up?' and if so asked, to give a standard reply, 'Not much.' I was always to be on time for appointments because, Muktar said, punctuality in America is money. A good way to start conversations was to ask, 'What do you do?' because Americans are obsessed with their careers. The more questions you ask of Americans, given their vanity, the less they will ask about you. Learn to speak loud and laugh a lot and look them straight in the eye, he said, because Americans are suspicious of dark-skinned guys with shifty eyes. No bribes. No bargaining. Be sure to shower daily and use plenty of underarm deodorant. Don't patronize women; treat them as equals. Feel free to admire the pretty ones with the phrase, 'She's hot!' You should call your brothers 'dudes.' With African Americans—always use that phrase, not 'blacks'—if the dude is flashily dressed, you can tell him that he looks 'fly!'

"'Remember,' he said, 'Americans have stereotypes about Middle East Muslims, and they all begin with the letter B. We are Bedouins *who act generous but who will stab you in the back at the first opportunity . . . and* bazaar *men who bargain and try to cheat you. Our women are* belly *dancers, modest in public, but exotic strip-tease artists behind closed doors. We're* backwards *or we're* billionaires. *And finally,' he said with a smirk, 'we're* bombers.*'*

"'We have our stereotypes of them too, I suppose,' I offered.

"'Oh, yes, I'm a student of that as well,' he said. 'Those begin with the letter c. They're cowboys and colonialists . . . conspiratorialists and consumers. They love their Coca-Cola. And remember this, Abu Tariq, most of all, they're cowards.'

"At an appointed time, Ahmad arrived at the safe house. With little fanfare, Muktar went to a closet and pulled out a vest. It had pouches, and wires and cigar-sized plastic tubes.

"'I ask everybody do this,' Muktar said, holding it up for me like a haberdasher to slip my arms through the sleeve openings. It was heavy, Karima, really heavy. Omar moved in with a loose-fitting light brown shalwar kameez and slipped it carefully over my head.

"'It's a ritual, Sami,' he said. 'Sort of an initiation.'

"I stood stock-still, dazed, uncomprehending. Was this really my public execution? They did not seem to be joking.

"'Follow Ahmad,' Muktar ordered with a wave of the hand and turned back to a document he was reading.

"The little shit put me in the back seat, and we drove into the city center, parking near Frere Hall. Ahmad motioned for me to follow him along Abdullah Haroon Road until the sparkling Marriott Hotel loomed before us. The imam pulled out his cell phone to check the time.

"'It's time for high tea, mate,' he said in an awful cockney imitation. We waited. Finally, a tourist bus slowly edged into the driveway.

"'*Good. Americans,*' *Ahmad said in a whisper. 'Walk slowly to the entrance, moving through those Americans. And then carry on down the street to the far side of the hotel.*'

"*And so, I walked like a zombie, one foot in front of another, and barely aware of anything other than the weight of the vest. I pictured Ahmad watching me approach the hotel and making my way through the American tourists. I could imagine his glee—since he despised me as much as I despised him—pulling out his cell phone and dialing the magic number.*

"*I knew what I was supposed to feel at this moment. If I was a good Muslim who wanted to go to heaven, in the gospel according to Osama bin Laden, I must kill Americans wherever I might find them and plunder their property and make big headlines. I looked at these pasty ladies ahead of me, perspiring in the February heat in their cotton print dresses, and their flabby husbands in their ridiculous Bermuda shorts.*

"*I tried to think only of you, Karima. As I got closer to them, I whispered your name. 'Karima, Karima, I love you, I love you, I love you,' over and over and over. And then I was among them, navigating through them, while inside I cringed and waited for a flash and darkness.*

"*And then, by some apparent miracle, I was through and still alive, and I found myself walking along the empty sidewalk, alone, confused, dizzy. And there beyond stood Ahmad, far down the street, leaning against a granite wall, smirking and chewing on a weed in amusement. Without a word, he nodded approvingly and led me to the car.*

"'Welcome, brother,' Muktar said matter-of-factly when we got back to the apartment. 'I've made a fresh pot of lentil soup.' Omar looked up from his computer and gave me the occult finger salute.

"On my final day in Karachi, they focused on the plan for the next few months. I was to work with Omar, the newly appointed emir, and obey his every instruction in the knowledge that he in turn was getting his orders from higher authority.

"'Obey God and all in authority over you,' Muktar repeated. He instructed me sternly, I was to restrain my contempt for Atta. Meanwhile, when I got back to Hamburg, I was to distance myself from the radical Muslims in the Al-Quds mosque. To my delight, I was ordered to shave off my scraggly beard. Then, Muktar handed me a plane ticket and an envelope with $5,000 in cash, as well as an eyedropper and a small bottle with a chemical to remove the Pakistani stamp from my passport after I arrived in Dubai. Ahmad was on tap to take me to the Quaid-e-Azam airport in the morning.

"'Will I have to be blindfolded again?' I asked.

"'No,' Muktar answered. 'But these neighborhoods are full of gangsters. So, keep your eyes wide open.'

"At sunset Ahmad came for prayers. As they had their foreheads to the floor, the little imam said, 'Now we will invoke Allah's guidance in relation to our brother, Abu Tariq al Lubnani, with the Salat-I-Istikhara, the decision prayer.

"'O Allah,' he intoned, 'if, in Your divine knowledge, embracing this man in our cause is good for my religion, my livelihood, my affairs, and my immediate future, then ordain it for me, make it easy for me, and bless it for me. If embracing him is not good for these things, then turn me away from him, and make me content with it.'

"*After a supper of mutton biryani and mango juice that Ahmad had picked up at a local takeout, we gathered on the floor in front of Omar's computer to watch an American movie called* Independence Day.

"*As the alien spaceships spread their shadows over New York, LA, and Washington, and the silly warrior president went into his Code Blue, their reactions varied. When the Americans ran through the streets like panicked chickens, when the sentimental, stupid old Jew invoked John Lennon, when the doofus cracker flew his bomb-filled plane into the belly of the beast, for family and love, and especially when a Christian seer held up a sign that read 'The End Is Near,' they took great pleasure. When Will Smith's wife did her pole dance as a stripper, Ahmad squealed with delight.*

"*But we didn't get through the whole movie, ya'youni. Halfway through, Muktar said, 'This is the important part.' The spaceship opened up and trained its death laser on the symbols of America, and one by one, they crashed down in flames: the Liberty Tower in Los Angeles, the World Trade Towers and Empire State Building in New York, and in Washington, first the White House, and then the US Capitol.*

"*As the dome and the pillars of the Capitol were crumbling, Muktar hit the pause button, and the image of the ruined monument to American democracy was frozen on the screen.*

"*Turning slowly to me, he trained his doe's eyes on me and said, 'This is your assignment, Abu Tariq al Lubnani. The Faculty of Fine Arts.'*

"*They looked at me, Karima, waiting for me to say something. I just looked back at them. I didn't know what to say.*"

Karima switched off the machine and rolled her eyes painfully across the ceiling. "Sami . . . Sami . . . Sami," she muttered to herself. She stared, dazed, at the industrial smokestacks far in the distance. *What am I to do?* she thought for the hundredth time. *What am I to do?*

She tried to collect herself and turned her attention back to the compartment. The man in leather had been watching her intently but quickly diverted his eyes back to his sports magazine. She pulled off her earphones.

"Are you getting off in Stuttgart?" she asked politely.

He seemed flustered by the question. "No, . . . ah . . . I'm going on to . . . Augsburg."

"Augsburg," she repeated.

"Yes, it's a Martin Luther town. The Augsburg Confession."

She shrugged indifferently.

"Never mind. You're probably not a Lutheran."

"No."

"You're Turkish, aren't you?"

"A bit more German than Turkish. But yes, I was born in Istanbul. How could you tell?"

"If you don't mind me saying so, I suppose it's your olive skin. Very lovely, mind you; don't get me wrong."

"Actually, I'm trying to recapture my roots. I have a cat named Roxelana."

"Roxelana?"

"Yes, she was the sultana of Suleyman the Magnificent."

"Really. In the harem, I guess. I've read about that."

"Actually, she was the sultan's wife. But you're right. She was also queen of the harem."

The interchange heartened her. Would a real undercover policeman dare to express such politically incorrect opinions in a public exchange with his subject? What would Kommissar Recht think?

"I think I've seen you someplace before," the man said.

"Really?"

"But I can't place it."

"I have a rather common face," she said.

"Oh, I wouldn't say that," he said. "No, definitely not. Not a common face at all."

9

WHEN KARIMA ARRIVED AT KAISERSTRASSE, clutching the plastic shopping bag with the lamb and condiments for their döner kebab dinner, she found her mother fidgety and light-headed. Her legs were bothering her again, and in the best of times, the discomfort made her cranky. Karima put away the meat in the refrigerator and knelt at her wheelchair. She snapped the leg rests out straight and began to massage her mother's sore legs with body oil. As Karima peered at this familiar, kindly, but tormented face, she thought her mother suddenly looked quite old. They spoke only the occasional pleasantry, holding off the big subject for later.

"You know, Mutti, I told a man on the train today that I was recapturing my Turkish roots."

"Perhaps you should also recapture your father's faith, my child. There is much in the Koran about mercy and forgiveness."

"I don't need forgiveness, Mutti."

"Mercy, then," her mother said. "I know you are suffering."

"What I need is peace, and I don't know if I can ever get over it . . . ever."

"Perhaps you should tell the police everything you know. That would be a start."

Karima could not bear to argue the point yet again, not with her mother, not with their secret. She said nothing, continuing to apply the oil and rub and rub and rub, as if she could rub away her own discomfort and terror. She could feel her mother slowly relax. The old lady lay there, reclined, her eyes closed, a slight smile on her wrinkled, fulsome mouth.

"The Americans have begun their public inquiry into the attacks," she mumbled finally.

"Yes," Karima answered. "I saw that in the paper."

"And they're sending the terrorists to that awful prison in Cuba."

"Yes, I saw that too."

"What a terrible place that must be . . . to be a prisoner there, I mean."

Rebuke and suggestion hovered in the air like a bad odor. There was nothing more to say. Slowly, without opening her eyes, her mother reached her hand into the pocket of her robe and handed Karima the tape.

"Are you safe, my child?"

"I don't know, Mama. I'm not sure."

"And what about me?"

"Yes, you're safe, Mama. You're not to worry."

It pleased Karima to fix the dinner just the way her mother liked it, for the old lady's pleasure was evident. She had arrived at an age where many things had to be done just the same way. Karima always went out of her way to make a ritual of it. She parked her mother in front of the television. And then she repaired to the kitchen to begin the dinner. On the balcony she rolled out the charcoal grill. There was still kindling from her last visit, she noticed. Returning to the kitchen to get the pilaf going, she glanced back into the living room to see that her mother had nodded off. Karima pulled the curtain slowly and noiselessly across the sliding door to block the evening sun that might disturb her mother's sleep. And then she went to her room.

As she sat on the bed, she looked around the walls filled with the relics of her childhood. "Those whom I have loved and lost," she whispered, "speak to me." As the voodoo rules for the evocation of the dead require, she repeated the phrase three times.

***

"Only ten days before I fall into your arms, my darling! Nine full days together! I count the hours. I kiss your hands, yahayati, and I even kiss the cat.

"I'm starting to get quite busy. So, I'm not sure I'll have time for much more recording. Things are getting hectic at the flight school, and Atta is as annoying as ever. I feel like punching him every time I see him.

"I begin simulator training tomorrow.

"I've been thinking about how close I came to not making it to this point. Sixteen months ago, after leaving Karachi, I had to change planes in Dubai, where airport authorities removed me from the line, deposited me in a small room, and interrogated me for four hours. A problem with my passport had alerted them, and I wondered if Muktar or I had botched things. In those hours I sat alone, sweating, locked in that room, while, presumably, they made calls to the CIA and German counterintelligence.

"If I had been compromised in Dubai, the whole operation might have been exposed. They would find out where I had been and who had been with me. But at last, they released me. I'm still not sure why. I'm not proud to say it, but by this time, I had become a pretty good liar. Muktar had been right. Look them straight in the eye. Relax. Laugh a lot.

"Back in Germany a year ago, we spent those four lovely months together, habibti. I made sure never to bring up religion or politics. We made love blissfully, like man and wife at last. And that was when it happened. You were pregnant. You seemed so happy. But I panicked. It will make more sense to you why now.

"Other things were going on that you didn't know. Regularly, Omar was gathering the group together at Marienstrasse for contemplation and preparation. As the newly appointed emir, he wanted to be sure that everyone's commitment in Afghanistan held firm. We sat around in a circle on the floor, and by candlelight, Omar focused our attention on one or another passage in the Koran.

"What a gang I joined! Atta, the Egyptian purist, hot with rage; Fatfat, the romantic dreamer; and Omar, the philosopher-leader. Ahmad, the imam, occasionally joined the circle. He always made a point of sitting next to me.

"Sometimes, I had the impression that these sessions were convened only for my sake. Things were different. It was no longer a study group. We were operatives now. Of the five of us, I was the only question mark. I had to be constantly reminded of the nobility of our mission. The Faculty of Fine Arts sounded so grand. They watched me closely for any hint of backsliding. I think they were mostly worried about you. Yet, they dared not confront me—they guessed that when the final moment came, I would choose you over them.

"One of those sessions, in April 2000, sticks in my mind. Omar focused us on the year 1421 AH and the month of Muharram, when Husayn, the son of Ali and the grandson of Muhammad, was martyred. Omar had chosen a passage from Sura 10 about the spoils of war. In his soft, mesmerizing voice, he read from the twelfth verse: 'Remember Thy Lord inspired the Angels with the message: "I am with you to give firmness to the Believers."' And then he turned to me.

"'Sami, you read the next line.'

"I read forcefully: 'I will instill terror into the hearts of the Unbelievers.'

"'Yes, terror in the hearts of Unbelievers. Good. Well-read. And Atta, the next words.'

"Atta almost shouted the next words: 'Smite ye above their necks and smite all their fingertips off them!'

"'Excellent. And Ahmad, you read the last bit.'

"'But I don't read very well,' he stammered. 'The sentence is long.'

"'Never mind. Do the best you can.'

"Ahmad stumbled over his words. 'That because they have made a breach with God and the Messenger, whosoever makes a breach with God and with His Messenger, surely God is terrible in re . . . re . . .'

"'Retribution,' Omar helped him. 'And I will read the last.'

"He closed his eyes, leaning his head back before he spoke the words without looking at the text. 'Therefore, taste it! And the chastisement of the Fire is for the Unbelievers.'

"Oh, Karima, if I could only taste it! I had become afraid. A vision of the Almighty sending his angels to alleviate my fear was attractive. Was such magic possible? The previous verse kept occurring to me! I kept turning it over and over in my mind. 'Remember, he covered you with a sort of drowsiness/to give you calm as from Himself to remove you from the stain of Satan . . .' That was me, the sleeper, covered with drowsiness, oblivious to his surroundings, tormented by the nightmare of Satan.

"In the meantime, I had applied for a new passport, saying I had lost the old one. Me and my 'carelessness.' We laughed about it. Omar and I researched flight schools and settled on one in Sarasota, Florida. In May 2000, we applied for our American visas. Mine came through quickly. But Omar's visa was held up, because they said his country, Yemen, was such a nest of terrorists. A month later he applied again, and again the Americans rejected him. By that time, Atta, as an Egyptian, and Fatfat, from United Arab Emirates, also had their visas. We three were in.

"But a disaster loomed. The Sheikh and Mohammad Atef had designated Omar as our emir. But if Omar could not get into the US, what then? In June, as I was preparing to fly to America as the avant-garde, the order I feared most came from Muktar in Karachi: unless Omar could somehow get into the States, Atta would be the emir.

"I still held out hope because Omar was going to England to find some homely, unwitting English woman to marry and get into America, hiding behind her skirt."

***

Döner kebabs were her mother's favorite. The meat had to be 100 percent lamb, for the matron disapproved of the cheap hamburger mixture that the street vendors passed off as authentic for the tourists. She preferred her tomatoes grilled rather than broiled, and the green peppers well-done. When everything was ready, it had to be served on a slab of pita bread, slathered with olive oil, with a side of pilaf.

When it was all done, and they sat down together, Karima found the meal intolerably long. Her mother talked on and on about her disability case. They were very close to settling now with her quack doctor, and the signs were positive. After Karima cleaned up, she knelt again in front of her mother and began to massage the sore legs again.

"I love you, Mutti," she said. "Thank you for everything."

An hour later Karima wandered into the living room and saw her mother fast asleep on the chaise longue. She slid the porch door open and saw that the embers were still hot. The night was chilly now, so she grabbed more kindling and threw it on the coals and watched the flames leap up. Then more coals. The smoke became thick and acrid. She gazed at the fire for a long time, extending her hands over the grill to warm them, as the coals became red-hot again.

And then she reached into her pocket and felt the cassette her mother had given her. Looking at the number, she saw that she had listened to it. She turned it over and over a few times. She wished she could think of a prayer, any kind of a blessing that was customary in saying goodbye. And then she cast the cassette onto the coals. The acetate curled and sputtered and writhed. She wondered which hot bubble might contain his last words on that tape.

"I am Sami Haddad, the one who could not kill a lamb."

Glancing at her slumbering mother again, she repaired to her room, rummaging about for the next unlistened-to tape. I'd better hurry, she said to herself.

"*My first flight in the Cessna 152. I was not the best student they ever had. But I survived the first round and got my first pilot's license that August. My instructor said she was proud of me. She appreciated my soft hands, she said . . . and my gentleness. When she handed me my citation, she said to the school director, 'He couldn't hurt a fly.'*

"*Atta and Fatfat were training at a different flight school in Venice, Florida, not far away. I didn't see much of them. We weren't supposed to have much contact with one another, only on occasions when it was absolutely necessary, which was just fine with me.*

"*Having seen a commercial on television about a US government program to support new farming ventures, Atta seized on an idea, as if the angel Gabriel himself had inspired him, to ask for a US government small business loan. He and Fatfat chortled about the audacity of it. The proposal was to pose as young aviation entrepreneurs who sought a start-up loan for a crop-dusting enterprise. With Muktar's permission, he would ask for $650,000 to buy a Cessna, remove all the passenger seats, and install tanks for the pesticide. Of course, pesticide was not at all what they had in mind. Atta asked me to accompany him to the loan office.*

"*At a cement building in Sarasota, we were seated before a veteran agricultural loan officer named Jones. She was a chunky woman with graying hair pulled back in a bun. Covering the wall behind her was a large aerial photograph of Washington, with the Pentagon in the center and nearby the Faculty of Fine Arts.*

"*Atta was immediately affronted. 'I cannot conduct business with a woman,' he announced.*

"*'Idiot, I thought. 'Please excuse my friend,' I piped up apologetically.*

'He's from Egypt. It's a cultural thing.'

"*She nodded her understanding.*

"'*I'm sorry, Mr. Atta,' she said. 'But I'm the manager of this program. If you're interested in applying for a loan, you will have to deal with me.*"

"'*You are but a female,' he said with disgust.*

"'*That is true,' she said patiently. 'But a female makes the decisions around here. This female.'*

"*Atta grunted. I smiled at her, showing how I appreciated her sufferance for my rude friend.*

"'*Do you wish to proceed?' she asked, gazing at the clock and glancing back at him.*

"*Atta nodded.*

"'*Very well.' She pulled out her application and a pen that bore the name of the local bank.*

"'*Your name is Atta, you said. A-T-T-A-H.'*

"'*No,' I jumped in. 'A-T-T-A—how do you say in America? Like "Attaboy."'*

"*She snickered. Atta didn't get it.*

"*The process was tedious and lengthy. As Ms. Jones asked her questions and scribbled, Atta fidgeted and jiggled his feet on the floor, making various guttural sounds of distaste.*

"'Why is there not more security for this building?' he demanded to know.

"'What do you mean, Mr. Atta?' she said. 'You were announced.'

"'Nobody searched me. I could be carrying a gun.'

"'I doubt that would do you much good, sir. We don't approve grants through stickups.'

"'Stickups?' Atta looked mystified.

"'We just push paper around here,' she persevered.

"'Well, what's to prevent me from going behind your desk, cutting your throat, and making off with the millions of dollars in that safe?'

"She put down her pen and gave him a stern look. 'Actually, there is no cash in that safe. Anyway, I wouldn't do that if I were you.'

"'Why not?'

"'Because, Mr. Atta, I'm a black belt in karate.'

"That seemed to arrest Atta's attention. 'I think I need that training as well. Can you recommend someone in the area?'

"'No, I can't,' she replied, irritated for the first time.

"After a pause he said, 'I intend to travel out of the country soon. Will my voyage affect my application?'

"'Oh, on vacation? Where are you going, Mr. Atta?'

"'Spain, Germany, and Czechoslovakia, if it's any of your business,' he said.

"'No, it shouldn't affect your application, unless you plan to slit a few throats over there.'

"Atta snorted.

"I decided that I'd better redirect the conversation. On her desk was a plastic football with a star on it. 'So you're a Dallas Cowboys fan, Ms. Jones?' I asked politely.

"'Oh, I see you're picking up on American culture, Mr. Hadley.'

"'Haddad. Haddad is my name.'

"'Oh, sorry, Mr. Haddad. After sixteen years in this business, I should be better with names, but foreign names throw me sometimes.'

"'Dallas Cowboys. America's team,' Atta said proudly.

"She nodded.

"'Their stadium has a big hole in the roof,' Atta said with a big smile.

"Ms. Jones continued to scribble.

"'Have you ever heard of Osama bin Laden?' Atta asked.

"She looked up. 'Osama bin Laden? Is that a character in Star Wars?'

"'No, he's not. Someday Osama bin Laden will be seen as one of the world's greatest leaders.'

"'Really?' she said without interest.

"Again, there was a lull as she scribbled. 'How much will you take for that photograph of Washington on your wall?' he asked. She turned around and looked at the Pentagon photograph as if it were the first time she had ever seen it.

"'It's not for sale,' she said.

"He took out an enormous wad of cash. 'Five hundred dollars,' he said, spooling out the bills.

"Her eyes widened in astonishment. 'I'm sorry, Mr. Atta. Your offer is generous. It's probably worth about five dollars. But the photograph is not mine to sell.'

"When we walked out of the meeting, I was fuming. We walked for a block or two without speaking. But my emir seemed quite pleased with himself.

"'What's so funny?' I asked bitterly.

"'That was just a big game in there,' he chuckled.

"'You won't be laughing when she reports us,' I said.

"'Me and that sharmuta were just having fun,' he said, still smiling. 'We'll really be laughing when we get that check.' And then he turned on me coldly.

"'Let's get one thing straight, Sami. I'm the emir of this operation. I know what I'm doing. Just keep your concerns to yourself.'

"Of course, we didn't get a check. A month later the rejection— without explanation—arrived in Atta's mail. He informed Muktar promptly that they would not be able to purchase a plane. Very well, Muktar replied through Omar. We'll have to rethink the nature of the operation. Up until this time, I thought our mission would involve small planes. Perhaps we might pack a plane full of explosives, shoe- horn Fatfat into the pilot's seat, and dispatch him to the White House.

"A few weeks later, Atta informed us that new instructions had been received from the Sheikh, through Mohammad Atef and Muktar. All three of us were to enroll immediately in simulator training for large commercial jets. Meanwhile, that fall, Omar applied for the fourth time for a US visa, and for the fourth time, he was rejected.

"I was stuck with Atta."

***

The following morning, Karima and her mother sat around the cramped kitchen table and enjoyed a leisurely breakfast. There was much to discuss. If her mother won her legal case, there would be many projects. So much had been deferred or ignored as too expensive in these three agonizing years of waiting for the court to render a favorable decision. Perhaps Mutti should move to a more spacious apartment closer in to town, or if she stayed put, this apartment could be repainted and spruced up and all the trash that had accumulated over these years could be discarded. They discussed color schemes and new furniture. They might hire a regular nurse and perhaps even a regular masseuse.

When Karima rose to clean up, her mother said, "Sit down, my child. We're going to grapple with your situation now."

The look in her mother's eyes startled Karima. A determination and strength that she had not seen in a long time was evident. The cast of her mother's face commanded respect and obedience. Dutifully, Karima sat back down.

"I smelled something burning last night," her mother said. "Did you burn that tape?"

Karima searched her mother's careworn face for a hint of disapproval. And then she nodded. "I did it on an impulse, Mutti. I'm sorry. It will probably get me into deeper water."

"What about the others?"

"Not yet."

"Now, you listen to me, my darling: we're going to get you out of this fix."

"But how? Mama, I'm so confused. I'm caught between two powerful forces, and I don't know how to get out."

"I'll tell you how," her mother said firmly.

"Can't we talk about this tomorrow, Mutti?"

"No, we're going to talk about it right now," she said firmly. "But first you must tell me everything about the police and about the terrorists."

The details poured out of Karima in a torrent. At last she could unburden herself to someone who really cared about her, and her relief was immense. When she finished, she looked into her mother's face.

"You see?" she said, fragile and brittle now.

"Okay," her mother said resolutely. "Calm down, my child. Listen to me carefully. This is what you're going to do."

For her return to Hamburg, Karima chose a slower route, as her mother had instructed, one that required a twenty-minute change in Göttingen and a layover in Hannover. At the main station, she bought a second-class ticket. When she came upon her seat, she found herself in a clutch of rowdy students returning to the university.

The students laughed loudly, tussled restlessly, and masticated their white-bread sandwiches with lip-smacking pleasure, covering the table that separated the four seats with moist crumbs. For a time Karima restrained her annoyance, maintaining her prim, professional composure, suffering the adolescent antics for as long as she could stand it. Finally, she could bear it no longer. Summoning up her best schoolmarm tone, she said, "Could you guys pipe down a little? I need to do a little work." They glanced at one another and giggled.

"Why don't you move over there?" one of them said, pointing to an empty seat across the aisle and poking his mate in the ribs. Gathering her dignity, Karima moved without answering. As she sat down, she noticed an Indian gentleman several rows back, sitting with his roly-poly wife, wrapped in a sari.

It seemed safe enough. When she put in a cassette, Sami's voice was flat and unemotional.

"Soon enough, you'll remember, my love, my father had a massive heart attack. Even though the pace of preparations in Florida was picking up, I could no longer put off a trip home. Without asking for permission, I informed Atta and took off for Beirut. For the next twelve days I scarcely strayed from my father's hospital bedside. With tubes protruding from his nose and monitors on his chest constantly beeping and flashing, he could barely talk.

"The parade of family members through the hospital was constant, including Uncle Assem. When he saw me by his father's bedside, he said, 'Excellent. The good son.' I nodded, pleased with his approval.

"Toward the end of the visit, I left for brief stretches, since, at last, father was resting comfortably. I had not been to Beirut for two years, and much had happened in the interim. After my training in Afghanistan, I saw my hometown differently. Taking a taxi to Mazraa Street, I wandered through the Palestinian market only a few blocks from my family's old apartment and there fell into conversation with a cheery Palestinian man on the street corner. Would he take me on a walk through Sabra? I asked. He gladly agreed.

"'We want everyone to see the squalor,' he said.

"We walked through narrow, muddy alleyways, and the man cautioned me to be wary of the frayed, exposed wires overhead and the stinking trash that littered the doorways. They wandered into a cramped school, and tiny boys shouted out greetings to the guide, clustering around his legs and competing to hold his hand.

"'What is their future?' I asked as we walked away.

"'It's very hard to say,' the man said. 'They have nowhere to go when they get older, and they will become very angry.'

"He was a doctor, he told me, unable by Lebanese law to practice either outside of the camp's confines or inside, for it was forbidden. It was a sunny, mild February day when we had entered the virtual prison, but we never saw the sun until we left. Omar and Muktar had been right: I had been blind, utterly detached from my surroundings in my youth, and from the reality of my manhood.

"We strolled down a street, crowded with stalls, where Syrian shopkeepers sold their cheap wares, and the urchins played in the mud puddles.

"'This is the street of the massacre,' the doctor said.

"'What massacre?' I asked.

"The sunniness of my guide's disposition vanished, and he looked at me in disbelief.

"'You lived here, and you don't know?' he said.

"'No, I'm sorry. I don't.'

"'In 1982 Sharon massacred seven hundred of our brothers along this street.'

"'Sharon, the Israeli general?' I said.

"The doctor turned full face. 'Young man,' he said, 'did you really grow up around here?'

"Toward the end of my visit, Uncle Assem invited me to ride out to the Bekaa Valley to see the plot of land the family had bought for us, Karima, where my relatives promised to build us a splendid house as a wedding present.

"Uncle Assem's big diesel car roared up the winding highway above the city past the pastel high-rise apartment buildings that dot the mountain slopes where wealthy oligarchs from the oil countries reside. At the summit we stopped for coffee at a roadside restaurant. After the coffee, Uncle Assem ordered shots of arak.

"'Drink this,' he said. 'It is called the milk of lions. Our ancestors in the mountains used to drink it and fight courageously.'

"The fertile valley stretched before us. Far to the south, above a low layer of cloud, loomed Mount Hermon. Once on the valley floor, Uncle Assem edged his car down the dusty main street of Al-Marj. Modern calligraphy of the Haddad name emblazoned nearly every store: the Haddad furniture store, the Haddad electronics store, the Haddad wedding gown store, managed by Uncle Assem's wife. And then he turned down a side street where lovely granite houses, tan and sunbaked, were positioned one by one in the Haddad family compound. At the end of Haddad Street was the grandest of all, belonging to Uncle Assem himself.

"'I never told you this before, Sami. But I am a retired brigadier general in the Lebanese security forces.'

"I turned to look at his strong profile. I admired him so much, Karima. I was proud that a Haddad had risen so high in the ranks for his valor and leadership and sacrifice. Was I living up to the ideals of this secret soldier? I wondered. 'No, uncle, I didn't know that,' I whispered. His revelation stoked my pride, but my fear also. What did the Lebanese security services know about our mission? With all his cunning, what had his uncle discovered after that visit to Germany? What would Uncle Assem think about my own warrior spirit?

"A little farther on, he stopped at an empty lot. From the back seat he unfurled the plans for our house. In a flash I saw our future spread out before me. I understood now that the family was only humoring my dream of becoming a pilot. They were sure that eventually I would give up my pipe dreams and return here with you, raise a family, and take over the leadership of the Haddad clan after father died. A comfortable life as a shopkeeper awaited. I tried to imagine how you could be happy here, far away from your roots, a European Turk toiling among disapproving Arabs. Could you ever be comfortable near hills dotted with caves holding Hezbollah rockets, only miles from the Israeli border and along their invasion route? I could not imagine it, any more than I could imagine myself happy in some drab suburb of Stuttgart, living out my life caring for your invalid mother.

"Uncle Assem prattled on about the kingdom of wealth and security and love that awaited us. As Uncle Assem talked, a vision of the Sheikh in Afghanistan rushed into my head.

"'You are living a great story, my son.'

Karima turned the tape machine off and picked up Dr. Meyer's report. Under the heading "The Challenges of a Gummy Smile," her eyes fell on the opening paragraph.

"Short and long teeth can detract from a patient's smile and may compromise cosmetic restorative procedures in the smile zone. Surgical manipulation of hard and soft tissues can enhance cosmetic appearance. Gummy smiles, ridge defects, and gum recession are candidates for this treatment."

She looked over at the hoodlum who was cackling to his mate, her eye falling with professional interest and secret pleasure on his gummy smile.

"Ideally, after successful surgery, when a patient smiles, the inferior border of the upper lip, should be at the gum line of the upper lip, with upper front teeth measuring 80 percent as wide as they are long."

She had met Dr. Meyer once. A tall, distinguished man with white hair and half-glasses, he stood at the top of their profession. She had put a question to him about ridge defects, and he had responded with the evident pleasure of a man who had once been a lover of attractive women. Karima had not read this particular paper of his.

At Göttingen the students and the Indian couple got off. Karima watched them disappear into the station. The station clock ticked down toward the departure time. Four minutes before the train was due to leave, she saw the pimply student run back through the station door and board the train again. A moment later he ran down the aisle to her.

"A man asked me to give you this," he said breathlessly. "He gave me five marks." He handed her a letter, then turned and ran back down the aisle and disappeared. She looked at the envelope. *Dr. Karima Ilgun. Confidential."* The train jerked forward.

Dr. Ilgun,

We know you have the holy tokens of Abu Tareq al Lubnani with you. For your good and that of your mother, do exactly as you are told. When you arrive in Hamburg, proceed to Bahnsteig 8 where the train to Koblenz will be ready to depart. Walk to the middle of the platform where you will see a circular trash receptacle next to an elevator. Deposit the tokens in the receptacle, immediately take the elevator up the main floor of the station and exit.

Omar

The image of her mother's cassette bubbling and curling into a liquid, viscous goo on the coals the night before, flashed through her mind. She had watched it curl and writhe from the heat, finally taking fire and transforming into a grotesque shape, before it became a cinder.

Two men were gazing at her across the aisle. She had not been aware of them before. One had a crewcut; the other wore the unmistakable costume of the BKA. Crewcut averted his glance.

Quickly, Karima ejected the cassette, glanced at them again, and then examined the cartridge carefully. She thought about what it covered: his training in Afghanistan, the meeting with Mohammad Atef, his weeks in Karachi with Muktar, his early months in Florida, his trip to Beirut. She stared wide-eyed out the window. *Well then*, she thought, *it is not exactly Mutti's plan, but close enough*. With a jerk, she rose to go to the restroom at the end of the car. Sauntering slowly by the two agents, she looked directly into their eyes and gave them a smile of recognition. They shifted their eyes to the passing countryside.

In the toilet she reached in her purse and pulled out a cigarette, her lighter, and a bottle of nail polish remover. And then she pulled out the cassette, laying it carefully on the stainless-steel sink. With evident satisfaction, she began to pull the acetate tape out of the housing, letting it spool into a Medusa-like tangle in the well of the basin.

The Americans really didn't want a human story. She was sure of it. It was much easier for them to think of Sami as a monster. She was doing them a favor. And al-Qaeda? Sacred relics of glorious martyrdom . . . never!

She watched the viscous drops of the nail polish remover ooze slowly out of the bottle and onto the tape. "Goodbye Sami," she whispered. Then she lit the tangle, jumping back as it burst into flame. The shrill, staccato smoke alarm went off. After a moment, she quickly doused the mess with water, squeezed it into a ball in a paper towel, and flushed it down the toilet. Then she sat down on the toilet, lit a cigarette, blew a smoke ring at the mirror, and waited for them.

In Hannover, the agents led her through the crowd on the platform. Crewcut guided her by the elbow, making no effort to spare her feelings at being made a public spectacle. They wound their way downstairs and through back corridors below the tracks. The rumble of trains overhead shook the walls. At the police office, processing the paperwork to fine her for smoking in the train took an age, and no one seemed to be in a rush. When they were done, they put her in a spare room with two chairs and a simple table. Had they not finished? Yes. Then why could she not leave and catch the next train? Orders.

In time, Kommissar Recht entered stiffly, followed by Sergeant Braun and the agent in the leather jacket, supposedly Augsburg bound, from her trip down. She rose to greet the vice kommissar as if he had come to deliver her from this unfortunate difficulty. Seeing the grim look on his face, she backed off into a more formal posture.

"You have been a naughty woman," Recht said.

"I'm sorry, Günther. I've tried to stop smoking so many times. Sometimes the compulsion is just too great. You can understand that. You know the pressure I'm under. I didn't know about the alarm. And anyway, you smoke those horrible French things."

Recht glanced at Braun. "Did you bring it, Sergeant?" he asked.

Braun nodded. Recht fished rubber gloves out of his pocket. As he snapped them on, he said, "I want you to empty the contents of your purse onto the table, Dr. Ilgun."

The usual detritus of a woman's purse scattered before them: keys, wallet, change purse, old bills, pocket mirror, cosmetics case, small scissors, lipstick, fingernail polish, nail polish remover. Braun handed the kommissar a small stick, and he began to pick through the debris.

"Does a woman's privacy mean nothing around here?" she demanded, half-heartedly. Recht said nothing. He picked up her wallet and began to go through the credit cards, money, and then the pictures. He pulled one out of the billfold and flashed it to the agent in leather.

"Recognize this guy?" he asked leather jacket.

The agent nodded. "The death pilot."

Recht regarded the picture as if it were a museum specimen, then glanced at Karima. "Okay, you can put all that stuff back. Now the briefcase."

She hoisted it on the table and took out the prospectus for the Fourth Annual conference, then her tape recorder, a few patient files, and three microcassettes. At the appearance of the cassettes, Recht showed keen interest, reaching his hand out to Braun. The agent handed him a microcassette recorder.

"Please be careful," Karima said. "Those belong to the hospital library. I only have them on loan. I don't suppose you've ever experienced the wrath of a librarian."

Again, Recht glanced at her with a trace of amusement. He slotted a cassette into the machine with the proud look of the sleuth who had just cracked his case. He hit the start button.

The disembodied voice said, "Correction of a gummy smile can have a dramatic and long-lasting impact on a patient's smile. The surgical procedure utilizes an incision to allow separation of the gum from the teeth, removal of a small amount of supporting bone and the replacement of gum tissues to expose the crowns of the teeth fully."

With each of Dr. Meyer's words, Recht's scowl grew darker. He looked up coldly at Karima, and she mugged a big, mirthless smile, pointing to her exposed gum line. Over Recht's shoulder, she could see Braun smirk. Recht ejected the cassette and put in the next.

"The management of a patient with a tooth-sized discrepancy in the so-called smile zone is a challenge to both the orthodontist and the restorative dentist. To evaluate, diagnose, and resolve the aesthetic problems caused by tooth discrepancy an interdisciplinary approach is recommended."

He discarded that tape quickly and went to the third.

"Since their introduction in the early 1980s, porcelain laminate veneers have become a popular treatment in the cosmetic dentist's armamentarium."

Recht switched off the machine, picked up her briefcase, and looked into the depths of its empty compartments. He examined the stitching and the Velcro. Anger and frustration mixed with embarrassment.

"Can I go now?" she asked sweetly.

Recht looked at Braun. The agent shrugged his shoulders.

"All right. You can go for now," Recht said. He glanced at the clock. "There's another train to Hamburg in fifteen minutes."

"In the future, Dr. Ilgun, please comply with the rules of the Deutsche Bahn," Braun said officiously.

Karima carefully put her things back in the briefcase.

"They ought to have special cars for smokers," she said with a pout, as if to put a fine point on the charade. "At least I don't smoke Gauloises," she said.

Recht turned toward the door without answering. "Do we still have a date tonight?" she called out after him. "I could bring slides of smile zones that need correcting." She glanced impishly at Braun. The man in leather seemed to take note.

"Yes," Recht said.

"Good. Ten o'clock. At my place, then. You bring the wine."

He nodded darkly. As she started toward the door and the detectives viewed her suspiciously, she stopped.

"Günther," she said, "I almost forgot. You might want to have this."

She pulled Omar's letter from her inside pocket and handed it to him.

10

AT 10:00 P.M. TO THE MINUTE, Kommissar Recht arrived at her apartment. He came across her threshold with a long face.

"I suppose you're quite pleased with yourself," he said.

Karima mustered a warm greeting to cover her nervousness. She had prepared a lavish spread to assuage his bad feelings. Scented candles flickered on her mantelpiece, and soft Ottoman music played in the background. She wore a casual, floor-length shift of red kelim design. She knew she looked gorgeous.

"I know I behaved badly today, Günther," she said, as she took his coat. "I *am* sorry. Will you accept my apology?"

He uttered a half grunt.

"Good," she said, taking his vocalization as an affirmative. "After all you've done for me, you did not deserve that."

"No. I did not deserve that treatment," he said, "especially in front of my colleagues."

She went to her pantry and reached for a shot glass and a bottle.

"Have you ever tasted arak?" she asked, pouring the clear liquid into the glass. "The Lebanese call it the milk of lions. They give it to their best fighters."

He gulped it down. "I prefer schnapps," he croaked.

At her kitchen table she put the goulash and wine before him and watched him eat in silence. "Tell me your news," she said at last.

He wiped his face politely and folded his napkin carefully.

"The good news first?"

"Please," she said. "I'd welcome some good news."

"For once we did things correctly," he began. He reached in his vest pocket and pulled out a sheet of paper. "This is classified," he said, "You can read it and give it back."

"What is it?"

"A police report."

She read:

At the call from Kommissar Recht from Hannover, five officers deployed to Hamburg Station. When the train from Hannover arrived at Bahnsteig 8, Agent A got off the train and made her way through the crowd waiting to board for Koblenz, deposited a packet wrapped in brown paper in the trash receptacle, and proceeded to the elevator and the upper floors. Two suspects were surveilled coming through the crowd. After looking around suspiciously, one retrieved the packet and started to walk away quickly as officers moved in on them. One was detained immediately, but the other took off running through the crowd down Bahnsteig 8 with the packet under his arm. An officer gave chase and tackled the suspect before he reached the stairs. Looking down at his prisoner, the officer said, "God is great," and the suspect spat in his face.

Karima looked up at him in amazement. "Who was my imperson-ator, Agent A?" she asked.

"The one known to you as Frau Weiner. She had taken off her wig. She's not much older than you. She's one of our best performers."

"Who are the prisoners?"

"Mere foot soldiers. When I got back to Hamburg, I interrogated them."

"Yes, and?"

"They cracked like an eggshell."

"What do you mean?"

"Later this evening, police in Duisburg arrested an African."

"An African?"

"Yes, a professor from Mauritania named Abu Musab. We think that he has been posing as Omar, that he was the one who left those messages on your answering machine and who wrote the instructions for your drop today."

"Omar is the Mauritanian?"

"We think that the publicity about you may have protected you somewhat from them."

"What about the real Omar?"

"We're sure now that he left Germany before September 11 and is somewhere in Pakistan. We have leads."

Karima exhaled deeply and slumped down on her couch. "What's the bad news?" she asked.

He shifted uncomfortably in his chair. "The note you gave us in Hannover mentioned sacred mementos."

"Yes."

"That confirms suspicions that I . . . and my colleagues . . . have long harbored."

Curiously, his formality pleased her. For all his fustiness, she saw him now as a consummate professional, and she admired that. It was a quality to which she aspired herself.

"What suspicions?" she asked.

"We believe you received more than merely a letter and a gold coin and an inscribed Koran and precious earrings from Sami Haddad right after 9/11. The postman who delivered your mail has approached us."

"Dear, sweet Herr Schmitt. He is a solid citizen."

"Yes. He described a bulky envelope. Indeed, he described its feel with considerable precision. That you would get a bulky package from Newark, New Jersey, only days after 9/11 aroused his curiosity. And then he read about your connection to Haddad in the papers. He was reluctant to come forward until now. To be honest, like a few others I could name, he felt protective toward you."

"Okay. What else?"

"A neighbor of your mother's in Stuttgart has been in touch with us."

"I might have guessed. I bet I know the biddy you're talking about. My mother has only a few friends left, you know."

"I would not make light of this, Karima."

"So, you have a curious postman and the gossip of an old blabber-mouth and a note from Omar."

"Yes. And a phone tap with Omar's demand for Sami's sacred relics. They were desperate to get whatever you had. Your gold coin and earrings did not make sense."

"And so, what is your conclusion?"

"We think you received some sort of tape recordings."

She took his plate without answering and drifted to the sink to soak the dish and silverware.

"Would you like another glass of wine?" she asked.

He nodded. She poured it, careful not to drip on her new tablecloth.

"Tell me something, Günther. Have you ever considered having that mole on your face surgically removed?"

He was content to let the conversation drift down side paths. She had not howled in protest at his mention of tapes. His detective's intuition told him that she would not posture or dissemble this night.

"My colleague at work refers to it as my signature. Someone else thinks I store my microdots there. I'm not sure why it fascinates people."

"I just thought women might find you more attractive without it," she said.

A long, awkward silence passed between them.

"Yes," she said at last. "It's true. Sami did send me tapes."

Recht felt his heart pound. Many confessions had come his way in his long career. Usually, they came as the fruit of a long, hostile interrogation when the subject was boxed in and when a confession was in the culprit's self-interest. This was different. It was voluntary, flowing from the heart, a confession of the best kind. He could not threaten her. This was what his American counterparts would scoff at as a "fishing expedition." Yet it felt now as if he had hooked his fish. Her story had to emerge naturally. If he coaxed the material out of her, it would be a real feather in his cap. It might even restore him to good standing in the office.

"Your favorite songs, I suppose," he said. "Sami Haddad reading the sweetmeats of Kahlil Gibran poetry."

"I didn't know you read poetry."

"Or some sort of sentimental, deathbed apology?"

"Sarcasm does not suit you, Kommissar," she scolded. "Since he mailed his package to me the night before the attack, I suppose you *could* call it a deathbed confession . . . except that he recorded his sentiments to me over the two months before the operation."

Her revelation floored him. Confessions from Haddad recorded over two months before 9/11! Unbelievable! The night before, when Recht had brainstormed about this meeting with the first kommissar, they had imagined tape recordings with a few sentimental tidbits. Nothing revelatory or actionable, perhaps a little elaboration on his farewell letter, just another piece of the puzzle, nothing that would be of any real interest to the Americans. Two months of recollections? It was unthinkable!

She paused. Now it was her turn to level a stare at him, searching for good intentions or bad.

"Günther, I think we should review our relationship."

"All right."

"Now that I have disclosed my secret to you, are you going to arrest me and throw me in jail? Put me on trial for withholding valuable evidence and send me to Guantánamo Bay? Dentists are not taught about their legal rights, except in cases of malpractice."

"Some would say that withholding vital tapes from the BKA and the Americans is a form of malpractice," he said.

"Unless the material is trivial or personal. If he sent me our favorite songs, or read sappy Kahlil Gibran love poems to me, that would have no legal or historical value, isn't that so?"

She continued to clear the plates, enduring his long silence stoically.

Finally, he said. "Why don't you let me listen to the tapes? Let me be the judge of their value?"

"I can't," she answered.

"Why not? We could make an agreement that would protect you."

"No, Günther, *I can't.*"

"Why not?"

"Because I have burned them."

Vice Kommissar Günther Recht thought he had experienced nearly everything in his long and varied career in criminal justice. But at this moment his shock was profound. Burn the tapes! Burn the most crucial evidence imaginable! How could she do such a thing?

"They proved my innocence," she was saying. "But you will have to take my word for it now."

"*Um Gotteswillen*, Karima! Do you know how many agents . . . here and in America . . ." he sputtered. "The entire BKA . . . a thousand FBI agents. . . if they knew what you have done. The Americans will be livid."

"Honestly, Günther, I don't think so," she replied calmly. "I don't think they're interested in the humanity of Sami Haddad. They're only interested in why their FBI and their CIA did not catch Sami and the others before they could act."

"You *burned* the tapes," he uttered again. "Of course! That accounts for the smell of burnt plastic in the train. How could I have been so stupid! The agents reported a smell of burning plastic mixed with your cigarette smoke."

She returned to the sink and began to wash the plates. The sound of rushing water was deafening to him. He was still shaking his head, more in anger now than in disbelief. "You burned the tapes," he whispered.

Her back was turned to him as she worked the detergent and brush. "Well, not all of them," she said.

She rummaged in the icebox for a pear and brought it to him with a knife. Why was it, he thought to himself, that peeling a piece of fruit had such a calming effect? He could feel his heart thumping.

"Not the last one," she said.

"The last one?"

"Yes, the one where he may tell me his decision."

"His decision?" Recht whispered.

"Yes, his decision to go forward or to desert the cause and run away with me," she said.

"You still have that tape?" he said, still trying to grasp what he was hearing.

"Yes."

He leaned back in his chair, speechless, as a year of his professional life seemed to pass through his mind in a flash.

"I could make you a promise," he blurted out finally.

She sat down across from him to hear it, her expression open, expectant, devoid now of artifice or duplicity.

"If you will let me listen," he continued, "I could promise not to reveal their existence to my colleagues and to the Americans, unless we agree together. I could swear that to you. I will put it in writing, if you wish."

"Oh, Günther, you are such a dear man."

He tried to modulate his tone. "I can't begin to imagine how hard this is for you, Karima. How have you borne this alone this far? You cannot bear it alone any longer. You just can't."

"You're not the first person who has suggested that."

"We could work together. I know as much about 9/11 as anyone. I can fill in your blanks. If we need to keep this confidential, so be it. If we decided together to go public, I promise that you'll be protected."

"I know you're an important man, Günther . . . Ober Kriminal Haupt Kommissar Günther Recht . . ."

"Actually, the oberkommissar is under me."

"Over or under, I doubt that you'd be able to control things if my tapes were made public."

"I could. I could."

"Besides, why does hearing Sami's voice excite you so much? It's morbid."

"Why does it excite me? Because I have been on Sami Haddad's trail for a long time."

She rose from the table and pushed in her chair. "I have an idea, Günther. Why don't you go outside and smoke one of those revolting Gauloises, and I'll think about it."

It was true. She had been alone in this quest, so utterly alone. For once, listening with someone might be a good thing. Gretchen? Or Gretchen's brother? Or her mother? They would not understand. Hadn't the time come to unburden herself completely? Maybe he was right. She could no longer bear this witness alone. Unless she wanted to go crazy.

Recht came back through the door almost tiptoeing. He glanced at her sidelong for a hint.

"Well?" he said.

She pondered the lumpy face of this man with whom she had logged so many miles since the catastrophe, and she felt a great storm of sympathy well up. She sat down beside him on her couch, hands over her face, and broke into uncontrollable sobs. He put his hand on her shoulder, and she collapsed into his arms. He held her firmly, as the convulsions came one after another, as if all the hurt and confusion and anger and shame of the past months had to come out wave after wave until it was all expended, and she could speak again.

"You're right. I can't do this alone anymore."

"Of course not. Nobody could."

"I thought . . . I thought . . . that his tapes were just for me. Just for me! Such an honor! He wanted me, only me, to know his whole story. How stupid I have been."

He held her silently, awkwardly, as if afraid of saying the wrong thing.

"I'm so far beyond anger now," she said. "But the shame . . . the shame . . . " She could not finish. "Do you think people will ever forget about him . . . and me?"

He held her at arm's length, his hands firmly on her shoulders, looking deeply into her eyes.

"Yes," he said emphatically. "Yes, they will forget. Not about the attack. But the Nineteen? They were forgotten even before they acted."

"But how can the attack be remembered, and not the attackers?"

"Oh, the masterminds may be remembered. Bin Laden, perhaps Atta. But not Sami. He's the one who failed. He's easy to forget. By his failure, the Capitol Building of the United States was saved. More than that. He gave the Americans a great story of heroism. That was his gift. Listen to the news reports and the political speeches about the brave passengers who stood up to 'terrorists' and to 'terrorism.' But not to Sami Haddad. The perpetrators are an abstraction."

"He's no abstraction to me."

"Nor to me." He paused. "Let's just sort this out together, Karima, just you and I."

"All right," she answered. "But not now. I can't handle any more tonight."

"When, then?"

"In a few days. Yes, in a few days. I promise."

"What will we be listening to? I'd like to prepare myself."

"You want a heads-up? Isn't that what the Americans call it?"

"Yes."

"Okay, his last three entries."

"What dates?

"July 18 and 19, and then the last one, August 8, I think."

***

Recht arrived early the next morning at headquarters, eager to avoid Braun, at least for an hour or so. If he was to have the chance to listen to Haddad's narrative of the last weeks, he needed to review the intelligence that his agency had developed on the same period. If they were more than wistful yearnings, the Haddad recollections might go right to the heart of the conspiracy. They would constitute the best evidence of motive, unfiltered, unadulterated, untainted. There was nothing else like that in the BKA files or in any files elsewhere. The truth was that neither the Germans nor the Americans had any real insight into the motives of the nineteen perpetrators, much less in the motives of the most interesting and vulnerable one of the bunch, the one who had almost pulled out of the operation.

Even though he was in a kind of unofficial probation for his cozy relationship with Karima and under tremendous pressure to produce the contents of Karima's package, the vice kommissar still sat, however precariously, atop the huge BKA task force that was investigating the Hamburg cell and coordinating with the Americans. It had been he who wrote the agency's summary report and sent it to Washington. He had been the one to sign the authorization to share secret information with the CIA and FBI. The BKA had done its work. His agency had responded promptly to every request by the Americans, but it had been a one-way street. Muaz the doctor, Bin Laden's number 2, had *not* been killed in December after all, and now the terrorist leader was making threats against Germany for helping the Americans in its "war on terror." Despite that, the FBI was refusing to share the intelligence gained from its separate interrogations. And Recht was disappointed in the way the Americans had used his information. The vice kommissar was mired in a state of chronic frustration.

In his modest office, with its gray walls and fluorescent lights, he leaned back in his leather chair and surveyed his domain. On the walls were reminders of a long and distinguished career: the picture of him as a rookie cop during the hostage crisis at the Munich Summer Olympics in '72, as a young inspector during the *Achille Lauro* hijacking in '85, and from the mad dash around Germany in '88 with the Gladbeck hostage crisis. It had been a good run.

September 11 was supposed to be its capstone. It was a great honor to be put in charge of the German investigations. Instead, it became a devastating embarrassment: the BKA had had the Marienstrasse apartment under surveillance for two years before 9/11. He was the man in operational charge and, therefore, was held responsible for the lack of action. They knew about Mohamed Atta and the man Sami called Fatfat. They knew that a Pakistani air force pilot had been part of the cell, perhaps the inspiration for the "planes operation," but they had lost track of him after he slipped out of Germany to the tribal areas of Pakistan.

Of course, the BKA had no actual details of the plot or its connection to America. But they knew the players (except Sami Haddad) and knew that they were dangerous. They had let them slip away without even adding their names to any watch list. To the German press, the agency blamed Germany's progressive legal system for overprotecting free speech, even in cases of violent criminal conspiracies. Few were persuaded. It was a black eye for the agency. No one had been officially reprimanded for these failures.

With some trepidation now, he pulled the file on the detention of Haddad in the Dubai airport on his way back to Germany from Afghanistan. He was the one who had taken the call in June 2000 about a young Lebanese connecting through Dubai from Pakistan on his way to Hamburg. Recht had listened to the suspicions of the Emirati authorities that the subject was al-Qaeda and had trained in Afghanistan. His passport had been altered, and he was giving contradictory and unsatisfactory answers during his four-hour interrogation. He had failed a lie-detector test. And he laughed constantly, nervously, almost randomly. What should be done with him?

It had been he, Günther Recht, the vice kommissar of the BHA, who delivered Germany's final recommendation: the suspect should be released for lack of evidence. Recht was a stickler for following German regulations and law to the letter. There was no probable cause of a crime. His legalistic approach had persuaded his colleagues. They had acquiesced in his arguments, and later, denied that they had done so, leaving Recht to hold the bag. The first kommissar had been especially reluctant in the decision.

That colossal error had initiated Recht's obsession with Sami Haddad, long before he met Karima Ilgun. Haddad's release and his central role in the attack weighed heavily on the vice kommissioner's conscience. Since 9/11, no one had overtly held his advocacy for Haddad's release against him, though he suspected that it was behind the first kommissar's chronically sour attitude toward him. The consensus persisted. Had Haddad been found, broken, and arrested, he might have led them directly to Atta, to the Hamburg cell, and to the plan for 9/11.

He could not share his disgrace with Karima. In the end, he knew he was far more responsible than she.

To overcompensate for his mistake, he had allowed himself to get too close to Karima. He had gone soft. His failure to report the existence of the Haddad tapes immediately would be grounds for instant dismissal. His pact of silence with her violated every rule of investigative practice. He knew the consequences. Perhaps it *was* time to go. It would not be so bad to retire to the Frisian Islands, and do a little fishing. He had always wanted to climb Mount Kilimanjaro. True, he would lose a significant part of his pension if he took early retirement. He was fifty-five—still young. He could find ways to be useful.

Now, he opened the top drawer of his filing cabinet, pulled out the FBI's "psychological profile" of Haddad, and stripped away the cover sheet marked *SECRET* in big red letters. The report was more than a hundred pages long, but he was not impressed with its contents. More a narrative of Haddad's movements and calls and expenditures than a psychological profile, it contained no insights into the villain's mind-set or motivations or conflicts. As a fact sheet, it had its uses, but as a psychological profile, it was garbage.

Recht knew that he had to overcome his anger over the destroyed tapes and make the most of what survived. Karima had said the tapes she would play for him were recorded on July 18 and 19. That was around the time that Atta had flown to Spain to meet Omar and work out the final details of the planes operation. A few weeks earlier, Haddad had flown to San Francisco in first class on a 757, the aircraft he flew on September 11. And then he had flown on to Las Vegas to rendezvous with Atta, where they happily swilled whiskey and cavorted at the blackjack table. Caught on casino surveillance videos later, the pair had had a great time. Sami had purchased a GPS for use on the operational flight. The receipt for it was in his file. These actions did not sound to Recht like those of a man gripped by indecision.

If Sami Haddad was really torn, even right up to the end, was his ambivalence sincere? Or was he trying to make himself look more sympathetic in Karima's eyes? Recht could argue it both ways. On the one hand was Haddad's inexorable path toward his terrible fate; on the other was al-Qaeda's verifiable concern about his commitment and reliability. The allure of Karima was their greatest worry, and who could blame them? In intercepted communications, marked TOP SECRET, Muktar had specifically written to Mohammad Atef that "if Haddad asks out, it's going to cost a lot of money." *Money* was code. The cost of Haddad's defection would be far greater than financial.

And the evidence showed that as they worried about Haddad, they were grooming al-Sahrawi to take his place. In an encrypted message, Muktar instructed Omar to "send skirts to Sally," meaning "send money to the Algerian." By the time Karima prepared to fly to Florida to see Haddad for the last time, al-Sahrawi had completed six months of flight training, including an intensive flight simulator course in Eagen, Minnesota. Al-Sahrawi himself had told authorities that when he finished his flight training in August, his instructions were "to proceed to New York." Why? The answer was obvious: clearly to be ready to assume the pilot's role if Haddad pulled out at the last moment. But Muktar considered Algerian to be a poor substitute.

Viscerally, the vice kommissar knew he had caused himself a

problem with Karima. All his professional life, he had known never, *ever,* to fall in love with your agent, and now the first kommissar had called him on the carpet for his indiscretions. His superiors knew that he was not involved in any romantic way. The notion was ludicrous. Recht was no lover. He was far too old and jaded and set in his ways for amorous indiscretion, though they imagined that he, like everyone else who came into contact with this stunningly beautiful woman, it seemed, had his fantasies. Rather, "the lover does not care for his beloved so much as he draws inspiration from her." Recht had come upon the line in his nightly reading of Nietzsche a few nights before.

And Recht *was* drawing inspiration from Karima. No woman in his limited experience or even in his imagination had ever been betrayed so cruelly. By helping her navigate Sami's recollections, interpreting his actions and statements, Recht hoped to prevent her from going insane. He had indeed become emotionally involved.

Now, against his better judgment, he had made her a promise. However impulsive, it was eminently practical: at the least hint of bad faith, she might consign these last tapes to the flames as well.

He turned to the section on Haddad's voluminous telephone records. The man had been a telephone obsessive, and the Americans had done well to track every call, most of which had employed prepaid telephone cards. Sometimes he'd called Karima three times in a day, clearly in search of moral support. Flipping to the end of the record, Recht wanted to see whether Haddad's last call had been to Karima— the three-times-I-love-you call. Could there have been a later one? Was it really true, as he had heard, that Haddad had called Omar in Germany from the cockpit itself? The unconfirmed report stated that as Haddad, somewhere over Ohio, turned the plane back toward Pennsylvania and set the course for Washington and the U.S. Capitol, he had shouted to Omar, "I can't do it! I can't do it!" and Omar had screamed back, "You must! You must!" But the report was unverified.

In the FBI's telephone logs, he saw no record of such a call, but the hijacker could have used another phone. Recht knew that in certain circles in the Middle East, this story was gaining credence. In other circles, Haddad was being held up as an Arab hero. In the hills of the Bekaa Valley, there was now an insurgent group called the Sami Haddad Brigade.

Recht reached for the al-Khatani and al-Sahrawi files. Haddad's tape of July 18 or 19 would have to mention their names, he surmised. What would Sami have to say about those hapless blunderers? The vice kommissar had enjoyed the slapstick of the al-Khatani story when he first heard it: a bumbling Bedouin arrives on a one-way ticket in Orlando with a wad of al-Qaeda cash, unable to fill out the US immigration form, unable to say why he was coming, unwilling to swear an oath that he was telling the truth, first saying that someone was waiting for him, then that no one was, while Atta waited outside, twiddling his thumbs. Recht chuckled darkly to himself. Here again the Keystone Cops of America had sent him home rather than detaining him. Then he checked the record. Yes, al-Khatani indeed had been captured in Tora Bora late in 2001 and was now in Guantánamo. But he had been brutally tortured and rendered useless.

And al-Sahrawi? He had been indicted in December and was headed for trial in US federal court, purportedly as the "twentieth hijacker." But Recht knew that al-Khatani was the twentieth, and al-Sahrawi was to be Haddad's backup pilot, the twentieth and a half. The elements of the Algerian's story seemed like a dark comedy to the kommissar as well. His remark to his flight instructors that he was not interested in learning how to take off and land a jetliner, only in how to control it in flight, was priceless. Recht had encountered many pathetic criminals in his day, but this character ranked high in his gallery of dim-witted blockheads.

As Recht reviewed the latest FBI intelligence on al-Sahrawi, Braun entered with a smirk. "Well," he said. "Did you have a good time last night, Kommissar?"

Recht scowled. "You have a dirty mind, Braun. Shouldn't you be busy with the Deutsche Bank case?"

"Come on, boss. Give. What happened?"

"Look here, Braun, if something significant happened, you would have no need to know it; 9/11 is my province. If I need your help, I'll tell you."

"In Hannover, your nighttime appointment with her seemed so promising," Braun pouted.

Recht glowered at him in silence.

"By the way, the man from the FBI is waiting," Braun said.

"Let him wait." Recht waved his assistant away and went back to the Al-Sahrawi file.

***

They each kept their promises. Two nights later Recht arrived at Karima's apartment at 10:00 sharp. This time there were no candles, no music, no food. Karima had collected herself, steeling herself for what was coming.

"Okay," she said. "Let's get on with it. I didn't sleep very well last night."

She shooed away the cat, and they sat together on her couch.

"Do you believe in black magic?" she asked.

He snorted. "I'm a Lutheran. We believe that life with God persists even after death, if that's what you mean."

"But do you think we can communicate with the dead?"

"I suppose it might be possible to be a Lutheran and practice voodoo at the same time. Martin Luther wrestled with the devil, after all."

"I'm not talking about Martin Luther."

"We also believe in perpetual judgment."

"What does that mean?"

"That judgment lasts forever, now and into eternity."

Christian theology confounded her, as much as did the fine points of Islam. She let it go.

"I have developed a ritual, Günther. It's silly, I know. Don't laugh. Will you humor me?"

He nodded.

She folded herself into the lotus position, laced her fingers in her lap, and closed her eyes. With a tinge of embarrassment, she whispered, "Those who I have loved and lost, speak to me now."

She switched on the machine, uncoiled her legs, and tilted her head onto his shoulder. Sami's voice filled their ears like an infection.

July 18, 2001

"And so, Karima, I'm at a fork in the road. One path leads to you. I've begun to think about withdrawing from this adventure. Its finality is just . . . too final. If I leave, then Atta will have his magic number, nineteen. Nineteen angels to guard the hellfire. Then he will be happy. I know they've got a backup for me. He's getting trained in Minnesota. He can do it instead.

"What would happen then? I've been thinking about that a lot. They would track me down. To the ends of the earth. I would never be safe. You, my family, all of us would be in danger. When this is over, whoever is still alive, whoever helped along the way, will be on the run. I must protect you.

"Maybe when we see each other, we'll talk about it. You would be shocked at first. But then, my love, you will be my rock of support. We could be brave together. I'm sure of it. Because you love me. That will be enough.

"And the other path . . . Atta does not share all the particulars with me, but I know we're four teams of five. The other teams are complete. Almost everyone is in the States. They know this is a martyrdom mission, but they don't know the details. Only my team is one guy short. Atta is in Orlando today to pick up my fifth.

"Ahmad has been shadowing me for weeks. Atta insisted that we room together. The little prick is insufferable. Seriously, I hate him. He's constantly waking me up to pray in the middle of the night. He goes out of his way to annoy me. And he sticks to me like glue.

"The others in my team are staying in Naples. They come from the al-Qassim in Saudi Arabia, where the Wahhabis are. I know them only by their warrior names. The guy from the al-Ghambi clan, his name means "might," "pride," and "invincibility." I hope so. He was in Chechnya. The other claims to be a descendent of the Prophet. I haven't met them yet.

"My fifth team member is that little Bedouin, al-Khatani, who bunked next to me in Afghanistan. Remember I told you how he used to dream of glory with Osama bin Laden and the Prophet himself? He'll be in the best physical shape. That will be a huge plus.

"Perhaps for once in my life I should finish something I have started. To really achieve something—what would that be like?"

Karima switched the machine off. "Perhaps for once in my life I should finish something I've started," she repeated.

"He was past the fork in the road, Karima," Recht said.

"Maybe," she answered. "I've listened to this passage over and over. He still has a chance to reject them."

"Maybe," he repeated. "Go on."

She pushed the play button. Haddad's first words boiled with anger.

July 19, 2001

"Karima! I CAN'T BELIEVE THIS! Atta came to my apartment tonight and said that stupid little al-Khatani had been turned back at the Orlando Airport. He learned this from Muktar. Since

al-Khatani had a tourist visa, they asked to see his return ticket. And he didn't have one. Then he showed them he had $2,800 in cash, and they said that was not enough for his stay. When they asked if he was being met, he said yes, then no. What a joker! Then they asked again, only under some kind of oath. He sputtered something incoherent.

"Then he lost it. Goatherd! He got hostile with them. The whole idea, I mean, the first principle is not to draw attention to yourself. Kalb! Asshole! What happened to all that training? And get this: he claimed to speak no English through the whole interview. So, they got an interpreter. But then they took him to the plane, sending him back to Dubai, and he stood there at the door of the plane and shouted at them.

"'I'll be back!' Idiot!

"And so, my team has four guys rather than five. There's no time to get a backup. Maybe this makes my choice easier. When I asked Atta what we do, he just shrugged his shoulders."

"Have you ever heard him that angry?" Recht asked as he switched it off.

"Once."

"When was that?"

"With my old roommate, Gretchen, in Greifswald. She was a theology student and a pretty good cook. We got together for a student dinner from time to time, and when Sami was around, they often discussed religion. She's a devout Catholic and very interested in the rituals of religion. There was only one rule: we were never to bring up Israel and Judaism. That was taboo."

"So, what happened?"

"One time they were talking about whether Muslims had a highly developed sense of right and wrong, or whether following the ritual of praying five times a day was enough. But the conversation drifted to the question of whether Islam was a violent religion. Sami became quite agitated, and he made some outrageous remark—I can't remember what exactly, something about jihad, probably. She was pretty well versed, and she challenged him on some important pillar of his faith. He was obviously wrong about it. And then, half-serious, she questioned whether he was a true Muslim or was just faking it."

"*Ach so!* She went right to the core of his insecurity," Recht said. "Whether he was really a true believer or just putting on a show."

"Yes. He exploded in a terrible rage. He turned on her viciously and said something like, 'Tonight we eat together, and tomorrow I will take you out of the picture.'"

Karima rose from the couch to get them a drink of water. She could feel his eyes on her back as she glided toward the kitchen.

"Why is he so upset with this al-Khatani business?" she asked, handing him his glass.

"It's pretty obvious, isn't it?" he answered. "With four instead of five, his team would have difficulty controlling the passengers. With Sami and Ahmad in the cockpit, that left only the two Saudis to keep forty passengers at bay. Sami seemed to understand that. He knew the Americans by this time, knew there was a good chance that there'd be some hero on board. His chances of success were severely diminished."

"*Success,*" she whispered.

"But isn't that the way he thought?"

"I don't know how he thought anymore," she mumbled.

"Don't you see?" Recht persevered. "All his life he'd had trouble finishing anything. He falters in high school, in dentistry school, in flight engineering school. He is always dropping out. Always needs help—from his professors, from his family . . . from you. The loss of al-Khatani must have felt very familiar to him. He saw the shape of yet another failure."

"I suppose that's the way it worked out," she muttered.

"Tell me what you remember about your two weeks together that summer."

Karima had replayed those two weeks in her mind so many times they had almost become a dream. Or actually, two dreams. She now could accept that she had loved half a man: the good Sami, the funny, playful Sami, the great dancer, and yes, great lover. In Florida, he'd taken her to his flight school to meet his instructors, to his gym to meet his personal trainer. They'd picnicked on the beach of Siesta Key. He'd flown her solo to Miami, where they'd partied in the bars and discos of Miami Beach. And he'd taken her downtown to see the skyscrapers.

From afar, she'd seen him through the glass corridor of the Tampa Airport, tanned and fit. He had frosted his hair, and his aviator glasses hung low around his neck by a pastel Croakie, a Tommy Bahama shirt hanging loose over his athletic frame. When he spotted her, he'd flashed his wonderful grin. She'd looked forward to being with him immensely. They were good at reunions.

That was the good dream. It was her fantasy that this was the total person—that this was the real Sami when he was free to be himself.

And then there was the nightmare.

She had not been at her best in late July. Her persistent summer cold with a hacking cough had interfered with the romantic moments, and she was feeling real pain in her throat—a sign that she would soon need that tonsillectomy. She had greeted him warmly, and they made love that night with all the excitement and enthusiasm of the past. But for the next three days she was under the weather, and when she got better, she announced that she could not take off the full two weeks from work. Her vacation days were depleted. They'd had their first quarrel.

While she rested, he receded into a corner and "worked" on her computer and took long walks. It was then, she found out later, he'd visited the website about "joining the caravan." Once she had risen from her bed, groggy and dizzy from her medication, and crept up on him for a surprise hug, only to see over his shoulder an image of an airplane crashing into a skyscraper in a Hollywood movie.

"Hey, Sami, nice going!" she had said with a laugh.

He'd turned on her with a crazed look she did not recognize, as if some terrible secret had been exposed. More than startled—she had terrified him. When she put her arms around him affectionately, he recoiled.

"You know, Karima," Recht was saying to her now, "he wanted you to save him."

"To save him?"

"Yes, to rescue him from the trap he was in. He knew he couldn't do it by himself. In his mind, he was putting the entire burden on you."

"But how was I to know?'

"There was no way for you to know."

"If only he had said something . . ."

"Yes, if only he had said something." Recht muttered. He didn't dwell on what might have flowed from that. "If he had only said something *actionable*."

From the moment of her witnessing him transfixed by the freeze frame of a burning skyscraper on his computer, Sami had withdrawn. He'd viewed her with suspicion, casting sidelong glances at her, acting as if he were a cornered animal. The tiniest tiff had turned into a raging argument. They'd quarreled and pouted and apologized and made love joylessly. The glow of Florida faded, and there they were again, almost an old married couple, up and down, hot and cold, guarded even in their happiest moments.

A few days before she was to return to Germany, Sami was again pacing his apartment, and Karima attempted to confront him.

"Sami," she had said, "sit down. I want to talk."

Warily, he'd obeyed.

"What's going on, Sami?"

"What do you mean?"

"You're so jumpy. Something's off. Something's wrong. We're not connecting."

He'd looked at her with a blank expression. "Well, you haven't exactly been at your best either."

"I'm sorry I've got this cold. I know I haven't been much fun to be around."

"No."

She could feel her heart pounding as she took his hand and kneeled in front of him.

"Sami, I want you to come back with me to Germany."

His eyes wandered to the window. "I haven't finished my training," he'd said.

"You could finish it there. These long absences are killing us. It's taking longer and longer to get back on the same page. You feel so far away from me."

"I'm almost done. Just a few more weeks."

"Are we still going to your sister's engagement party in Beirut?"

"When is that, again?" he asked.

How could he not remember? Her family was planning a big celebration. They had talked about it often. "Late September," she said. "September 26."

"Late September. Yes, of course, I should be finished by then."

Again, she'd fixed her eyes on his. "Sami, look at me. If you want to finish your training here, I want to stay in Florida. I've already talked to my supervisor about a leave of absence. We could be together in the next month until you get your certificate."

"You would abandon everything for my sake?"

"Not forever. We could fly on to Beirut for the wedding, and then afterwards, figure out what to do next."

She'd thought she'd seen panic in his eyes. "It would be wonderful to have you with me, *yahabibti*," he'd said. "But it's just too complicated. Really, I have to focus."

Recht listened to her story impassively. "There are things you don't know, Karima," he said.

She did not hear him, still possessed by *might-have-dones* and *should-have-dones*. As she worked herself into hysteria, it was as if she had taken this entire history of the attack on her shoulders. "Aren't they saying that the dissension in Florida between Sami and Atta had posed the greatest threat of all to the plot?" she shrieked. "Aren't they saying that if only Karima Ilgun had turned him from his course . . . If only I had gone to the authorities . . . If only I had exposed it all? If only—if only—if only . . .."

"Calm down, Karima. STOP. Get ahold of yourself." Recht grabbed her by the shoulders. "None of that is true! You are not a clairvoyant!"

And then she grew quiet, turning away from him with a terrifying calmness.

"If only I had not had that abortion," she said in a soft voice. "If only I had had his child."

"What on earth are you talking about?" Recht said.

"He drifted away from me after that."

"He was drifting away anyway!" he protested.

"No, a child would have bound him to me. He would never have abandoned me . . . and his child. Our child would have made the difference."

She burst into tears and fell into his arms.

"There are things you don't know," he said again, holding her tightly. "There are things you just don't know."

***

When Recht came to her door the next night, Karima ferociously blocked his way.

"What things?" she demanded.

"Excuse me?" he replied, startled.

"What things don't I know?"

Recht looked at her quizzically.

"Günther!"

He raised his hands in supplication. "Give me a chance to catch my breath, will you?"

She stepped aside, put her hands on her hips, and watched him shuffle to the couch. As he sat down, he exhaled loudly.

"I don't think it's fair," he said.

"What's not fair?"

"That you won't let me smoke while we talk about such profound things."

"Okay, talk. If your talk is good, I'll let you smoke afterwards."

They eyed one another warily. "Okay," he said gruffly. "Let's get on with this."

She switched the machine on. No words came at first, only far in the background the throbbing, repetitive chant of an Arabic singer. Karima recognized the Hamas anthem, and the phrases *the wolf has entered your house, the law of the jungle decides the fate of man,* and *the only solution lies in the tenets of the Koran.*

Sami's first words were flat and cold. Before he was through his first sentence, Karima heard a tone that she had heard only once before, that night in Greifswald, when he'd said to her Gretchen, "Tonight we eat together. Tomorrow I will take you out of the picture." Recht, too, recognized that tone. He had heard it before too, through the static of airborne communications, cockpit to passengers, recorded on the ground by the Cleveland air traffic control center. For more than a year that voice was burned in his brain.

"Ladies and gentlemen. Here is your captain speaking . . ."

August 8, 2001

"I've been back for three days. I'm putting my doubts aside once and for all, preparing myself for my own personal Battle of Badr. I am purifying my soul.

"Do not be sad. By your love, you tried to turn me away from this course. I absolve you of any responsibility in my historic act, yahayati. I proclaim your innocence, and I love and admire and honor your strength and your virtue. I do this entirely on my own. This is my choice. I alone am responsible.

"My oath binds me to Osama bin Laden. I'm guided by the trust that has been placed in me. I am the instrument of my people. At last, I connect myself with the history of my clan and my region. I have not been a good Muslim. I have failed in my duty to my faith all my life. Including my duty to jihad. By this act, I end my inner struggle.

"Omar says that doubt and inner guilt and anxiety are vanities of the unbeliever. These feelings are un-Islamic and must be laid aside. If the fatwa of Osama bin Laden is wrong, if I kill Americans wrongly, thinking, just because Osama bin Laden said so, that it was my duty as a good Muslim to do this, then the blame lies not with me but with Osama bin Laden. I will be absolved of all crime, as merely a courageous warrior in a misguided cause. And my victims will go immediately to heaven and live in joy through eternity.

"I am ready for my Day of Judgment. Whatever will happen is inevitable. Whatever happens is God's will, for His hand is everywhere.

"Farewell, Karima, my love, my life, my heart.

"Atta has returned from Spain and his meeting with Omar. Our targets are finalized. My target is confirmed. The Faculty of Fine Arts.

"The date is set as well: a lollipop, a slash, and two toothpicks."

***

Karima slumped back on the couch, drained and dizzy.

"That's all? That's the end?" she whispered.

"On your tapes, perhaps, but no, that is not the end," Recht answered.

"What else could there be? He was lost. He was lost after his visit with me."

"No, my dear, he was lost long before that."

"You can have your smoke now," she said ruefully.

"Let's take a walk, Karima. There's a full moon."

They walked along narrow winding, cobblestone byways toward the heart of the city. At a cross street, she stopped and looked at him. "See, you hounded me, Günther. You put me on trial. I told you I knew nothing."

"That is not the end," he repeated.

The air was moist with the promise of spring, bringing new life and new possibilities. Strollers were out in force. Well-dressed, elderly gentlemen with their well-coiffed ladies meandered along arm in arm, taking the night air. As she noticed them, Karima took Recht's arm as well.

"We are an odd couple," she said.

When they reached the river, they stopped to gaze out at the silhouettes of the sailboats, secure in their overnight moorings. After a long silence, he finally spoke up.

"I have said many harsh things to you along the way," he said.

"Yes."

"I was just being a policeman, challenging you, hoping to discover your secret."

"You accused me of being responsible for the entire catastrophe of 9/11."

"Yes. That was unfair. There are others far more responsible."

She did not seem to hear his last remark. "What else don't I know? You must tell me."

He paused. "Well for one . . . after your visit to Florida, Sami did go back to Germany briefly."

"He went back to Germany . . . after me?"

"Yes, Atta drove him to the Tampa Airport. For them to be seen together broke all their operational rules, but they knew that Sami's possible defection was a major crisis. And on the other end, Omar met him in Dusseldorf and spent hours with him. They threatened him. They let him know in the most graphic detail what they would do to him and to you and to his family and yours if he pulled out. From that point forward, through his whole visit with you, and all the way into the cockpit for Flight 93, he was driven by fear."

"Not by commitment or his oath or any sort of ideology?"

"That is so."

"How do you know this, Günther?"

"What was your answer to the judge? 'I know it in my heart.' They were gangsters, and I've had a lot of experience with gangsters."

"But what about his oath, and the trust placed in him, and setting aside his doubts?"

"I don't believe a word."

"Not even his reprieve of me?"

"Oh yes, I believe that. But the rest? He was trying to put a noble face on it. It was more comfortable to present himself to you as a hero to the Arab peoples rather than the frightened, cornered, tormented wretch he was."

"He spoke of martyrdom."

Recht stopped to extract another cigarette from his crumpled pack.

"You can't stop martyrs. All you can do is reduce their number. I read that line once in a novel," he said.

"He seemed to have come to terms—"

"Oh, please," Recht responded in annoyance. "He was not ready for his Day of Judgment."

"But they had a backup," she insisted. "You said so yourself. They had this Algerian."

"Al-Sahrawi is a loathsome little maggot, totally unreliable. They had only contempt for him and were trying to figure out how to terminate him with the most extreme prejudice. Zacarias Al-Sahrawi was no Sami Haddad. They were right to worry."

In the distance they heard a tugboat's horn and then the clang of a buoy, bouncing in the sharp waves of the North Sea.

"Listen. On August 29, Sami was in Washington. He had come to scout his target, and for some reason to apply for a Virginia driving license. He had never seen the US Capitol before, except in the movies. He and Ahmad strolled down Pennsylvania Avenue, and they fell in with a group of tourists."

"Tourists?"

"Yes. From Kansas. They listened to a guide speak of the Capitol as America's "Temple of Liberty" and how George Washington laid the cornerstone, and the guide quoted Lincoln saying that 'if the people see the Capitol going on, it is a sign we intend this Union shall go on.'"

"Abraham Lincoln? During the American Civil War?"

"Yes, that's when they were finishing the Capitol. The Kansas couple were in the group, and we have their statements. The husband remembered the two Arab men on their tour—one handsome, the other small and ugly. The handsome one kept fiddling with a device. At first, the husband thought it was a cell phone, but then he saw it was a GPS. As the group meandered up a walkway, the husband remembered remarking to the Arab visitors about how beautiful the Capitol is, and his wife leaned over to them and said, 'it's beautiful because of its idea.'"

Recht stole a glance at Karima. She trudged on, staring straight ahead. Finally, she said, "Poor Sami."

"He was thinking about only one thing," Recht said.

"One thing?"

"About what it was going to be like to see the ribs of that dome right in front him through the cockpit window."

"Do you think he was insane?"

"Not entirely. He made one last attempt to get someone else to stop his 'caravan.' He rented a car in Washington."

"I read about that. They found a copy of *Penthouse* magazine in the trunk."

"I would not take that personally, Karima. Listen to what Atta did on his last night. He left his Koran in the strip joint where he was throwing down one scotch after another."

"I don't care about Atta," she said.

Recht nodded his understanding. "And on Sami's drive toward

Newark," he continued. "he hiked his speed up over 140 kilometers an hour north of Baltimore. Of course, he was stopped by the police. Even on an interstate in America, that's going to get noticed."

"You think he was trying to get arrested?"

"Yes. For the second time."

"Second time?"

"Yes. The first was in the Dubai Airport."

"You think he wanted more than just a speeding ticket?"

"All he got was a ticket and a lecture."

"But what about his checklist? The part about scuttling the mission and landing the plane safely?"

"I doubt he had the skill to pull that off, and I think he *knew* he didn't have the skill. We've talked to his trainers."

"Including the one in Sarasota?"

"Yes, she was hard to find. She fled to Australia. She confirmed that Sami was not the brightest bulb."

The night fog was moving in from the North Sea. Karima pulled her jacket tightly around her.

"He wrote me that letter on the last night."

"Yes . . . as he took a break from studying the cardboard mockup of the cockpit panel of a Boeing 757 that they found in the dumpster of his motel afterwards. At that point, Karima, you were an afterthought."

"But he called me from the airport."

"That call was his last act of treachery toward you. He knew the call would be traced."

Again the mournful, clang-tinged wail of the foghorn drifted across the dark sea.

"You have thought a lot about his case, haven't you, Günther?"

"Yes."

"What else do you know . . . that you haven't told me about?"

He paused. "I had the chance to stop him too," he said finally. "But I didn't." She seemed not to have heard him. "I am far more responsible for 9/11 than you are," he said emphatically. Still, his confession did not seem to register. In the dim light of the nearby street lamp and the glow of the distant searchlight on the piers across the way, he stopped and looked at her. He started to speak and then hesitated.

"What else do you know, Günther?" she repeated.

"The cockpit . . ."

"The cockpit recording?"

"Yes . . . from the voice recorder . . . from the flight data recorder . . . from Shanksville."

"You have heard it?"

"Yes."

"*Um Gotteswillen*," she whispered.

"It's horrible," he said.

She sat down on the cold grass and covered her eyes with her hands. A tugboat moved away from the distant pier with a roar of its powerful engine. He sat down next to her.

"I want to hear it," she said.

"I'm not sure—"

"Do you have it?" she asked.

"Yes."

"Then I want to hear it. I *insist* on hearing it."

Slowly, half-reluctant, half-eager, Recht rummaged through his pocket and pulled out a microcassette player.

"You understand English, *nichtwahr?*"

She nodded. "You wanted me to hear it, didn't you, Günther?" she said.

"Yes."

Forcefully, he switched it on. Haddad was making his first announcement. "Ladies and gentlemen, here is your captain speaking. Please sit down. Remain seated. We have a bomb on board. So, sit!"

Recht switched it off again. "Are you okay?" he asked her.

"Yes. What's happening?"

"Sami and Ahmad had stormed the cockpit. The other two musclemen were herding the passengers to the back of the plane. Sami and

Ahmad had knives at the throats of the pilot and copilot."

Recht took hold of her hand and held it tight. "I warn you. The next five minutes are very difficult," he said.

She nodded. "Go ahead."

They listened to the sounds of mayhem. *Sit down. Shut up. No. No. No. Lie down. Please. Please. Please. Down. Down. Down. I don't want to die. No. No. Please.* Gurgles and then Ahmad's squeaky little voice in Arabic, "That's it. I finished. Everything is fine."

Then a different voice. A flight controller in Cleveland.

"United 93."

Sami's voice again, in English, with Arabic cadence and German syntax. "Here is the captain. I would like to tell you all to remain seated. We have a bomb aboard, and we go back to the airport. We have our demands. So please remain quiet."

"United 93," the controller's voice crackled again. "I understand you have a bomb on board. Go ahead." Ten seconds went by. The controller again: "Center exec jet 956. Did you understand that transmission?"

A different voice. "Affirmative. He said that there was a bomb on board."

"That was all you got out of it also?"

"Affirmative.

"Roger."

"What's going on, Günther? Center exec jet? I don't understand what's happening!"

Recht switched off the recorder. With the slow deliberation of a veteran policeman, he laid out the facts. Forty-five minutes into the flight, Haddad took control of the plane over Ohio. He forgot to turn off the communication link to the ground, so the controllers and a private jet in the vicinity—executive jet flight number 956—could hear his warning to the passengers. With the pilots dying at their feet, Sami turned the plane to a southeasterly course and set the GPS with the coordinates for the US Capitol: N3853.3W7700.3.

Meanwhile, their two musclemen held the passengers at bay in the rear of the plane with box cutters and mace. Because Flight 93 had departed nearly half an hour late, and only a few minutes before the first plane hit the World Trade Center tower . . .

"Wait a minute," Karima broke in. "It left late? I thought they grounded all flights after the first plane hit the World Trade tower?"

"Yes. If Flight 93 had been delayed another five minutes, it would have been grounded."

Recht plowed on. The Flight 93 passengers knew from their cell phones what had happened in New York and began to call their families. Seeing this, one of the musclemen announced in a loud voice that the passengers might as well call their loved ones because it would be the last opportunity they would have to speak to them.

"*Um Gotteswillen*," Karima mumbled again. "How do you know this?"

"We have the calls of the passengers."

Recht switched the recorder on again. For the next ten minutes, there was a garble of unintelligible sounds, thumps, electrical switching, snatches of Arabic, and in the background, the liquid sounds of life ebbing away. A voice said clearly in Arabic, "In the name of Allah. I bear witness that there is no other God but Allah."

"Who was that?" Karima asked.

"Ahmad. They were now twenty-nine minutes out of Washington, and the third plane had just hit the Pentagon."

Several minutes later, the revolt began. Recht surmised that Ahmad saw several passengers rise up through the pinhole window in the cockpit door.

"Is there something?" Haddad shouted.

"A fight," Ahmad shouted back.

"A fight?"

"Let's go, men," Ahmad shouted. "Allah is greatest!" Suddenly, there was a distant sound that became increasingly louder, of something heavy being rolled up the aisle, along with the shouts of two American males. "Oh guys. Oh no," Ahmad shouted his unintelligible alarm.

Recht hit the pause button. "We know from the flight data recorder that at this point, Sami, sensing the impending attack from the cabin, pushed forward on the control column as hard as he could and put the plane into a steep dive. This probably threw the passengers against the ceiling, creating almost a zero-gravity environment. And then he pulled the column back for a steep climb. He was such a novice. He was exceeding the tolerance limits of the plane, and it could easily have broken apart."

"Did it work?" Karima said.

"No. Listen." He turned the recorder on again.

She could hear the banging and the shouting, and she heard Sami scream, "The ax! Get the ax!"

Amid the confusion, Ahmad screamed, "Stay back! Stay back!"

And Sami, "They want to get in here. Hold. Hold from the inside. *Hold!*"

There was more banging and a cracking sound, as if plastic and metal were giving way.

And then, in an eerie voice, Haddad said, "Is that it? Shall we finish it off?"

"No! Not yet!" Ahmad screamed.

"When they all come in, we finish it off."

"There is nothing."

Recht turned off the machine again. He and Karima sat on the cold ground, breathing heavily. Trembling, Karima asked, "What did he mean, 'There is nothing'?"

"I don't know," Recht answered. "I've wondered about that myself . . . many times."

"You've listened to this many times?"

"Yes. Nothing. Nothingness. I don't know. We need a Hegel or a Heidegger to explain it." And then he turned back to her. "Can you handle the end?"

She took his hand and held it tight. "Yes, play it."

It had become just noise to her now. A few words were intelligible:

cockpit . . . roll it!. . . oxygen. . . . engine . . . until she heard Sami say, "Is that it? I mean, shall we put it down?"

And Ahmad said, "Yes, put it down."

Seconds went by. Ahmad shouted more forcefully. "Put it down, *kalb*! Put it down, I say." And more seconds, as the banging became louder. And finally, Ahmad screamed. "Give it to me, then! GET OUT OF THE WAY! Give it to me! Get away! Get your hands off there!"

A few more seconds passed. There was the sound of rushing wind. Ahmad started to chant.

"Allah is the greatest. Allah is the greatest."

In the last moment, Sami, the passenger at last, joined him. "Allah is the greatest." Then—silence.

They sat there for a long time, listening to the gentle waves lap against the sea wall.

"He couldn't do it in the end," Karima said at last. It was more a statement than a question.

"No," Recht replied. "He couldn't do it. Ahmad did it."

They got up and wandered aimlessly, losing track of time. Karima leaned on his arm, wobbly at times, as they walked, an occasional wave of nausea washing over her. He tried to be stout and strong, but he did not feel strong. They were joined now in their mutual culpability.

"What is to become of me, Günther?"

"I don't know," he said. "You will have to decide. I have some decisions to make too."

"Am I still a person of interest to the BKA?"

"No. I will have some explaining to do. And then I will no longer be a person of interest either."

"I feel like a castaway."

"We're both castaways now."

"I'm thinking I might move to Turkey. I would feel safe there."

"You could take one of those unpronounceable names."

"Yes. Build a new life in some small, remote village."

"How about that conflict between the German and the Turk in you?"

"I'm older now."

He nodded. "Yes, we've all aged in the last year."

"Someday, when I'm stronger and have more distance, I might go to America. Visit Washington, and even, if I could find the strength, go to Shanksville."

"Oh, I don't know, Karima. I'd think twice about doing that."

He reached in his pocket and pulled out Sami's last cassette. The thin, acidic strips came out of the housing with a whine, and Recht broke them strand after strand. The tangle gathered around his large, yellow fingers until it became a nest of gibberish. And then he took the Flight 93 tape and did the same, so that Sami's confessions and his final act were intertwined. He reached to the ground, scooped up a handful of mud and pebbles, and squeezed the jumble into a ball. And then he threw it into the North Sea.

Together they watched it sink beneath the froth.

EPILOGUE

SIX MONTHS LATER, a few weeks after the first anniversary of 9/11,
Vice Kommissar Günther Recht arrived early for his last day of work and
lingered in his car for a leisurely smoke. The daunting modernist building
in front of him, where he had spent the last years of his professional life
and fought so many battles, seemed like a medieval fortress that morning,
with its prongs emanating from its central donut and its base raised in a
berm. It reminded him of the walls of Vienna that held back the Turks in
the sixteenth century. He looked up at his office window. How he wished
he could have had the office at the end of the hallway, with its panoramic
view of the woods, but that belonged to the first kommissar.

A day earlier, Recht had turned over all his classified documents to
counterintelligence and endured his final debriefing. There had been

significant developments in the past months. Osama bin Laden had escaped from Tora Bora, and his trail had gone cold. Al-Sahrawi had been indicted in America as the twentieth hijacker and faced the death penalty. The real Omar had been captured in Karachi, and Muktar in Rawalpindi. Their interrogations in various US secret prisons formed the basis of current knowledge about the plot and plotters. But Recht was not impressed with the reports of their interrogations, and he bluntly said so to the first kommissar.

The vice kommissar disapproved of the Americans' harsh methods. The operatives had been tortured unmercifully, and as a result, the principals were either vegetables or crazy. Omar was now a raving paranoid, afraid of his own shadow, addicted to psychotropic drugs, given to loopy disquisitions on the state of the world. He had lost himself in food and was now immensely fat. In one proceeding at Guantánamo Bay, Recht reminded everyone, Omar had to be chained to the floor like a rabid dog. Was that any way to extract useful information? he asked. Muktar, after repeated waterboarding, was confabulating incredible tales that glorified himself at every step. His information was ridiculously unreliable. No wonder there were such gaping contradictions in the assertions of the two captives, Recht told his debriefers. If only they had had Sami Haddad's tapes. But of them Recht said nothing.

His colleagues listened politely. Their minds were elsewhere. America had shifted its focus from 9/11 to Iraq, and their priorities had shifted as well.

The ceremony for his early retirement was slated for noontime in the central courtyard of the headquarters at Bruno-Georges-Platz. Folding chairs, about twenty of them, had been set up near the sculpture of the iron eagle seal of the German Republic. Flags of the department, the province, and the nation stood like sentinels behind a simple podium amid some recycled potted plants. Colleagues from his thirty years of service had been invited. The first kommissar had been sent around a directive that everyone in the office was expected to attend.

The small audience gathered promptly at noon. Braun, his head clean-shaven now and a big smile on his face, sat grandly in the front row. He had been temporarily appointed acting vice kommissar until someone more senior and more accomplished could be sent to take over.

When everyone was seated, Recht scanned the audience for Karima. He had written her an awkward little letter in which he had wondered how she was coping. He wanted her to know that he personally had signed the order to remove her police protection. He hoped her mother had won her case. And then, if by any chance she were free, he would be pleased if she could attend his retirement ceremony. The food for it was costing him a pretty penny. Not only that, he had a nice surprise for her.

The speeches were dignified, if a little flat. Law enforcement officials, especially those in the secret services, are not given to soaring rhetoric. The high points of Recht's career were ticked off seriatum, ending with Kommissar Recht's "remarkable" management of the complicated 9/11 investigation. This occasioned a few muffled snickers in the audience. First Kommissar Schuh, in his brief remarks, gave his deputy credit for the arrest of dangerous domestic terrorists. If Recht was not exactly beloved, he was respected and even liked by some of his colleagues.

Through the fog of comfortable words, Recht's mind wandered. He did not believe that Karima would ever find a way out of her unknown place, no matter where she had gone. Phantoms would torment her for the rest of her life. While her guilt might lie dormant, some random event would trigger a memory like a grotesque, clown-faced jack-in-the-box. Because he was a policeman, he had helped her define where her culpability did *not* lie—but her problem was no longer with the law. Merely to say that she was not guilty, in the legal sense, was the easy part. In the face of such daunting shame, he recognized that his paltry efforts to protect her had been fleeting. And he had his own secret shame to deal with. He had escaped official reprimand, but he had been unable to compensate for his errors or exculpate himself for his own failures.

When he left her that last night, his mind had drifted, like a good German, to questions of soul and spirit. He admired her strength, her resilience . . . and also her suffering. In the Nietzsche that always lay close at hand on his bedside table, he had read that suffering did not make a person better, only more profound. Perhaps that was her path forward, not to the good life, not to happiness, certainly, but to an affirmation of life over death and guilt. He believed in the power of forgetfulness, for her and for himself. It was a way to deal with bad judgments and bad decisions. Karima would have to find her own way now, as would he.

He also thought about the impact she had had on him. His entire career had been spent in the company of criminals and, more recently, terrorists like Sami Haddad. It had given him a sense of superiority. He strove for a kind of private, personal nobility even as he wallowed in the swamp of evil. To disperse the odor of the riffraff, he read Goethe and listened to Beethoven and tried to appreciate Bizet's operas because Nietzsche had said they were brilliant. When his superiors berated him for being condescending to his staff, and when he felt awkward in the presence of women, he convinced himself that exceptional men always found it difficult to connect with ordinary people because they were different and found familiarity to be tasteless.

But Karima Ilgun? He almost felt humble around her at the end. She had gazed deeply into the abyss and had not flinched when the abyss stared back at her. Her situation *was* beyond good and evil. She longed for a resolution, but there was none to be found, nothing either he or Haddad could present to her in a neat and tidy bow. As Recht let the speeches of his soon-to-be former colleagues and associates wash over him, as speakers lingered on one or another crisis he had solved (or failed to solve), crimes of history committed by the malignantly evil or credulous and misguided, he thought of Karima, somewhere, trying to start a clean new life in an unknown place, and remembered again his Nietzsche.

When he got home after the ceremony, his letter to her was in his mailbox. It had been returned unopened. On the front were the words: *UNBEKANNT VERZOGEN* . . . moved away to an unknown place. *Yes*, he thought, as he turned it over several times, *unbekannt verzogen*. He knew the feeling.

One has to be strong to forget.